Vintage Trailers and Blackmailers

Vintage Trailers and Blackmailers

A
JULES KEENE
GLAMPING MYSTERY

Heather Weidner

LEVEL BEST BOOKS

First published by Level Best Books 2021

AUTHOR PHOTO CREDIT: Studio FBJ

First edition

ISBN: 978-1-68512-036-8

Cover art by Level Best Designs

This book was professionally typeset on Reedsy.
Find out more at reedsy.com

To Stan, Mom, and Dad,
thanks for all the love and support!

Praise for Vintage Trailers and Blackmailers

"In *Vintage Trailers and Blackmailers,* the calm of Jules Keene's Blue Ridge Mountain camper resort is disturbed when a man's lifeless body is found in the woods. What follows is a cozy mystery full of blackmail, secrets, mysterious strangers—and handsome security guy, Jake Evans. Jules and her loyal pup Bijou are in for a suspense-filled adventure. I love the warm and friendly characters and the twists and turns in this new down-home, mutt-loving series."—Susan Van Kirk, Author of The Endurance Mysteries and *A Death at Tippitt Pond*

"Jules Keene is focused on her vintage trailer camping resort, but when a dead guest is discovered in the woods and her aunt is questioned, Jules decides to help catch the killer. She must stop the culprit, keep her guests satisfied, grow her business, run for president of the town's business council, and stay alive when the bad guys come after her. This book is a joy to read."—Jackie Layton, Author of the Low Country Dog Walker Mysteries

"Packed with action and filled with "Oh, man, I didn't see THAT coming" moments, this first installment in the Jules Keene Glamping Mysteries series will not disappoint. And Weidner made glamping sound so glamorous that I think I'll take my husband up on his suggestion to go camping...but only if it's Fern Valley Camping Resort style!"—Jayne Ormerod, Author of *Goin' Coastal*

"Smart and persistent businesswoman Jules Keene puts on her amateur sleuth hat to track down murderers at the upscale Fern Valley Camping Resort, set in the beautiful Blue Ridge mountains. The bad guys have met their match in this fast-paced mystery."—Frances Aylor, Author of Money Grab

"Heather Weidner's *Vintage Trailers and Blackmailers* is an exciting addition to this year's cozy mystery line-up. Fern Valley Camping Resort, with its refurbished vintage trailers and tiny houses, is as enjoyable as can be, but don't be fooled, this book is all excitement. I don't know how she combines charm with a fast-paced story but I'm so glad she did."—Lane Stone, Author of the Pet Palace Mysteries and the Tiara Investigations Mysteries

Chapter One

Monday

Jules Keene had been so focused on making the gift bags look fabulous that she didn't hear her aunt approaching until Roxanne dropped her Gucci purse on the counter with a clatter.

"What in tarnation is going on here? It looks like the gift-wrapping counter in a nineteen fifties department store." Roxanne stared at the sea of red and purple tissue paper covering every available surface of the office of their family's vintage trailer campground. Clad in a pink fuzzy sweater, tight designer jeans, pearls, and a perfectly coiffed blond bob, Roxanne looked more in vogue than anyone else. As usual.

Jules pulled her long red curls up into a ponytail. "It's gift bag central. We're assembling them for this weekend's Classic Car and Camper Cruise-in."

Starting Thursday, hundreds of classic camping enthusiasts were expected to descend on their sleepy little one-stoplight town of Fern Valley, nestled in the Blue Ridge Mountains west of Charlottesville, Virginia. Twenty years ago, the downtown had been boarded up. But now, the area boasted a variety of eateries, a bookstore, several art galleries, wineries, and the fifty-acre Fern Valley Luxury Camping Resort. Jules and Roxanne catered to visitors looking for solitude, luxury, and outdoor adventures in refurbished trailers that were updated on the inside but vintage on the outside. Jules used her degree in interior design to add special details for their guests. She themed and stocked each camper for swanky vacations for the glamping craze, which turned out to be profitable for the family business.

"Where's Bijou," Roxanne asked, "under all that paper?"

"No. I left her at home this morning. She'd have had a field day with all the wrapping paper and bags."

Bijou was Jules's six-year-old Jack Russell Terrier.

The bell on the front door tinkled. Roxanne and Jules stepped out in the public space that included the general store and guest registration.

"Hello, may I help you?" Roxanne asked the couple who approached the counter.

Their three boys bounced around the store like small tornados, jostling camping supplies, books, and flyers of nearby attractions.

"Boys!" The man's deep baritone voice echoed in the store.

The three children closed ranks behind their mother and stood soundlessly.

"Hi, we're Jill and John Riley, and these are Michael, Daniel, and Rex."

"T-Rex," the middle child with the blond buzz cut added.

Jules smiled. It was always more fun when there were kids at the resort. "Welcome. I'm Jules Keene, and this is my aunt Roxane Mallory. You're in for a week of fun." She clicked a few keys on the computer. "We have the nineteen fifty-nine Airstream reserved for two weeks. Here's your key. It's number A-5, and this is your welcome package. Breakfast is served from six to ten in the lodge. If you'd like to book a tour or need ideas for things to do, please let me know." Jules processed the man's credit card. "If you'll follow me, I'll show you where your Airstream is."

Jules held the door for the family and then trotted down the front steps into the bright sunshine. The long, covered porch, lined with rocking chairs and a swing at each end, served as the perfect spot for those seeking relaxation in the shade.

They walked down a sidewalk past the parking lot, bordered by a split-rail fence. The flower beds overflowed with Virginia bluebells, and the dogwoods and mountain laurel looked like they were ready to burst into bloom at any moment.

"Here we are," Jules said. "All of our trailers have a wine chiller, refrigerator, and microwave. Most everyone eats in town for lunch and dinner, but if you need takeout or delivery ideas, we can help. There's no cooking except for the microwaves. The trailers have been refurbished and upsized to accommodate today's travelers."

"This will be fine for us," Jill Riley said.

"We also have camping and sporting gear available for you to check out in the office. Please enjoy our wooded trails, croquet course, and rocking chairs on the front porch. And we have recipes and supplies if you want to try a campfire and our world-famous s'mores. Let me know if you need anything." The sun glinted off the iconic silver camper. Jules used her hand to shade her eyes.

"We will," Jill replied. "This is lovely."

"We're gonna have a campfire and go fishing," said the tallest boy, who looked about ten.

The smallest child chimed in with, "And ride horses. I hope we see a bear! And maybe Big Foot."

Jules smiled. "If you do, let me know."

The dad unlocked the door, and the boys clamored up the two steps and bounced around inside.

On her way back to the office, she passed Ira Perkins sitting under the awning on the patio of the 1947 Robin Hood, a smaller, bean-shaped camper, perfect for a single guest. Jules had themed that trailer in honor of the famous outlaw/hero from Sherwood Forest. Mr. Perkins, who Jules guessed was in his early sixties, had arrived two months ago and paid in advance for an eight-month stay to finish writing his book.

"Hello, Mr. Perkins. Beautiful day, isn't it?"

"So far. But I saw you over there with a bunch of kids a few minutes ago. I hope they don't ruin it for me. I came for solitude. And I won't tolerate shenanigans."

"There shouldn't be any issues. But let me or my team know if you have any concerns."

"Oh, I will. This is my writing retreat. I don't like interruptions. I DO NOT wish to be bothered. I was here first."

She smiled and waved as she meandered through the trailers and back to the office. *He must be a temperamental writer.* He always had some mild jab or complaint to voice.

Jules dismissed thoughts of her grumpy guest as she climbed the wooden steps to the porch to survey the vintage campers. A lot had changed around here since she was a little girl. She and her father had slowly removed all of the traditional campsites and replaced them with vintage trailers before he died three years ago. The property still had hookups in a field she called the meadow on the other side of the barn for events like this weekend's cruise-in, but the vintage trailers were now the campground's selling point. People wanted a nice retreat for their weekends and vacations. Her vintage trailers had been modernized for comfort with posh amenities.

She missed her parents on days like this. Since her dad's death, Roxanne and her son were Jules's only living relatives. And Bijou, her dog, was the only good thing to come out of her divorce from The Idiot. Jules shook off the nostalgic feeling and leaned forward to open the office's screen door.

Roxanne sauntered out of the office with a wine bottle and two glasses. "Hey, kiddo. Everything's closed up in there. There aren't any other guests scheduled for today. I'm heading out. I put the phones on the night answering service, and Emily will be in tomorrow morning to cover the front desk. See ya later." She sashayed down the path toward Mr. Perkins's trailer.

Jules's eyes widened.

Her feisty aunt and the ornery Mr. Perkins? Jules would have to get the scoop on that.

Chapter Two

Tuesday

Late in the morning, Jules slid into the seat at the table in the lodge that also served as the social hall for the resort's large events. The tall ceiling with its exposed oak beams reminded Jules of a European ski resort. An oversized stone fireplace stood sentry at one end of the hall, while a bank of windows on the opposite wall showcased the view of the woods and the blueish mountains in the distance. The last guests had cleared out and headed off for their day's adventures. The lone person in the big room was her employee, Jake Evans.

"Coffee?" Jake placed one of the two steaming mugs in front of her. The muscular thirty-something had worked on and off for Jules's family since they both were teens, and he now handled maintenance and security for the campground.

"Thanks. All quiet last night?" Jules added creamer and stared out the wall of windows at the mountains.

"Yep. I did the last of my rounds at eleven-thirty. Everyone was tucked in and behaving."

"Good. All the trailers are reserved through the weekend. And we have the cruise-in on Friday. All the spots at the meadow are taken as well."

"A full house. Your special events keep 'em coming in. Did you book extra security for the weekend?"

"I did. If we stay full for the rest of the summer and fall, I'll add extra guys for weekend security. That should give you a break."

"Thanks." He smiled, and Jules noticed the glimmer in his green eyes. "I like the overtime, but it'll give me time to scout some new projects." Jake had helped the team that did the restorations for the campground, and now he was itching to try a project on his own.

"You work too hard." But it was nice to have him around.

He had moved into one of the small cabins on the back of the property last year when she added security to his duties. On premise security was a good trade-off for free rent in case there was ever a situation.

"I've got to go check on the office. Aunt Roxanne should be in by now."

He grinned and stifled whatever he was going to say.

"What?"

"Nothing. Your aunt is a free spirit." He smirked.

"What brought that on?" Jules looked at her well-worn fingernails.

"Uh, nothing really." Jake paused. "She was visiting with guests last evening."

Jules's tried to maintain a poker face. She wasn't the only one who saw Roxanne's stop at Mr. Perkins's trailer.

She rose from her seat, cleaned off her side of the table, and then waved goodbye to Jake.

The sun warmed her face on her stroll across the property to the office. It would be a great day for a walk in the woods, but her list of unfinished tasks drew her like a magnet toward her desk. She needed to complete this month's newsletter and do some artwork for next week's social media posts.

Jules, still thinking about her new marketing ideas, backtracked to her cabin to get Bijou. The white and brown Jack Russell Terrier greeted her with a yip. Jules leaned over to pick her up and got a face full of puppy kisses instead.

"Hey, sweetie, ready to go to work? I'm sorry you had to stay home yesterday. Everybody missed you."

Bijou answered by circling Jules's feet and running out the door. She enjoyed the warm June morning as much as Jules did. On the walk to the office, the dog had to smell everything and bark at a bird.

CHAPTER TWO

It looked like most of the guests had left for the day. Jules made a mental note to pull out the two hammocks in case anyone wanted to relax under the trees. She also decided to bring out the badminton net for pickup games.

Bijou bolted after a butterfly. Giving up on the fluttering insect, she trotted up the front porch steps and whined for the door to be opened.

"Hey, good morning," Jules yelled as her eyes adjusted to the cool darkness of the store.

The Jack Russell Terrier zoomed around the displays and ran off in search of Roxanne, who always had a treat or two in her desk drawer.

"Hi, Jules." Emily Owens, a diminutive teen, worked part-time at the campground. She arranged camping and first-aid supplies on the rack closest to the registration counter.

"How are things going?"

"Great. I went to the French film festival at the Bijou Theatre with friends last night."

Jules had such fond memories of the former Lowe's movie palace in town. With its balcony, huge, red velvet curtains, and ornate art deco furnishings, the Bijou was her favorite place to watch movies. The name meant jewel, and it was perfect for the small dog that ruled Jules's house and heart.

"That sounds like fun. Thanks for restocking. When you're done, would you check on our Instagram and Facebook accounts?"

"Sure. I love getting paid to do social media." The teen headed to the counter, and her ponytail bounced in time with her gait.

Jules disappeared into the workroom, where her aunt flipped through a pile of manila folders. "Hey, how goes it?"

Roxanne shared her office chair with Bijou, who had already settled in for a mid-morning nap. "Everything's humming along. It's all under control."

"Love it." Jules settled in at her desk.

"Oh, you got a call about a group outing..."

A loud bang and shouting echoed from the front of the store. Bijou barked, and Jules and Roxanne rushed to see what all the commotion was about. Roxanne pulled the bottom part of the Dutch door closed behind her to keep Bijou out of the fray.

Mr. Perkins slammed his fist on the counter and spilled one of the brochure displays. His beet-red face matched the color of his ballcap. "Listen to me. I came here for quiet, and I will not be subjected to those hooligans. You will do something about it right now, or you will refund all of my money. Those kids are out of control. They keep knocking on my door and running away. And they peek in my windows. What are you going to do about this, young lady? You don't look old enough to work here. I want to talk to your boss." He poked his finger close to Emily's nose. "I want quiet and my privacy!"

Before she could reply, Roxanne strode forward. "I'll take care of this. Mr. Perkins, you do not need to shout. We will be happy to assist you."

"This, this young lady rolled her eyes at me. I don't appreciate the sass. I've paid good money to stay here, and I demand to be heard." He pounded on the counter again with his fist, shaking more of the display items. "I oughta teach those kids a lesson. They run around unsupervised. Maybe if one or two of them disappeared for a little while it would teach their parents something about making their kids behave, and it wouldn't be so loud around here."

Shock flashed across Jules's face at the threats to other guests, especially those directed at little kids. She opened her mouth to retort, but Roxanne's voice dominated the room.

"Listen here, Ira. You need to calm down. You can't yell at our staff and threaten to kidnap little children. It's time for you to go back to your writing and pipe down."

"You listen to me, woman. Don't tell me what to do. I know my rights." Mr. Perkins spat the words at Roxanne as he shook his fist and grimaced.

Before Jules could intervene, Roxanne leaned across the counter toward Mr. Perkins and pointed a finger at his nose. "I heard what you said. And I hope, for your sake, you were just popping off. We all heard you. And we'll take care of the noise issue. You make sure you steer clear of that family and those kids."

"Don't patronize me, woman. I had enough of you last night. You overstayed your welcome with all your yammering. And if this kid thing isn't resolved to my satisfaction, I'm going to reconsider my extended stay."

Roxanne's cheeks flushed, and anger flashed across her face.

Mr. Perkins turned on his heel and stormed out, slamming the screen door.

Roxanne bounded across the store and yanked the door open.

"Well, old man. Last night wasn't a thrill for me either. You're not the conversationalist you claim to be. And don't come barging in here hollering at my staff and threatening little kids, or I'll make you disappear and not think twice about it."

Jules peeked over her aunt's shoulder to see several guests, including a pair of bird-watchers and Lester, the groundskeeper, watching the drama. She hoped everyone would move on and forget the outburst. Upset guests who left bad reviews were one thing she didn't need right now.

Roxanne huffed back in the office and slammed the door.

Chapter Three

Wednesday

Jules opened the office door, and Bijou made her entrance like a firecracker. Jules grinned. Nothing was ever quiet with a Jack Russell.

Jules dropped her black messenger bag on the desk in the back and flipped through the mail.

"Hey there. Anybody home?" Roxanne swooped in with a to-go coffee cup and a bagel.

Bijou greeted Roxanne with a favorite tennis ball. Roxanne tossed the ball for the little dog as she held onto her breakfast with the other hand.

"Morning," Jules said. "I talked with the parents of the three boys, and I moved them to the nineteen seventy Airstream Sovereign on the other side of the campground. The boys should like the fishing theme. And I haven't heard anything else out of Mr. Perkins. You?"

"No. I haven't seen hide nor hair of the old buzzard since he embarrassed himself yesterday. And I have nothing further to say to him. He can enjoy his own company since he thinks so highly of himself."

Jules straightened the items on the counter. "Okay. If he comes back, call me. I'll deal with him. I know you're protective of Emily, but..."

"I know. My mouth took over when my brain didn't kick in. He got on my last nerve. I guess I probably shouldn't have raised my voice at him, but he was asking for it."

Make that threatened him. But she refrained from correcting her aunt.

"I'm going to check out the grounds. Call me if you need me. Bijou, keep Aunt Roxanne company while I'm gone."

The dog bounced around the office like a pinball.

Jules strolled out and jumped in the golf cart parked under the carport behind the store. The warm weather was perfect for a tour of the grounds with a three-hundred-sixty-degree view of the Blue Ridge Mountains. The wildflowers had popped, and the color mixed with all the greenery. Jules loved this time of year.

She drove the cart around the vintage campers, where most were already filled with guests. Some empties stood ready for weekend occupancy. She stopped for a minute before rounding the corner to survey the grounds. No guests in sight. She didn't see Mel or Crystal Carson either. They must still be in the kitchen. The mother-daughter team cooked breakfast in the lodge and cleaned the trailers. Nothing but peace and quiet and the occasional cicadas.

As she made her turn to check out the maintenance area at the big red barn, a bloodcurdling scream echoed from the edge of the woods. Jules slammed on the brakes and made a quick turn. She mashed the accelerator, and the cart lurched in the direction of the noise.

Jules stopped at the edge of the tree line as one of her guests, Mrs. Charlene Fillmore, came running out of the woods with her hair and sun visor askew. The septuagenarian bent over with her hands on her knees. She took a moment to catch her breath. "Jules, call the police. I tripped over a body in the woods."

"A body? Where?"

"Over by that copse of trees. Trudie and I were birdwatching, and I stumbled over a root and fell on him."

"Are you okay?" Jules punched 9-1-1 on her phone.

"I'm better than he is. He won't need an ambulance. He's been there a while. And there's a big hole in his chest. Pretty gruesome."

"Where is Mrs. Greenbaum?"

"Trudie stayed back there so I could find the spot again. Plus, she insisted someone needed to preserve the integrity of the crime scene. If you ask me,

I think she watches too many detective shows on TV."

Jules said, "Hello. This is Jules Keene at the Fern Valley Luxury Camping Resort. We need the police. One of my guests found a body in the woods. Yes. We'll wait here and make sure no one disturbs it." She clicked off and said to Mrs. Fillmore, "Police are on their way. Are you sure you're okay?"

"I'm fine." She was catching her breath. "I used to be a nurse in the army. I've seen a lot worse. We were looking for a woodpecker we heard off in the distance. And then boom. I tripped over a root and fell on the guy. I didn't expect to see a body in the woods today in that condition." She fanned herself with her hand.

"No, I guess not. Or any time." Jules clicked her walkie-talkie. "Jake. I'm expecting the police. I'm over with Mrs. Fillmore near the woods by the barn."

"Be there in a sec."

"Hey, if you could hang out at the office and keep folks contained over there, it'll help when the police get here."

"Ten-four."

She was surprised Jake didn't ask any questions. A police visit to her campground was a rarity. She would get the third degree from her team when she returned to the office.

Jules and Mrs. Fillmore waited in silence in the golf cart for what seemed like hours. When Jules's walkie-talkie squawked, both women jumped.

"Boss, Sheriff Hobbs just rolled up. I sent him your way down the back road. He should be there in a minute."

"Thanks, Jake." Jules climbed out of the cart.

The black and white sheriff's car kicked up dirt and gravel as it approached on the maintenance road. The cruiser stopped next to the golf cart, and, before the dust settled, the burly, middle-aged officer built like a wrestler climbed out.

"Hey, Jules. Ma'am." Sheriff Hobbs plopped his hat on his head and approached the women. "Dispatch said you all found a body."

"I did." Mrs. Fillmore raised her hand and jumped out of her seat. "Follow me. He's over there a ways by those trees. I fell over him. Trudie is waiting in the woods so no one disturbs him further."

The elderly birder took off like a shot. Jules had to jog to keep up with her. The sheriff made a call on his cell phone and then trotted to catch up to the women.

Jules's eyes adjusted to the darkness of the forest. The coolness of the woods or maybe the thought of the dead body made her shiver. She shook off feelings of doom and tried to concentrate on following Mrs. Fillmore and not stumbling.

After dodging branches, Mrs. Fillmore stopped suddenly, and Jules almost ran into the back of her.

"Trudie, Trudie..."

"I'm over here," said a faint voice that came from the left.

"They're over there." Mrs. Fillmore caught her breath. "He was leaning against the back of that tree, but I might have knocked him over when I tripped."

"Mrs. Greenbaum, are you okay?" Jules asked.

"I'm fine. I'm glad to see you all. He's not much company. A lousy conversationalist."

Jules and Sheriff Hobbs stepped around the exposed roots and a shirtless man slumped over on his left shoulder.

"Yep. That's him." Mrs. Fillmore leaned in closer.

"No one has been back here since we found him," Trudie Greenbaum added. "I know it's important to preserve the crime scene, right, Sheriff? I tried to keep my footprints to a minimum. And I didn't touch anything."

Sheriff Hobbs smiled wryly. "Thank you. I need for you all to go back to the cart and wait for the forensic team. When they get here, send them this way. After I secure the scene, I'll get your statements."

Jules turned and looked at the very-dead Ira Perkins, clad only in a red satin thong.

She hoped her mouth wasn't hanging open. This was the last thing she expected to find this morning at her resort. The rational side of her brain said to stay calm and keep everything in order. The other half wanted to run screaming from the woods to hide in her office.

After the initial shock subsided, Jules and the two bird-watchers picked their way through the woods to the golf cart. Mrs. Fillmore claimed the front seat, and Mrs. Greenbaum slid in the back.

Time dragged on. Finally, another police car barreled down the maintenance road and skidded to a stop, slinging dust and gravel toward the women. Mrs. Greenbaum coughed and waved her arms around.

Deputy Charles Dempsey climbed out, hitched up his pants, and stuck his Smokey Bear hat on his balding head. "Ladies, Sheriff Hobbs asked me to get your statements while he's investigating. Ma'am, if you'll step over near my car," he pointed to Mrs. Fillmore, "I'd like to ask you a few questions. Uh, and you two, please don't discuss anything while we're gone. This is an active investigation."

Mrs. Greenbaum rolled her eyes and put her hands in the "don't shoot" position. Mrs. Fillmore followed the deputy to his car.

Jules turned around and faced the woods, hoping to catch a glimpse of the sheriff. What in the world was Mr. Perkins doing in the woods in his underwear? This could destroy her summer business. This season was key because it positioned her to make payroll for the rest of the year. She let out a deep breath and tried to be patient.

After both bird-watchers had talked with Deputy Dempsey, he waved Jules over. He leaned on his dusty cruiser.

"Hey, Bubba. How's it going?" Jules asked.

"Fine. But I go by Charles now in my professional life. I haven't been Bubba since high school."

He might be Charles to everyone else, but he would always be Bubba to her.

"So, how did you find out about the deceased?"

"I was making my rounds this morning, and I heard a scream. I found Mrs. Fillmore near the woods, and she told me she and Mrs. Greenbaum had found a body."

"Did you recognize the victim?"

"It's Mr. Ira Perkins, one of my long-term guests."

"When did you last see him alive?" Charles stared at her.

"Yesterday. He stopped by the office."

"What'd he want?"

"He was upset some children were making too much noise. I took care of the problem and moved the other family across the property."

"I'm gonna need to talk to your staff and maybe some guests. Definitely that family with the kids." Deputy Dempsey chewed on his bottom lip.

Jules thought about Aunt Roxanne's outburst and stiffened. Would the police read more into it than there was? "Not a problem. Do you need me anymore? I'd like to take these ladies back to their accommodations. They've had quite a morning."

He nodded and glanced past Jules. A forensic van sped down the maintenance road toward them. He keyed his radio. "Sheriff Hobbs. Forensics is here."

"Ladies," Jules said. "Thank you for your patience. Deputy Dempsey's done, so I can take you back to your trailers."

"Do we have to leave?" Mrs. Greenbaum asked. "It's just getting interesting. And we may be able to assist."

"Yes, let's stay," Mrs. Fillmore chimed in. "They may need to question us again. And our husbands won't be back for hours. They went fishing."

Jules doubted the need for more questioning, but curiosity got the best of her as three forensic techs, with all their gear, trudged into the woods. She and the two birders sat in the golf cart, hoping to get a glimpse of some of the action. So far, the only thing that heated up was the temperature.

An hour later, a black van from Johnson's Funeral Home bounced down the gravel road and parked next to the police cruisers. A few minutes later, a red SUV pulled in next to the collection of emergency vehicles. Jake was doing a good job of keeping the rest of the guests and staff away. She hoped he didn't have to lock Aunt Roxanne in the back office with Bijou.

Jules's stomach rumbled and reminded her lunchtime had come and gone. "Ladies, are you ready to head back? I need to check in with my team." After two reluctant nods, she turned to Bubba. "Charles, we're going to head back to the office. Let me know if you need anything."

"Will do. The sheriff will be over when he's done here. Don't leave the premises."

Jules put the cart in reverse, and it lurched backward. Mrs. Greenbaum saluted, but Charles didn't seem to notice.

Dodging the emergency vehicles and the van, Jules bumped the cart across the grass toward the office.

"Jules," Mrs. Greenbaum said sheepishly. "I'm sorry I ratted your aunt out to the police, but he kept peppering me with questions. And I guess I cracked. I had to mention the altercation she had with Mr. Perkins yesterday. You know, it's important when they look for motives."

"Aunt Roxanne said a lot of things, but that doesn't mean she would kill anyone." Jules hoped her smirk didn't give away her feeling of dread. "That's okay. They have to investigate everyone in order to rule out the innocent." She hoped Sheriff Hobbs would get to the bottom of this soon. What kind of damage control would she have to do for the resort's reputation?

Jules drove the women to their trailers, a 1948 Palace Royal and a 1947 Westcraft Coronado. The former, decorated to highlight Virginia's birds, was perfect for Mrs. Fillmore and her husband Wyatt. The Coronado boasted a wildflower motif for the Greenbaums.

Jules waved goodbye to the women and floored the golf cart. She parked behind the store and raced inside. Before she could get to the computer with the security camera feed, Lester, Roxanne, Jake, and Bijou pounced on her. The humans wanted details. Bijou wanted a hug. It was hard to follow all the lines of questioning when everyone spoke at once.

Roxanne put two fingers in her mouth and let loose with a whistle that echoed through the building.

"Okay. Okay. One at a time. I can't even hear myself think in here with all this yammering. Jules, what's going on?" Roxanne asked.

"Mrs. Fillmore and Mrs. Greenbaum found Ira Perkins in the woods this morning."

"Was he lost?" Lester asked in his southern drawl.

"No. They found him dead." She left out the part about what he was wearing.

Roxanne looked dazed, but she didn't say anything. She picked up Bijou and hugged her.

"Remind me to let Mel and Crystal know," Jules said. "I'm sure they're still over at the lodge. Roxanne, the police know about your altercation with Mr. Perkins yesterday, so I'm sure the sheriff will be around later to talk to you. I'm going to look at the footage from yesterday's security feed. Jake, did you see anything out of place on your rounds last night?"

"No. It was quiet. Even that trailer with all the kids. The only odd thing was an older green truck on the side of the main driveway about ten-thirty. It was gone when I checked on it a little after midnight."

Jules settled behind her desk and clicked through the camera feeds as the others huddled behind her. At four thirty-five yesterday afternoon, the camera caught Mr. Perkins walking to his Corvette. He returned to the same parking space at eight twenty-five that evening. Only Bijou expressed her disinterest by curling up on her pink bed next to Jules's desk.

For twenty minutes, they watched guests come and go from the parking lot. Satisfied that nothing was amiss, she checked the other cameras near the lodge and the meadow.

Jake, Lester, and Roxanne lost interest and wandered back to other areas of the resort.

After another hour of looking at the security feed frame by frame, Jules couldn't find anything that stood out as unusual. A little after ten, according to the camera's timestamp, an older dark Chevy truck with a light-colored roof pulled in through the open gate. Before it reached the parking lot, it veered off on the edge of the entrance road. A thin guy with a dark hoodie climbed out and walked into the woods. At eleven thirty-eight, the guy jogged out of the woods, threw something in the truck bed, and backed the truck down the driveway. The truck didn't have a front license plate.

She replayed the clip and let out a heavy sigh. She was sorry about what had happened to her guest, but the resort didn't need this right now. Cancellations and people linking the resort to a murder could be devastating. Bad publicity, even if it was unwarranted, was hard to recover from.

Jules heard Lester say "Hi, Sheriff Hobbs. She's back in her office." Jules stood.

Bijou growled and ran to the door.

"Hello, Sheriff. Would you like some coffee?" Jules asked.

The sheriff opened the bottom of the Dutch door and leaned over to pet the terrier. He looked ten years older than he had this morning.

She sniffed his pants leg and followed him through the office.

"Coffee would be good."

Jules popped a cup in the coffee machine. "How do you take it?"

"Black's fine."

She slid a clean mug in and pushed the button on the machine.

He eased his tall frame into the guest chair in the corner of Jules's office that doubled as the work area for the staff. "Forensics is finishing up in the woods. They need to go through the trailer next. I'll need a key."

"Sure. You ready now?" Jules unlocked the lockbox on the wall by the door and pulled out the key to the Robin Hood.

He took several sips of his coffee and set the mug on her desk.

She followed the sheriff out of the office. Roxanne gave her a sideways glance that Jules ignored.

"Aunt Roxanne, could you get coffee and sandwiches for Sheriff Hobbs and his team? I'm not sure how long they'll be here. They've missed lunch," Jules said.

"Be happy to." She winked.

Jules wasn't sure what the wink was for. Roxanne was probably being her flirty self.

Jules and the sheriff trekked over to the vintage trailers.

He pushed the button on his walkie-talkie. "Charles, what's your ETA? I'm at the camper, and I still need to talk to the staff."

The deputy replied, "The funeral home folks and the medical examiner left a few minutes ago. We're headed your way."

"Door's unlocked," he said to Jules as he turned the handle.

She peered around the sheriff, who filled most of the trailer's doorframe. The curtain rod hung down to the floor.

Shredded cushions and pillows littered the floor, tables, and counters. The fluff looked like a snow bomb went off in the trailer.

Jules let out a sigh. It took a lot of time and money to decorate these trailers. She hoped it wouldn't be out of commission for an extended period of time. Backing down the steps, she plopped in one of the patio chairs under the green-and-white-striped awning.

The sheriff joined her as the forensic team and Deputy Dempsey parked in the guest lot. Two men and a woman in jeans and navy golf shirts with "Police–Forensic" emblazoned in bright yellow on the back walked up the path. Each toted two black cases. The taller tech nodded to the sheriff. Deputy Dempsey hustled up the path a few minutes later.

"Deputy, please stay here. I'm going back to the office with Jules."

The rotund deputy caught his breath like he had something to say. He paused and remained quiet.

"My aunt should be by soon with sandwiches."

"'Preciate it," the sheriff said.

Charles nodded with more energy than she'd seen from him all day.

Jules picked up her pace to keep up with Sheriff Hobbs, who strode down the sidewalk.

"Mind if I use your office? I want to talk to your folks who had contact with Mr. Perkins." He walked toward the office as if Jules didn't have a say in the matter.

"That would be me, Aunt Roxanne, Jake, Lester, and Emily. But Emily's off today. Bijou's back there."

"The dog's fine where she is. Let's start with Jake."

Jules found Jake leaning against the front counter. "The sheriff would like to see you. He's in the office."

Jules woke up the computer in the front to catch up on email while she waited for law enforcement to vacate her office.

The door creaked open about twenty minutes later. Jake called for Lester. Jules wasn't impressed with the investigative process so far. It had been a lot of waiting. Nothing like the action in the cop shows on TV.

About fifteen minutes later, Lester bellowed for Roxane to replace him. Jules jumped when his voice pierced the quietness of the store.

Her aunt sauntered into the back office. They heard, "Well, hello, Sheriff," as she closed the door.

Jules busied herself with verifying the bookings for the week and working on the next newsletter.

Roxanne finally emerged. "Bye, Sheriff," she called over her shoulder. "Let me know if you need anything else."

Sheriff Hobbs followed her out. "Jules, do you have access to Dropbox?"

She nodded.

"Please make me a copy of all the camera footage for this week. Here's the contact information."

She took the yellow sticky note. After some clicks, she said, "Okay. Done."

"When the forensic team is finished, I want to turn Mr. Perkins's trailer back over to you."

She followed him through the main doorway.

"Where is the family with the active kids?"

"On the back row. The one in the middle." Jules pointed to the far side of the campground. "Come on, I'll show you."

After pointing out the family's trailer, they continued on and stopped outside the Robin Hood trailer. Two forensic techs packed their equipment. Charles sat in one of the patio chairs and tapped his phone. He stood when he saw the sheriff and rammed his phone in his pants pocket. The third technician climbed down the steps to the patio.

Roxanne appeared with a cardboard box full of sandwiches, apples, cookies, and canned drinks.

Deputy Dempsey descended on the food while the other technicians waited behind him.

Sheriff Hobbs looked at the forensic techs. "Done?"

"Yes. Everything will be sent to the lab in Richmond today," the female technician said.

"Good. We've got what we need for evidence. Jules, here's the key you gave us. Please box up anything left that belongs to Mr. Perkins. I'll come by tomorrow to pick it up."

"What about the guest key Mr. Perkins had?" Jules asked.

"I don't remember seeing it. Johnson, check the log. Any keys?"

The taller male technician flipped through a notebook. "Nope. No keys. Not even car keys."

"I'll get Jake to change the locks. We'll gather Mr. Perkins's things and work on putting the camper back in order. We're cleared to clean up and get this back in circulation?"

"We have what we need. You're good to go," Sheriff Hobbs said.

She pulled her walkie-talkie off her belt. "Jake, when you get a minute, can you come over to the Robin Hood?"

The radio squeaked and crackled. "Be right there."

"Sheriff, what do you want to do about Mr. Perkins's car?" Jules asked.

A pained look flashed across his face. "Which one is it?" He glared at Charles.

"The red Corvette over there under the oak tree." She pointed behind her.

"Charles, get the techs to photograph the car. I'll call Zeke for a tow. Stay with it until the truck gets here." He walked over to the classic car as the others grabbed bags and joined him.

Jake pulled up in the golf cart and parked by the split-rail fence. "How much damage to the camper?"

"I can't tell. It looks like everything is strewn about. Now there are black smudges where they fingerprinted. Could you change the lock on the Robin Hood today?"

"Not a problem." He examined the dented door.

It took Jules longer to reorganize the vintage trailer and assess the damage than it did for Jake to replace the lock. By then all law enforcement had left and quiet had returned to the resort.

"Need some help?" He tested the door handle.

"Yes, please. You can take these suitcases and the two boxes back to the office. Please lock them up in the back. I should be done in a few. Mel and Crystal will need to give this one a good scrub. Mr. Perkins wasn't the neatest guest."

"You okay?" He stepped closer to her.

"Just tired. I didn't realize how much Mr. Perkins had crammed into this small space in such a short time. And it's odd I didn't find any notes or a computer. For that matter, there weren't notebooks or pens either. It didn't look very writerly."

"Maybe the police took all that?"

"It's weird. You'd think there'd be something related to his book in the stuff he left. But at least the only real damage was the destruction of a couple of cushions and two bed pillows. I can get those repaired. The curtain rod was an easy fix."

She filled a trash bag with the pillow stuffing and carried the last box and the two cushions outside and set them on the patio table.

Jake pulled the cart around to the little patio. "Figured you'd need it to transport the last of the stuff."

"Thanks." Jules shut the camper's door and shook it. "I think I can fix the couch cushions. The two pillows didn't make it."

He loaded the bags and boxes, and she jumped in the front seat. Jake dropped her off at the office. "I'll take this stuff to the dumpster. Let me know if you need anything else."

"Will do. I'm hoping for some calm. We've had enough excitement around here."

"Big plans for tonight?" he asked.

"Dinner and a movie with Bijou. You?"

"I'm working on my Mustang before rounds tonight. It needs an oil change."

Jules smiled. His candy apple red Shelby was his pride and joy.

Jules put the last box of Mr. Perkins's belongings with his suitcases and locked the closet door. She sunk into her chair to collect her thoughts. The physical damage to the trailer wasn't as bad as she first suspected. Maybe that would be the end of it, and they could get back to running the resort.

Roxanne barged in and interrupted Jules's thoughts. "Hey, Sheriff Hobbs called. He'll be back tomorrow. And Jane Jenkins called. She wants to interview everyone for next week's edition of the paper."

"I don't want to talk to her right now. I'm going to refer everything to Sheriff Hobbs's office. I can see Jane trying to get the scoop on a murder. Plus, she slants the story to highlight anything that might be juicy or salacious."

"Since Roger took over the paper, he never lets her do the news. She likes to wallow in the gossip and the dirt. Jane the Pain is always trying to weasel her way into a big story," Roxanne said.

"Nobody here should talk to her. This could backfire on us, especially if she's looking for dirt. We need a quick staff meeting. Let's get everyone up here."

"I'll round 'em up. Emily won't be in until tomorrow. We can tell her then." Roxanne pulled out her phone and sent a flurry of texts.

By the time Jules washed up and straightened her hair, her team had assembled in the back room.

"Thanks for being so flexible for an impromptu meeting. As you're all aware, one of our guests, Ira Perkins, was found dead in the woods this morning by Mrs. Fillmore and Mrs. Greenbaum. I'm sure the sheriff'll have more questions for us."

"Besides the security footage, I'm not sure there's more we can tell him," Jake said, and Lester nodded in agreement.

"Mom and I were cleaning up after the breakfast rush and prepping for tomorrow. We had no idea anything was going on." Crystal Carson twisted her long blond braid as she spoke.

Her mother wrung her hands. "Poor Mr. Perkins. What a sad ending."

Roxanne frowned but didn't say anything.

"Jane Jenkins is interested in covering the story. Right now, I think it's best if we refer all questions to Sheriff Hobbs. The police should be the ones to contact his relatives and release the information. So, far as the resort goes, all media inquiries are to be directed to the sheriff's office. Any questions? And let me know if any guests have concerns about their safety or stay."

"That's a good plan," Roxanne said. "Jane has a habit of sensationalizing things for a better story."

Lester raised his hand. "Do you think any of us are suspects?" His gaze landed on Roxanne.

"The sheriff hasn't cleared anyone as far as I know, but I don't think any of us had anything to do with Mr. Perkins's demise." Jules looked around at the faces.

Roxanne fidgeted but remained quiet.

"Any word on how he died?" Mel looked at her fingernails.

Lester said, "Bubba said he was shot in the chest and found in his fancy red underpants in the woods."

Mel covered her mouth and crossed herself.

Roxanne picked up Bijou and started petting the dog. She looked lost in thought.

A loud thunk emanated from the store. Bijou jumped down, barking. Jules and the others followed the Jack Russell Terrier into the store.

Jane Jenkins scrambled to get up. A shelf had collapsed nearby. Boxes of bandages and ointment littered the floor near the doughy reporter with the bowl-cut gray hair.

"It looks like that ol' buzzard was leaning on the shelf, eavesdropping on us," Roxanne said.

Jane bustled out the door and slammed the screen door.

Lester picked up the shelf and restacked the first-aid supplies.

"Great." Jules heard a car start in the parking lot. "So much for not talking to the press. We have to assume she heard everything."

Chapter Four

Thursday

Instead of tossing and turning until the alarm buzzed, Jules grabbed a yogurt and a banana, and at three forty-five, she and Bijou headed to the office to plow through the work that didn't get done yesterday. Bijou wasn't having any issue sleeping. She curled up in her bed and snored softly.

When the sky turned an orangey-pink, Jules paused and rubbed her eyes. She had spent the last hour going through the security footage. Camera by camera and frame by frame. Nothing looked out of place except the strange green truck Jake had spotted.

Jules stretched to ward off the kinks in her back. The sun came up over the mountains, and the birds started their morning serenade. Bijou snorted and rolled over in her bed.

Roxanne wandered in about an hour later and dropped her pale pink Michael Kors bag on the other desk. "Hey, there. You're here early this morning."

"I couldn't sleep, so I decided to get some things done. I wanted to make sure all the paperwork was current before the rush tomorrow. Emily's scheduled today and tomorrow, right?"

"Uh-huh. She'll be here both days to help with the evening guest registrations." Roxanne busied herself with straightening her desk. "And all the gift bags are ready to go when the cruisers check in. Find anything more on the cameras?"

"How'd you know I was looking at the feeds?"

"I know you. You're not about to let this go if you think you might find something."

"Well, it did happen on my property. I should try to get all the facts that I can. I need to make sure my guests are safe."

"Did you see anything interesting?" Roxanne made herself some coffee and smiled at her niece.

"Sort of. The cameras caught the green truck Jake noticed on his rounds. I couldn't see the license plate. What about you? You spent a lot of time with Sheriff Hobbs. What'd he focus on?"

"Oh, everybody mentioned that fight I had with Ira, and the sheriff wanted details. It was nothing but me blowing up at Ira when he acted like a jackass. I had no more contact with him after that. It was just a big misunderstanding." Roxanne sank down into the other desk chair and flipped open several files. She fell silent, and Jules returned to her laptop.

Around ten, Roxanne stood and stretched. "I'll be right back. I'm going over to see if there are any breakfast leftovers. You want anything?"

"No, thanks." Jules grabbed her phone and scanned through her emails. Something creaked in the store area. Bijou barked, and Jules jumped. She looked up to find Sheriff Hobbs, blocking the doorway.

"Good morning, Sheriff. How are you? Can I get you some coffee?"

"No thanks. I can't stay long. I'm here to pick up Ira Perkins's things."

"They're back here." Jules pointed to the closet. "Were you able to contact his relatives?" She unlocked the door and pulled the items out.

"We found a neighbor and the manager of his apartment. An ex-wife is listed as an emergency contact. We're still trying to track her down."

"Here, let me help you with those." Jules grabbed the smaller suitcase and a box.

"Call me if you find anything else."

"Sheriff, my plan is to refer any media questions to your office."

"That's probably best."

"I had a staff meeting yesterday, and we found Jane Jenkins creeping around in the store. She was listening at the door."

He furrowed his brow but didn't reply.

They descended the porch steps. The warm breeze ruffled their hair. The fresh mountain air distracted Jules for a moment.

"The paper comes out on Tuesday," Jules said. "I'm curious about what she'll focus on."

"She hasn't been by the station yet. I'm sure she'll turn up. I wouldn't worry too much. Roger rules the newsroom with an iron fist. He'll rein her in. Thanks for the heads-up, though."

She followed Sheriff Hobbs across the lot to his cruiser. He grabbed what she was carrying and put them in the trunk.

Jules's cell phone rang as the sheriff drove off. She clicked the button. "Hello."

"Hey, this is Mel. Crystal and I found something in the Robin Hood. Can you come over here?"

"Be right there." Jules jogged over to the small trailer and found Crystal scrubbing the kitchen.

"Hey, Jules." The blond woman continued to scour the metal sink. Her long braid had been twisted up in a clip, and loose tendrils popped out at all angles.

"What's up?" Jules joined Mel in the bathroom that had been expanded from the original trailer's design.

"I found something when I was cleaning. It fell on the floor. It was duct-taped to the back of the commode."

Crystal peeked around Jules. On the black and white tiled floor between the toilet and sink next to a wad of silver duct tape lay a silver thumb drive.

"Do you have disposable gloves?" Jules asked.

"In the cleaning caddy. Crystal, hand her a pair," Mel said.

Jules took one of the gloves the younger woman offered and scooped up the thumb drive. With the other glove, she grabbed the piece of duct tape. "I'll call the sheriff." She wondered if they had found Ira Perkins's novel.

Gingerly carrying the gloves and their contents, she hurried back to the office. She plugged the thumb drive in and tried to access it on her laptop.

A garbled message popped up on her screen. Jules let out a heavy sigh. She needed a way to get a look at what was on this device.

Gwen popped into her head like a lightning flash. She hadn't talked to her former college roommate and computer guru, Gwen Pierce, in a while, but maybe she could help. Jules grabbed her phone and flipped through her contacts. If anyone could access the contents, it would be Gwen, who went by the moniker Pixel for her forays into the dark web. Curiosity got the best of her. Jules wanted to see what the thumb drive contained before she handed it over to Sheriff Hobbs.

"Gwen. Uh, Pixel. How are you? This is Jules."

"Hey, girl. What's up? I haven't heard from you in ages."

"Work gets in the way. I know this is out of the blue, but I need a favor. Can you meet for lunch?" Jules asked.

"Lunch would be good. Today?"

"Sure. You name the place. My treat."

"How about the Topsy Turnip on the downtown mall? Will one o'clock work for you?" Pixel asked.

"See you then." Jules slid the thumb drive and the gloves in a plastic bag and dropped it in her purse.

Roxanne returned with a carton. Bijou darted toward her, following the bacon scent wafting from the container.

"Smells good," Jules said. "I'm headed out in a little while to meet Pixel in Charlottesville. You okay with things here? Only a couple of the cruise-in folks have Thursday check-in times."

"Don't worry about it. Bijou and I have things under control."

Jules puttered around her desk until it was time to leave. "I'll be back as soon as I can."

Roxanne and Bijou were snuggled in the office chair, cruising the internet.

After a short ride through the mountain roads, Jules found a parking spot on the roof of the parking deck in downtown Charlottesville. She locked her silver-and-black Jeep Wrangler and headed for the stairs. The Topsy Turnip sat nestled between an antiquarian bookstore and a new-age jewelry shop on the downtown mall, in an area of several city blocks closed to vehicle traffic.

Jules opened the restaurant's door. A tiny string of bells tinkled a happy sound. Her eyes adjusted to the dimness as she waited in the small foyer. Wooden tables sported tin lanterns with candles, and straight-back chairs, painted in a variety of pastel colors, covered every inch of the narrow floor space. Colorful paintings of cows, giraffes, and windmills dotted the walls.

"Please sit anywhere you like." The hostess in jeans and a gauzy tunic had bangle bracelets that jangled when she waved her arms toward the seating area.

Jules looked around but didn't see Pixel.

"Thanks. My friend should be here soon." Jules ordered an iced tea and perused the lunch menu, containing lots of vegan choices.

A few minutes later, Jules spotted Pixel at the door.

"Hey, there. How are you? You look great." Pixel dropped her leather backpack in the chair next to her and eased into the seat across from Jules.

"You too. It's been too long." Jules

"I know. Work has been all-consuming lately. What have you been up to?" Pixel flipped through the menu.

"Mostly work. That happens when you live where you work."

"I do some crazy hours, too. And I'm teaching now as an adjunct at the University of Virginia. I really like it. It's different from my normal job. Anything else going on other than work? Dating anyone?" Pixel asked.

"Nah. After my divorce from The Idiot, I've sworn off dating for a while. You?"

"I go out occasionally but nothing serious. I had a date for ComiCon, but it wasn't much to write home about. He showed up in a Power Rangers costume." Pixel wrinkled her nose. Before Jules could comment on what little she knew about that world, Pixel said, "I would have liked a superhero better."

Jules laughed.

The waitress popped in to take their orders. After she had picked up the menus and retreated to the kitchen, Jules said, "I need your help. Something bad happened this week."

Pixel pushed her purple-tipped black hair behind her ears. Concern flashed across her face. "What's up?"

"We found one of my guests dead in the woods. He was wearing only his shiny red unmentionables. I think one of the only leads the police have is he had an altercation the day before with my aunt. I know she had nothing to do with it. But who knows what the police are thinking? It was tragic. And this is going to sound bad, but I'm not sure what kind of backlash this is going to have for the resort. I can't afford to lose any bookings right now."

"What do you know?" Pixel asked.

"My security guy noticed a green truck near the main entrance, but it was gone when he made his rounds. And then my cleaners found a thumb drive in the camper of the victim this morning. The guest who was killed had said he was a writer. The weird part was there was nothing in his stuff that looked like he was working on a manuscript. And he didn't want the thumb drive found easily. It was taped behind the toilet. I tried it on my laptop, but I couldn't open the files. I was hoping you could look at it for me."

"Sure. No problem. I live about three blocks from here. We can walk to my place and check it out if you want. You might have a copy of his great American novel."

"That would be a relief. I wanted to take a peek at the contents before I turned it over to the police."

"Hopefully, I can help."

The waitress returned with their orders.

Between mouthfuls of the avocado and sprouts sandwich, Pixel said, "You think your aunt's really a suspect?"

"It's hard to tell. She had a shouting match with the victim that spilled out on the lawn, and they said some unflattering things about each other. And she kind of threatened him. Several people mentioned the fight to the police, and they questioned her longer than they did anyone else. I'm trying to do damage control."

"Maybe we'll find something that'll take the focus off your place and your aunt."

"I hope so." Jules polished off her ham and baby Swiss sandwich and dug into her pasta salad.

After passing on dessert, the two women walked through the bustling shopping area to Pixel's apartment, a few blocks near High Street.

"It's this one," her friend said.

They climbed the older house's stone steps to the wrap-around porch.

"I'm on the second floor. I moved in about three months ago, so it's still relatively new to me."

"I like the Victorian flair."

"It's a quiet neighborhood, and I can walk to just about anything. Come on in. My downstairs neighbors travel all the time, so I usually have the whole place to myself."

Jules followed her up the interior wooden staircase. She ran her fingers across the intricately carved banister. Pixel opened the heavy oak door to a large loft area that spanned most of the top floor of the old house. A bicycle and an old filing cabinet stood guard near the door. Her computers and gear took up space on a long wall in the living area. Pixel flipped a few buttons and sat down in the black office chair. "Okay. Let's see what we can see. Have a seat."

Jules pulled a teal ottoman closer to Pixel's desk. She handed her friend the bag with the glove and the thumb drive. "Now for the pièce de résistance."

Pixel slid the glove on her right hand and extracted the device. She used the bag to remove the cap on the thumb drive and plugged it in. She clicked the keys for a few minutes. "I'm going to copy the contents. Then you can have it back for the police."

After more clicking, Pixel handed the bag with the thumb drive to Jules, who dropped it in her oversized zebra-print purse. "Okay. There are a few spreadsheets. This doesn't look like a novel to me." She wrinkled her upturned nose. "This one has model numbers and dollar amounts that appear in different colors. There is also a folder on here that's encrypted. It's going to take me some time to get into this one, if I can. I'll copy these files and send them to you. And as soon as I can get into that other folder, I'll call you."

"I appreciate all of your help."

"Hey, what are friends for. You bailed me out a couple of times over the years. Okay. The files are copied. You can download them at your leisure. I'm curious to find out what's encrypted."

"Thanks. I have to be getting back. I have guests arriving for our classic camper cruise-in."

"Sounds like fun. My scooter's downstairs if you want me to give you a ride back to your car."

"It's a nice day. I can walk. I've already taken up too much of your time."

"I hope you find something useful on these files. You sure about the ride?"

Jules nodded and hugged her friend. "See you soon."

She strolled back to the downtown pedestrian mall full of all kinds of eclectic stores and shops, a beehive of activity in a college town. Jules wanted to hang out longer, but her curiosity about the file contents pulled her back to reality. She needed to return to the resort to check on the arrivals.

Retrieving her Jeep, she headed home, knowing she'd have to call the sheriff about Mel's find and explain why she hadn't turned it over right away. But she had a little while until she had to face the music. Jules pushed thoughts of law enforcement to the back of her mind and enjoyed the curvy roads on the way back to Fern Valley. She rolled down the windows in the Wrangler and blasted her favorite '90s station. Sitting at the town's only stoplight, she made a quick decision to pop into Lula Belle's for boxed dinners for her team. They would be working late today, and dinner would be a nice surprise.

She pulled open the glass door of the cozy restaurant. Sunshine beamed through the windows decorated with yellow and white gingham curtains. The focal point of the store, a long glass counter, was stocked full of sandwich fixings and gourmet sides like southern potato salad and Lula Belle's pimento cheese that made Jules's mouth water as she waited behind a couple of out-of-towners who ordered "Cawfee." Guests filled all of the restaurant's round tea tables and heart-shaped white metal chairs.

The Fords, a husband and wife team from Roanoke, bought Lula Belle's from the original owner when she retired a few years ago. They kept the classic recipes and slowly added their own touches to the menu.

CHAPTER FOUR

"Hey, Jules." Mitch Ford waved with one hand while wiping down the counter. "What can I do for you on this lovely day?"

"Could I get four boxed sandwiches with sides and a gallon of your strawberry lemonade?"

"Sure. What kind of sandwiches?"

"How about turkey, ham, roast beef, and pimento cheese."

"No problem. Give me a few minutes. Why don't you sample the dark chocolate peanut candy Donna made last night?"

"Yum." Jules picked up a dark chocolate blob filled with peanuts and popped it in her mouth. "Delicious."

Donna breezed in from the back with two trays of the couple's famous cheese stick crackers. "Hey, Jules. How's life at the campground?"

"It's busy, but that's a good thing. And these chocolates are wonderful."

Donna's eyes sparkled. "Thanks. And keep the folks coming to town. We love the business."

"Will do." Jules looked at the candy the Fords had stacked on tables near the cash register. The little lunch counter, a favorite among locals, now included event catering and gifts.

"Here you go." Mitch Ford stacked boxes in a shopping bag.

His wife disappeared in the back.

"I hope you get lots of visits from my guests this weekend." Jules handed him her credit card.

Mitch smiled. "I put some coupons in the bag if you'd like to share them with your guests."

About fifteen minutes later, Jules rolled up into the driveway. A large wooden sign and a tree-lined drive greeted resort visitors. She followed the maintenance road to her cabin and parked in the garage.

Balancing the bag of boxed sandwiches, the lemonade jug, and her purse, she walked across the field. After she managed to get the store's screen door open, she nodded to Emily, who was on the phone. Jules dropped the bag on the counter in the office and petted Bijou.

Emily stuck her head in the back office.

"How's it been?" Jules asked.

"Not bad. Roxanne went with Jake to make sure everything was okay at the meadow. They should be back soon. I love that so many of the cruisers show up in costumes. It's been fun checking them in. I saw Elvis, and he liked his gift bag."

"I brought boxed sandwiches in case anyone is hungry."

"Oh, yum. Lula Belle's is the best. And you got strawberry lemonade. Jules, you rock."

As Emily checked out each of the sandwich boxes, Roxanne and Jake came in through the back. Jake stomped several times to shake the mud loose from his boots.

"How's life at the meadow?" Jules asked.

"Fine. No issues. By my last count, there are about fifteen couples left to check in between tonight and tomorrow." Roxanne pulled cups and napkins out of the cabinet.

"Twelve," Emily chimed in.

"I picked up dinner from Lula Belle's. Anyone hungry?" Jules asked.

Emily grabbed the ham sandwich box and retreated to the kitchenette area in the back.

"It's been a long time since breakfast. Thanks." Jake selected the roast beef.

"You okay with turkey?" Roxanne asked.

"That's fine. Take what you want," Jules said.

"Nobody around here makes a better pimento cheese spread than Lula Belle's," Roxanne said.

The room fell silent as the group munched on the sandwiches made with thick, homemade bread. The Fords had packed each box with pasta salad, garlic cheese sticks that crunched with just a hint of cayenne pepper, grapes, and a gooey brownie.

The bell on the door tinkled at about the same time most of the food disappeared. Bijou jumped immediately to attention.

Emily slid out and pulled the bottom of the Dutch door closed. "Oh, hi, Deputy Dempsey. May I help you?"

"Is Roxanne Mallory here?"

"I'm back here, Bubba. What can I do for you?" She opened the Dutch door and faced the deputy.

"Ms. Mallory, I need to talk to you for a minute." He scowled.

"Well, go ahead. I'm right here."

He shifted his weight from one foot to the other. "I need you to come in for questioning." The deputy fidgeted and then stepped forward into the back office.

"What?" Her voice rose an octave. "Bubba, I have things to do. Can't it wait until tomorrow or Monday?"

"It shouldn't take long. The sheriff sent me over here to bring you in. He's got more questions."

"Are you arresting her?" Jules took several steps toward the deputy.

"Uh, no. But the task force wants to talk to her. Now, please come with me." He stepped back from Jules.

Roxanne drew up to her full height in her red three-inch Manolo Blahniks and stared at the deputy. "Do they really need to see me tonight?"

"Yes. Sheriff said now. Please follow me."

Roxanne sighed heavily. "Emily, hand me my purse, please."

"Wait a minute." Jules pointed her index finger at the deputy.

"It's okay, Jules. It shouldn't take long. I don't have anything else to tell them. Thanks, Emily." Roxanne took her red Gucci Soho bag and sashayed to the door.

"Wait up. You'll have to ride in the back. County policy doesn't allow civilians up front in official police vehicles." Deputy Dempsey lumbered after her.

"I will do no such thing, Bubba. You can follow me to the county courthouse. I will not be paraded through town in the back of your squad car. And, Jules, please call the lawyer and have him meet me at the station." She headed to her white Mercedes.

The deputy trotted down the stairs after Roxanne. Jules reached for her cell phone to call the family attorney. Hopefully, he would know someone who could help Roxanne if her chat with the sheriff turned into more than a few simple questions.

Chapter Five

Friday

Jules had called and texted Roxanne repeatedly after Deputy Dempsey came for her yesterday evening. Not a peep from her aunt. Jules tossed and turned all night, thinking the worst. When the sun started peeking through her blinds, she jumped in the shower. At least being in the office would make her feel like she was doing something.

"Come on, Bijou. Let's go to work." She grabbed a muffin.

The Jack Russell Terrier bounced around until Jules snapped on the leash and opened the door.

The cool morning air enveloped them on their walk to the office. Nothing stirred on the classic-trailer side of the resort. She made a mental note to check on the meadow later after the sun had made its full entrance over the mountains.

Jules put a cup in the coffee machine and sat down while her computer booted. "Bijou, what are we going to do about all this? I know Aunt Roxanne had nothing to do with Mr. Perkins's murder."

She opened her laptop and took a bite of her banana nut muffin. There had to be a clue in the files from the thumb drive. Jules zeroed in on the spreadsheet. The first column was filled with numbers and letters separated by dashes. Another column contained phone numbers. Dollar amounts in red, black, or green stood out in the last column. She copied one of the number-letter combinations and pasted it in Google. An entry for a company called MedPro popped up on her screen. She put in four others, and several different medical devices appeared. All from MedPro. They turned out to be serial numbers for pacemakers, insulin pumps, and implantable cardioverter-defibrillators. What was the color-coding on the dollar amounts? And who bought this many medical devices? She thought Ira Perkins was a novelist. It was time to do some research on her odd guest.

Bijou danced at the Dutch door.

"Hey, puppy. I hear ya." Her aunt freed her hand from her purse and several shopping bags.

"Roxanne, I'm so glad to see you." Jules grabbed her aunt and hugged her. "You didn't answer any of my texts. I thought Bubba threw you in the slammer."

"Sorry, kiddo. Didn't mean to make you worry, but I got home late. The lawyer didn't get to the police station until after eight, and I refused to answer any questions without him, and that made Sheriff Hobbs fume. Then I found out from Henry I didn't even have to stay. I should have walked out. You'd like Henry. He and I grabbed a late dinner after he determined I didn't need a lawyer."

"Henry?"

"Henry Osburn. He's the criminal lawyer Karl sent over. An interesting guy. Mid-fifties and divorced. And my phone died sometime during the evening, so I didn't get any of yesterday evening's messages."

"You're giving me gray hairs." Jules sighed.

"You're a redhead, like my mother. Gray doesn't show for a long time. Be thankful." Roxanne leaned over to pat Bijou. "It wasn't a total waste of time. I've got a date with Henry this week. We're going to Richmond for some art opening."

"Only you would get dragged down to the police station in a murder investigation and end up with a date with your would-be lawyer. Since you're here, I'm going to head over to the meadow and check on our guests." Jules shook her head in disbelief at her social butterfly aunt.

"Hey, there's an FBI agent on the sheriff's task force. He's kinda cute. I'm sure he'll be around soon to ask questions. Bijou and I will keep things on an even keel here," Roxanne said.

Jules drove the golf cart by the lodge, toward the meadow, and then down the path that ran through the woods. A few guests walked along the paths that ran from their campers to the lodge, where a hearty breakfast of quiche, muffins, or gooey chocolate-chip pancakes awaited.

When she drove out of the verdant woods, the meadow burst into a kaleidoscope of color. Silver teardrop campers, tiny tow-behinds, dotted the landscape as far as the eye could see. All of the guests had decorated their areas with lights, flags, and lawn gear. A fun city had sprung up overnight. People strolled about and greeted friends. The smell of bacon wafted through the air and overpowered the usual scent of pine trees.

The teardrop campers, shaped like their name, were about eight or ten feet long, depending on the model. Each slept two adults snuggly with room inside for only a bed. The trailers that could be towed with a car had a pop-up door at the back that opened into an outdoor kitchen area.

Jules parked the cart near a tree and walked around to check on her guests. The classic cars ran the gamut from souped-up roadsters to hot rods from a bygone era. She spotted Jake seated in a lawn chair at a campsite. He waved her over.

"Hey, this is my boss, Jules Keene," he said to the older couple. "She's the one who made all this possible. Jules, this is Al and Terri Patterson. They drove down here from Connecticut."

"It's nice to meet you." Jules faced the little party. "You came all that way for this event?"

"Yes, and no." Al smiled. We pick three or four teardrop meet-ups each year, and we combine them with our vacations. We're going from here to Myrtle Beach and then to Florida."

"We're so glad you decided to stay with us here in the Blue Ridge Mountains," Jules said.

"Would you like some coffee or breakfast?" Terri asked.

"No thank you. I should get back to the office. If you all need anything, please let one of us know."

"Jake's filling us in on places to see around here," Al said. "He's a great tour guide."

"He can do just about anything." Jules patted Jake on the shoulder.

He looked at her and smiled.

She waved to the cruisers and continued her stroll through the campsites.

A lot of the guests had put a great deal of time and money into their cars and campers. Her favorite was a gold Studebaker with the personalized license plate, MIDAS, that towed a gold teardrop trailer that glinted in the morning sunlight.

Pleased that the resort was filled for the weekend, she headed back to the office. Jules sank into her chair to do some more poking around the files on Ira Perkins's thumb drive. Maybe this was research for his story, but why would he go to all the trouble of hiding a thumb drive in the trailer's bathroom? It didn't make sense.

After hitting a wall with the medical device spreadsheets, she shifted gears and started searching for Ira Perkins. She found lots of entries, but only one matched on LinkedIn for an Ira Perkins from Alexandria, Virginia. Oddly, it listed him as a network engineer and then later as a network security administrator, first at a contracting company and then for MedPro. She couldn't find any information about him being a writer.

Grabbing her phone, she texted Pixel. **Can you research Ira Perkins from Alexandria? Google didn't yield much.**

Not a problem. Still working on the encrypted file. Love challenges, came the response.

Roxanne approached the back and hung over the bottom portion of the Dutch door.

Jules set the phone on her desk. "Hey. What did Ira Perkins tell you about himself?"

"Not you too. I'm tired of answering questions about that old goat. Absolutely nothing happened between us. We had a couple of drinks and talked late one evening. The police keep harping on my relationship with him. There was no relationship. We had drinks and some boring conversation. That was the extent of it."

"I'm curious. All I know is he said he was a writer, drove a red Corvette, and paid for an extended stay with a credit card. And he had sort of a northern accent."

"New York. He said he was originally from Brooklyn. During the dot-com bubble, he moved south for a job and stayed. He told me he was working on a novel that was sure to be a bestseller, and he didn't want to be disturbed. He said his work was going to get a lot of attention."

"Did he say anything about his job? Did he take a leave of absence?"

"I don't know. From his blabbering, it sounded like he was a wealthy man of leisure who had quit work to write a book. He said he found us online and the mountains were the perfect inspiration for his creativity. He liked the small-town life around here."

"Anything else?"

"He was a bore who did the majority of the talking. It was mostly about who he knew, how rich he was, and how smart he was. He liked eating at Lula Belle's and Pop's in town. And he told me he planned to extend his stay here." Roxanne rolled her eyes.

"Something's not right about his story. According to the internet, he's a network security administrator. A computer guy. His LinkedIn site hasn't been updated in about a year. And where did the newfound wealth come from?"

"Don't know. He kind of hinted he'd come into his fortune and that his life was going to be so different." Roxanne reached for a mug and a teabag.

"Something's fishy. Do you think you can keep everything humming here for a couple of hours? I need to run some errands in town."

There was more to Mr. Perkins than he let on. Jules needed to do some more checking into him, and the ride into town would give her time to plan her next steps.

"Take your time," Roxanne said.

Jules bent over to pet Bijou. "You be good for Aunt Roxanne. I'm sure she's got some treats around here somewhere for you."

At the magic "treat" word, Bijou's ears perked up as she looked around for her reward. Roxanne picked her up, and they shared the desk chair while Bijou nibbled on a bacon-flavored goody.

"See y'all later," Jules said. "Do you need anything from town?"

"Nope. But you'll need to make a run to Sam's Club next week for supplies. We're low on sunscreen already," Roxanne said.

"Okay. Make a list, and I'll go Tuesday or Wednesday." Jules picked up her purse and phone.

After a quick drive through town, she found parking in front of the courthouse and city office complex. The small jail and the courthouse bookended the sheriff's office. Lots of green space bordered by full oaks made it a nice park area in the middle of Fern Valley's business district.

Jules walked up the cement steps and pushed open the glass door. "Hey, Millie. Is Sheriff Hobbs around?"

"Well hi, Jules." The older woman had a bleached bouffant hairdo. Her cat-eyed glasses dangled from a silver beaded chain. "What brings you to town?" She flipped through a stack of papers and highlighted something.

"My cleanup team found something at the resort that I think the sheriff should look at."

"Sure. I'll buzz him as soon as he gets off the phone. Have a seat over there." She pointed behind Jules.

Jules slid onto a beige plastic chair that looked like it had been here since disco was the rage. She entertained herself catching up on email until Millie yelled and made her jump.

"Jules, Sheriff is finally off the phone. He'll see you now. Turn left at the corner, and his office is the first one on the left." Millie buzzed open the door.

Jules found the correct door and tapped lightly until she heard a faint, "Come in."

"Hi, Sheriff Hobbs," she said. "Mel and Crystal found something in Ira Perkins's trailer."

"Have a seat."

She dropped in the black captain's chair in front of his wooden desk. His dark-paneled office smelled like a cross between peppermint and pipe tobacco.

"Whatcha got?"

"When the ladies were cleaning the trailer, they found this taped to the back of the toilet tank."

He reached for the bag she produced. "The gloves were there, too?"

"No. I used those to pull off the tape and pick up the thumb drive. I was trying not to mess up any prints." She looked at her shoes.

"Thanks. I'll get the team to look this over. Maybe it'll open up another avenue of investigation. Notice anything else?"

"Nope. Life at the resort is back to normal. Except for Bubba, I mean Charles's visit yesterday."

He cleared his throat and stared over his desk at her. "Did he do something inappropriate?"

"Uh, no. But he told Aunt Roxanne she had to come in for questioning, and he wouldn't leave without her. You can't really think Roxanne killed one of our guests. You've known her and my dad since grade school."

An almost smile crept across his face. "Sorry if Charles was a little too aggressive. He gets excited easily. He usually handles traffic issues and school crossings. We haven't had a murder here in over ten years. There's a task force looking into this with support from the state police and the feds. Roxanne answered most of our questions. I don't think we'll need to talk to her again."

"I'm sure she'll be relieved to hear that. Have you talked to Jane Jenkins or anyone at the paper yet?"

"We had a short chat."

"This is bigger than a church craft sale or the annual chili cookoff."

"I know. She doesn't get to cover hard news much. I hope it doesn't take on a life of its own. We'll see what Tuesday's edition brings. Thanks for dropping this off. Tell Roxanne and Jake hello for me."

"Will do." Jules stepped out into the hallway. Her phone binged with a text.

What's your ETA? Something odd is going on, Roxanne texted.

Be there in a few. What's up?

Her aunt didn't respond, so Jules zoomed off in her Jeep to the resort. Her stomach did a flip-flop. What now? The short ride seemed like an eternity for the anxious Jules.

As promised, within a few minutes, she bounded up the stairs and burst into the store. Not seeing anyone up front, Jules jogged to the office. "Bijou, Hey, baby. What's going on? Where's Aunt Roxanne?"

The dog's bobbed tail wiggled.

The back door opened. Roxanne came in with a large cardboard box.

"What's up?" Jules put her hands on her hips.

"I had to get some more flyers from storage."

"No. I mean your text."

"Oh yeah, that. Right after you left, this guy came in. He was about thirty, tall, and too much on the skinny side for my taste. Looked like he hadn't been out in the sun in a while. Anyway, he came in and said he was Ira Perkins's nephew and he was here to collect his things," Roxanne said.

"What did you say?"

"I told him the sheriff took everything."

"That's it?" Jules asked.

"No. Then he asked to rent Ira's camper. I told him it wasn't available because it needed a good cleaning and then he left. He said he'd go into town to see Sheriff Hobbs."

"Interesting. The sheriff didn't mention a nephew. He said he was having trouble locating the next of kin. An ex-wife, I think. How did the guy act before he left?"

"He seemed okay. He didn't act angry or anything. The whole thing was weird." Roxanne set the box on the counter. She pushed a stray strand of hair from her eyes and refilled the rack of brochures for local attractions.

Jules wondered about the nephew and instantly grew suspicious. "Did the guy give a name?"

"Nope, but that wasn't the strangest thing. About twenty minutes after the first guy left, another guy with dark hair came in. And he said he was Ira's nephew. He was here to collect his belongings, and he thanked us for being kind to his uncle. This guy was short and stocky. And this one chattered incessantly."

"Two nephews? On the same day?" The hair on the back of Jules's neck stood up, and butterflies danced around her insides. This was no coincidence.

"Yep. I sent them both to see the sheriff."

"Did the second one have a name?"

"None that he offered. He acted jittery," her aunt said. "He kept looking at his feet and fidgeting."

Jules frowned. Time to check the security cameras again. "I'll call the sheriff to give him a heads-up."

"Already did." Her aunt rummaged through the drawer and pulled out a nail file. "He'd like any video you find."

Jules scanned the video feed. Finding the clip, she watched the first guy park his green truck on the main road and hike to the office. But the camera didn't catch a clear view of the license plate. So why did this guy keep coming back to her place?

A little while later, a gray Honda Civic pulled in and parked. A shorter guy jumped out, and he spent several minutes checking out the property. It looked like he was going to walk around the grounds. He stopped and paced in front of the store. Then the camera caught him stepping on the porch. Jules flipped to another camera. It captured the first guy as he walked down the main road to his truck. She couldn't see a license plate. Jules checked the other cameras. In another shot, the shorter "nephew" walked toward the vintage trailers and made a phone call. After he pocketed his phone and walked around the grassy area, he climbed in the gray Honda. Jules copied down the license plate number for that vehicle.

A surge of adrenaline pumped through her veins. Jules should report this to the police and let it go. But she couldn't resist the chance to do a little snooping on her own. After all, it happened on her property. She reached for her phone and texted Pixel. ***Could you check a plate for me? Virginia XBT-394 Gray Honda.***

Her phone beeped. **No problem. Should be quick.**

Jules replied with a smiley face and set down her phone. A twinge of guilt about poking around zipped through her, but she assuaged the feeling by sending Sheriff Hobbs the video clip. She had no intention of sitting back and waiting to see what would happen next.

Chapter Six

Saturday

Jules jolted out of a deep sleep. She lay still, listening for what had interrupted her rest. Her cell buzzed on the nightstand. She blinked and fumbled for the phone. Bijou stirred in her doggie bed in the corner. The time flashed 2:38 AM. Phone calls in the middle of the night were never good. "Hello."

"Sorry to wake you, Boss, but something's up near the vintage campers," Jake said.

"I'll be right there."

"It's the Robin Hood." He clicked off.

Jules sighed and threw on a sweatshirt and jeans. She stepped into her sneakers and pulled her long red hair into a scrunchie. "Stay here, Bijou. I'll be back as soon as I can." She hoped the trailer wasn't jinxed.

Grabbing her phone and keys, she locked the door and jogged across the damp grass to the trailers. Jake stood on the patio of the trailer where Ira Perkins had stayed.

"What's up?" she whispered.

"I was doing my last security check, and something looked odd over here. The door was askew. The lock's broken, and the door's off one of its hinges."

"Did you go inside?"

"I waited for you."

She pulled on the door handle and flipped on her flashlight application on her phone. "Not again."

The entire trailer had been tossed. Several of the cabinet doors had been torn off and the contents strewn around. Someone had shredded all the cushions and throw pillows, and the kitchen cabinets and contents of the drawers had been dumped on the floor.

She stepped back out on the patio and phoned the sheriff's office. After disconnecting the call, she turned to Jake. "They're going to send Charles over. It may be a couple of hours before forensics can get here." She dropped into a patio chair to wait.

"I didn't notice anything out of the ordinary when I came through here about ten-thirty. And no strange vehicles."

"What are you doing out so late or early? You know what I mean."

"I finished up around ten-thirty and went to the barn to work on a project. On my way home, I went over to check on the hired security at the meadow. Everything's quiet over there."

"Good. But you're always working. We'll talk about that later." She adjusted her ponytail holder.

"I'm fine. I don't mind keeping an eye on things for you."

Jules raised an eyebrow. She didn't want to take advantage of her employees, especially the ones who lived on the property. He should have a life outside of the resort.

"It's pretty clear Ira Perkins wasn't who he said he was. Roxanne said two guys came by yesterday for his things. Both claimed to be his nephew. Suddenly, there's an interest in Ira Perkins's last address. And now this." She wasn't sure whether it was the cool morning breeze or thoughts of the hidden thumb drive that made her shiver. She pulled her knees toward her and curled up in the chair.

"Did the nephews show up on the security feed?" Jake asked.

"I got clips of them coming and going. One was the green truck guy who parked on the main road again. The shorter guy parked his Civic in the guest lot. As soon as the deputy gets here, I'll go check the cameras again."

About twenty minutes later, headlights from the police cruiser bounced off the trailers as the deputy pulled in the main driveway and killed his engine. Charles slammed the car door and ambled over to the trailer.

Charles waddled over to the pair. "Up kinda late, aren't ya?"

"We've had a break-in," Jules said. "Jake called me when he discovered it on his rounds."

"Did you go in?" Deputy Dempsey asked.

"Far enough to see it's been ransacked," she said.

"Sheriff said I'm to stay here until forensics arrives. I'm securing the crime scene." Charles looked around the patio area.

"Do you need anything?" she asked.

"Nope. I'm fine." The deputy made himself at home in the patio chair Jake had vacated. Charles pulled out his phone and started tapping. "You got guest Wi-Fi?"

"Yes. Type 'Robin Hood' for the password. If you need anything else, I'll be in the office."

The deputy nodded but didn't reply. He stared at his phone.

"I'm going to do a lap around the classic campers. I'll meet you in the office when I'm done," Jake said.

"If you're going by the cabins, could you pick up Bijou? I left her at home, and I'm probably going to be in the office for a while." Jules tossed him her keys.

They parted at the camper. She jogged to the office's back door and punched in the security code. While her computer woke up, she made a strong cup of coffee. This morning might require at least two.

She started at the ten o'clock point on the security feeds and scrolled through all the cameras. The one at the main gate picked up a green truck a little after twelve-thirty. The driver had pulled off the asphalt on the main entrance like before. A little later, she noticed a guy in a dark hoodie trekking through the parking lot by the trailers. A smaller guy with lighter hair trailed behind him. The cameras didn't catch their exodus. She looked through the earlier footage again.

The door opened, and Bijou bounded in with way too much exuberance for this hour.

"Hey, puppy. Did you go for a ride with Jake?" She scooped up the Jack

Russell Terrier and kissed her on the head.

"Find anything?" Jake asked.

"The same truck near the front gate. Then two guys walked through the parking lot."

"Two? Did you catch him or them leaving?"

"No. I'm going through it again to make sure I didn't miss anything." Jules scrolled through the video.

He started the coffee maker and then pulled Roxanne's chair next to Jules.

Jake leaned over her shoulder for a better view, and she smelled his spicy cologne. They spent the next hour pouring over the footage. About two-fifteen on the timestamp, two guys jumped in the green truck and exited down the main driveway without the headlights on. Jules copied the evening's feeds and uploaded the file for the sheriff. She rubbed her eyes and Jake yawned.

"This is odd. There are two guys this time. In an earlier clip, it looked like the shorter guy's hair was lighter. So, all I have is one is taller than the other." She shrugged. "Roxanne said the other guy claiming to be Ira's nephew was a short guy with dark hair."

"I wonder who they are?" He yawned again.

"You don't have to stay up. I can hang out here until the forensic team gets here. Bijou's a good guard dog."

He laughed as they looked at the snoring dog in the pink puffy bed. "You sure?"

"Yep. We're fine. It's no use for both of us looking like we howled all night."

"I'm going to catch some Zs. I'll be back around eight." He patted her shoulder as he turned to leave. His hand lingered long enough for Jules to notice, but thoughts of the three trespassers jolted her back to reality instead of dwelling on what Jake's touch meant, if anything.

Jules had an uneasy feeling about this guy who popped up too frequently at the resort at night. And now he had a friend with him. Was the shorter guy the second nephew? Or was there a third guy?

Jules opened a new document in Word and made a list of everything she knew. She saved the file and then went back to the spreadsheet. He had to be up to something to make people keep coming back to the campground. She knew deep down that two alleged nephews were looking for something, probably the thumb drive. She stared at the numbers. There were names, model numbers, phone numbers, and color-coded dollar amounts. Why medical appliances?

She made another cup of coffee and researched each entry. She added a notes field to her copy of the spreadsheet and filled it with what she found.

A little after eight-thirty, Roxanne came in. Bijou ran to greet her.

"Hey there. You're up early again. And why are the police back? Is it that dreaded Ira Perkins again? Why can't we just put him to rest?"

"Jake spotted a break-in on his rounds. Guess which trailer? Mr. Perkins keeps popping up in our lives. Someone broke the door and tossed the contents again. There were two guys caught on camera. This time, it looks like the intruders tore up the inside of the camper."

"What could that old hyena have that would make someone so determined to keep coming back? And why so many nephews? Let me see the clip,"

Jules clicked on several keys.

Roxanne leaned over her niece's shoulder to get a better look. "Play it again."

Jules reversed it.

"It's dark. I can't quite say for sure, but that second guy doesn't look like the second nephew I talked to."

"It doesn't look like our guest was writing the next bestseller, either."

"So he was using us as a place to hide out?" Roxanne mused.

"Maybe. But he didn't act like he was hiding. He went into town a lot. Is Charles still out there?" Jules asked.

"Yep. It looks like he's got company with the forensic folks."

Jules let out a heavy sigh. "I want all this nastiness to die down. I hope it doesn't have an adverse effect on business."

"A couple of guests have asked about it, but I don't get the sense anyone's too bothered. Mrs. Greenbaum and her friend became instant celebrities after discovering Ira's body. I saw them holding court over at the lodge during a game of cards. I'm sure they both have stories to take home with them. Hey, it'll be a vacation they'll remember for a long time. Maybe you could do a mystery-themed event for Halloween?"

Jules wrinkled her freckled nose and shook her head. "I'd like to forget it, if that's possible. Say, what's the plan for today?"

"The cruise-in folks are having a jam session tonight in the amphitheater. Anyone with an instrument or who likes to sing is invited to join them. And tomorrow night is family movie night. Emily is showing *The Aristocats* and *Finding Nemo*. Jake said he'd put up the screen tomorrow evening and move the popcorn machine over there."

"Both sound fun. I'm going to walk over to see what Mel has for breakfast. Can I bring you anything?"

"Yes, please. I didn't eat breakfast this morning. I'm starved." Roxanne settled in at the other desk.

Twenty minutes later, Jules carried two cartons of chocolate-chip pancakes, with syrup and bacon, up the steps from the carport to the office. Bijou greeted her at the door with a sudden interest in the enticing scents escaping from the cartons.

Between bites, Roxanne said, "This is good. I haven't had chocolate-chip pancakes in years. I'll finish payroll today. And I'll have some checks for you to sign."

The bell on the door chimed. "I'll get it." Roxanne jumped out of her seat like she was expecting someone.

Bijou barked.

"Good morning, Kelly family. How are you all?" Roxanne asked from the front of the building.

Jules didn't hear the answer.

"Here are brochures on local caverns, the waterfall, and horseback riding. We have an equipment closet in the back. You can check out any of the fun stuff. What can I get you?" Roxanne paused. "Well, y'all come back when you're ready. We're in the office until five. If you think you'll want it after that, I can check it out to you now. We have iron skillets and all the fixings for s'mores. All you have to do is take it over to the fire pit and enjoy summer yumminess. I even have a copy of our world-famous recipe.

Chocolate, marshmallows, and graham crackers. There's nothing better on a summer evening."

"Thanks," a female voice said.

"Have fun on your adventures. Outdoor movie night is tomorrow. Bye."

Jules polished off the rest of her breakfast, and Roxanne returned to her desk and her pancakes.

Jules opened the spreadsheet again. Three major kinds of medical appliances with a variety of model numbers jumped out at her. The phone number column had area codes from all over the country. Why was this information so important to Mr. Perkins?

Bijou growled, breaking Jules's concentration on the data. She looked up as Deputy Dempsey entered the store.

"Hi, Charles. What can I do for you?" She opened the bottom half of the door and made sure Bijou stayed put.

"Forensics is done. The camper door is off the hinges. Do you want to come out and see it before we leave? You know, to secure your property."

Jules followed Charles to the Robin Hood trailer. The front door, hanging askew on one hinge, had seen better days. Inside the little trailer, it looked like a hurricane had jostled the contents. Smudges from the fingerprinting dotted every surface.

"Hey, Charles," Jake said from the patio area. "You all done here?"

"Yep. But you need to do something with this door."

"Hopefully, I can repair it. It's original to the nineteen forty-seven trailer, so it's going to be hard to get another one. If there is another one."

Jules joined the men outside. "Jake, do we have a big trash bin that's empty?"

"I'll get you one. How bad is it?"

"It's worse than last time." Jules sighed and looked around the outside of the trailer.

Jake stuck his head inside the trailer. "Whoa. Somebody was looking for something important. I'll be back in a little while to help you."

"Charles, we'll take care of the door. Please thank the sheriff for me. This time, I saw two intruders." Jules tried to emphasize the point by staring at the deputy.

"I'm heading out. I'm sure the sheriff will be in touch with you." The rotund deputy didn't seem impressed with her new information.

Jules stepped into the chaos inside the little trailer. After snapping some photos, she returned the contents of the cabinets and drawers and then loaded the dishwasher with the plates, cups, and utensils.

"Jules. Hey, Jules."

"What's up?" She stuck her head outside.

Jake brushed his longish hair out of his eyes. "I've got a trash can here for you. And I told Mel to add this to her cleaning list tomorrow."

"It's going to need more scrubbing. And I've probably got another hour or so to get this mess straightened."

"I'm going to see if I can repair this door. If not, I'll secure it, and we'll figure out our next steps. Holler if you need help." Jake unloaded a large trash can and returned to the campground's ATV.

"Will do." Jules returned to the cleanup. The cushions on the built-in sofa and the throw pillows, along with the comforter and bed pillows, had been sliced and the stuffing strewn around the small room. The camper looked like the inside of a snow globe with all the fluff.

Jules spent the next hour filling the trash can and restoring order to the little trailer. She made a mental note to get a copy of the sheriff's report for her insurance claim. She had a lot of work to do on this one before she could put it back in the rental rotation.

She dropped the last load in the trash can as Jake approached in the four-wheel ATV. He had the camper's door in the back-cargo area.

"Hey," he said. "I was able to bang out the dent and repair the hinges. It's not perfect, but I think I can get it to hang correctly and lock."

"Fingers crossed." She dusted pillow filling off her jeans.

He aligned the hinges and rehung the door and did some tapping and pushing. "Voila!"

"Jake, you worked magic on that. Thank you. That would have been costly to replace the vintage door."

"Glad to be of help. I'll take the trash to the dumpster. Let me know if you need anything else." Jake loaded the rolling trash can in the back of the metallic gray ATV.

Jules's phone dinged with a text from Pixel. **Found something interesting. Meet me today? Can you come to C-ville?**

Lunch?

Bagby's at 1:00, Pixel replied.

A little after one, Jules grabbed a small wooden table in the back. Bagby's, a local favorite, sat next to a 1960s gas station and a laundromat. The wood paneling and the 1970s décor didn't match the foodie menu that attracted university students and locals.

The petite Pixel breezed in the front door. Jules rose and hugged her friend.

"Sorry I'm late. I got a call as I was leaving. Have you ordered yet?" Pixel asked.

Jules shook her head.

The two women made their way to the counter. Jules ordered the "Green Turkey" with cream cheese, sprouts, and avocado, while Pixel settled on the "Groovy Californian" veggie sandwich.

They waited while their lunches were prepared and then took their drinks and food to Jules's table in a back corner across from the counter, where they could talk in private.

"I had to do some work to find that license plate you saw on your security tape, but I finally found it. Here." She handed Jules a hot pink sticky note. "Normally, it's not that hard."

"So, who's Kevin Bailey?"

"I knew you'd ask. He's a freelance reporter in his mid-thirties out of Washington, D. C. He has bylines in a lot of newspapers and blogs. Investigative stuff. And he drives a gray Civic."

"I wonder what he wants with Mr. Perkins?"

"Call him and ask. Oh, and I've been banging hard on your encrypted folder. I didn't have much success, but I called in some big guns. After a late-night session, we broke through." Pixel's brown eyes sparkled with a devilish gleam.

"I'm sorry it was such a pain."

"My friends like chances to show off their skills." Pixel pulled a black thumb drive from her pocket and passed it across the table.

"What do I owe you?" Jules took a bite of her sandwich.

"Nothing. It was kind of fun. Glad to help."

"I can't thank you enough. The police are working on it, but I want to know what the dead guy was up to and why he picked my resort for his extended stay. So, what did you uncover?"

"There's a poorly written play or script in one of the folders. I got bored with it, so I stopped reading. And then another folder has some bank records, mostly transfers."

Jules swallowed hard. What was Mr. Perkins doing? "I think there's more to Mr. Perkins's activities than a list of medical products." She sighed and closed her eyes for a few moments.

"The bank is in the Cayman Islands," Pixel whispered excitedly.

Butterflies awakened in Jules's stomach. She had seen enough movies and true crime shows to know the Caymans were always connected with dodgy, if not illegal, transactions. She couldn't wait to get back to the office and explore the new files. She should probably let Sheriff Hobbs handle it, but it wouldn't hurt to check it out first. Plus, he had a task force working on it. He probably already knew about this.

Pixel interrupted Jules's thoughts. "So, anything else going on with you?"

"No. Just work. I have a whole meadow full of classic cars and restored trailers. And all my vintage trailers' bookings are solid for the summer. That's good news. What have you been up to besides breaking encryption on a dead guy's folder?"

Pixel's grin made her look like an imp. "Your guy's folder was pretty sophisticated. Somebody worked hard to keep people out."

"They didn't count on your friends."

"We like to think of ourselves as the guys in white hats, even though we cross the line sometimes. We try to right the wrongs and help the underdogs."

"Real life avengers..."

"It's funny you should say that. One of the guys is a full-time hacker and part-time RLSH, Real Life Superhero."

"Huh? That's a thing? With tights and capes?" Jules hoped she didn't roll her eyes.

"Yup. They dress up as their alter ego and fight crime on the streets. He has a costume he wears. It's kind of a purplish bodysuit. His mother made it for him."

"Okay. Sounds kinda dangerous." Jules wrinkled her nose. "People really do that?" She popped the last bite of her sandwich in her mouth.

Pixel nodded her head vigorously. "The police see it as silly and vigilante. He's gotten in fights a couple of times. And he got arrested once. I think he does it for kicks. They were thrilled when I told them we were helping crack the code on a folder of a guy who had been murdered."

"How many people did you tell?" Jules stared across the table at her friend. Her cheeks heated. She worried too many people knew about the file.

"I didn't give specifics. I can trust these guys. There's honor among hackers. They believe they're fighting for truth and justice. It was a race to see who could break the encryption first. After that, the fun wore off, and they lost interest. They didn't really care what was inside your folder. A spreadsheet and a bad script wouldn't hold their attention for more than five minutes, if that. For them, the fun was cracking the encryption. This morning, they're working to uncover who did the siren prank in Los Angeles. Somebody hacked into the emergency alert and set off alarms all over the city."

"I don't know what we've stepped into, and I was trying to keep the people who know about it to a small group. Somebody has trashed my trailer twice looking for something. Probably Mr. Perkins's files, and I want to know why they keep coming back. There's got to be something valuable they're looking for," Jules said.

Concern flashed across Pixel's face. "Be careful. And don't get in too deep. If there are accounts in the Caymans, there's money involved. Usually big money that someone wants to hide in offshore accounts."

Chapter Seven

Sunday

After a quick shower, Jules grabbed a banana and fed Bijou kibbles. She poured coffee into a to-go cup. "I'm gonna check out the meadow. Wanna go?"

The terrier heard the magic word and turned her head. Her ears pointed straight up.

Jules snapped the red leash in place. Bijou led the way to get the golf cart. The terrier jumped in and claimed the shotgun seat. The perfect weather made Jules want to have an outside adventure in the mountains. A hike or a bike ride would be the best way to spend the day. She reminded herself she needed to do more research on Mr. Perkins's files. So, she had to settle for tooling around the meadow with her furry sidekick.

She and Bijou bumped along the path through the woods. On the other side, many of the guests were busy breaking camp, while others lounged in chairs, enjoying their morning coffee and breakfast.

She waved to the Pattersons, who were sitting with another couple under a copse of oak trees. Jules slowed the cart, and Bijou barked her greeting.

"Shhhh!" Jules said to the dog. "How are you all doing?"

"Great," Al Patterson said. "You ordered up some fantastic weather. We appreciate it."

"I hope everyone enjoyed their stay," Jules said.

"We did," he said. "This is Tim and Kathleen Love from Cleveland. This is

Jules, the proprietor." He pointed toward the golf cart.

"It's just fabulous here. We're definitely coming back. We had so much fun in town at the craft beer tasting. And I bought the cutest little gifts for friends," Kathleen said.

"What do you all have planned for the day?" Jules pushed her bangs out of her eyes.

"Just enjoying the company right now," Al said. "We'll have lunch in town and head south today."

"We're going to go the other way to see the grandkids in Philadelphia before we head home," Kathleen said.

"Safe journeys! Let me or my team know if we can do anything for you. We'd love to have you back for another visit. Nature puts on a spectacular show in the fall."

Terri Patterson said, "We'll be sure to tell all our friends about how much fun we had."

Jules smiled as she put the golf cart in gear and waved at the couples as she headed around the loop to the rest of the campsites. Nothing looked amiss. Driving around the outer ring, she completed the circuit and headed down the maintenance road through the woods to the barn area.

Outside the barn, Lester gassed up the industrial mower. He saluted as she circled the lodge and the vintage trailers. A couple of families wandered to and from breakfast and their trailers. All quiet in Fern Valley. Life seemed to be back to normal.

She parked under the carport. "Come on, girl. Let's see what we can find in Mr. Perkins's files. Maybe today's our lucky day."

Bijou headed straight for her bed and her mid-morning nap while Jules zeroed in on the coffee maker for a refresh.

For the next two hours, Jules poured over the dollar figures in the two spreadsheets. She matched a handful of the green numbers to the bank list, but most entries were unique to each document. "Green for money," she said to the sleeping dog. "So, what do the black and red stand for? It's got to mean something." She stood and did several yoga poses to ward off the kink in her back. "Credits and debits?"

"I don't know what it means." Jake entered through the back door and darted toward the coffee maker.

Jules straightened up, embarrassed he had caught her stretching and strategizing with Bijou.

"The meadow is about half empty. When everyone clears out, Lester and I will start the cleanup. When Crystal finishes with the bath houses, I'll lock them up. You don't have anyone else scheduled for the meadow tomorrow, do you?" He put a mug under the spout and waited while the machine heated his coffee.

"Not until next week. There's a scouting campout arriving for a few days. We're expecting about a hundred and twenty-five teenaged boys and about fifty chaperones. They'll be tent camping."

"We haven't had tent campers since that folk festival last summer." Jake leaned against the counter.

"That was an interesting event, our own little Woodstock. Thanks for spearheading the cleanup efforts today."

"The cruise-in folks were fairly self-sufficient and quiet. A nice bunch of people."

"I saw the Pattersons this morning. They said to thank you for all of your help."

"I didn't do anything special. They needed a jump. Their car battery died."

"I appreciate it, and they did, too." Jules stacked her spreadsheets and straightened her desk.

Jake grabbed his coffee, patted Bijou on the head, and disappeared out the back door, leaving Jules with her thoughts.

The unreconciled spreadsheet numbers bothered her. She fished out her cell phone and dialed the first red number on the spreadsheet. It didn't take long to get a "this number is no longer in service" message. She dialed two more with the same results. On her fourth try, she got a live person.

"Hello," said a sleepy voice.

"Uh, Mr. Cain, Mr. Joseph Cain, please."

"You've got the wrong number. I don't know a Cain. Stop bothering me," he groused.

"I'm very sorry. I'll update my records." She clicked off. "Hmmmm. What do you think, Bijou? I think the red ones are outdated numbers. We can cross them off the list." Before she could continue to the next set of color-coded phone numbers, the bells on the door tinkled.

"Hello," said a female voice. "Anyone here?"

"Hi, Mrs. Fillmore. What can I do for you?"

"Sadly, Wyatt and I are checking out today. We had a lovely time. It was one of our most exciting vacations. And when we get home, we'll pick dates and get our reservations in for next year. Trudie and Bert are heading out today, too. I wanted to pop in and say thank you for a great time. And we did manage to spot a few birds."

"Very good. I'm glad you enjoyed your stay. We hope you'll come back."

"We'll definitely be back. Your resort is top-notch. And this is one adventure we won't forget. I've been telling everybody about all the fun here. I'll post pictures on Facebook as soon as I get back. Well, I've talked your ear off. Thanks again for everything. Here are our keys. And I have Trudie's, too. Oh, I left the iron skillet from our s'mores last night in the camper. I'll go back and get it."

"That's no problem. We'll pick it up this afternoon when we clean. Have safe travels. I look forward to seeing you all again soon."

Mrs. Fillmore waved on her way out. Jules closed out the paperwork on the two trailers and added them to Mel and Crystal's cleaning list. Before she could return to Mr. Perkins's numbers, the bell rang again. This time, a young couple with two toddlers came in. The youngest made a beeline for the first shelf full of brightly colored snacks. The father scooped him up, and the mother grabbed the older child by the hand.

"Hi, we're Anna and Sid Holmes. And we've got a reservation for the week."

"Welcome, Holmes family. I'm Jules Keene, and we have a reservation for you all in our vintage nineteen fifty-three Redman's New Moon trailer. It's famous for being the model Lucille Ball and Desi Arnaz used in the movie, *The Long, Long Trailer*. When we restored this one, we decked it out in honor of *I Love Lucy*."

"Lucy, Lucy," piped up the little girl with blond curls and apple-round cheeks. She clapped both of her pudgy hands.

Jules smiled. "I love Lucy, too. And I left a copy of the movie in there in case you haven't seen it. Here's your resort welcome package, a list of things to do around here, and the breakfast schedule. If you need anything, please let me know."

"Thank you so much." The wife handed Jules her credit card while her husband flipped through a brochure of local attractions.

"Here you are," Jules said after the charge cleared.

Bijou barked, and the little boy yelled, "Puppy!"

"That's Bijou. She works here, too."

"Doggy! See the doggy," the toddler begged.

"Sure, if you have a minute. Bijou likes to jump, so I'll hold her." Jules opened the bottom of the Dutch door and picked up the wiggly dog.

The little girl squealed, and the little boy patted the dog's head.

"They love dogs. Bijou is such a cute name. Mandy, tell her about your doggie."

"Edgar lives with us. He's big," Mandy said.

"Actually, he's almost a horse," her mother replied. "He's a Great Dane."

"Edgar's my friend." Mandy waved to Bijou.

"And now you have a friend named Bijou. She's a Jack Russell Terrier," Jules said.

"Okay, guys. Let's go find our trailer and then head into town," Mrs. Holmes said.

"You're in D-5, the last one in that row. If you all need sporting equipment or campfire gear, let us know. We have it all available for you here," Jules said.

"Bye, Bijou." Mandy waved over her shoulder.

Jules set the dog down in the back and closed the bottom half of the door. "Hey, there. You were a good girl. I'm gonna put you on the website."

Jules returned to the spreadsheet. Taking a deep breath, she picked up her cell phone and dialed the first number printed in black.

"Hello," Jules said. "Mr. Thompson, please."

"Speaking."

"Mr. Thompson, this is uh Tammy Shields from MedPro. I was calling to see if your insulin pump was working okay." Jules ran her finger across the row with Mr. Thompson's information.

"It's fine. I have no issues. Except for the medical bills. But I guess you can't do anything about that."

"I wanted to check on you and our product and make sure all is well. I'm glad to hear you're not having any issues with it. Thank you for your time."

She made four other calls to names and numbers in black. Everybody seemed satisfied with his or her device. So far, her snooping had yielded nothing but wrong or disconnected numbers and a bunch of satisfied clients. Investigative work was harder than she thought it would be. If she didn't turn up anything soon, she would give up on Mr. Perkins and let Sheriff Hobbs figure it out. It was none of her business, but inquisitiveness got the best of her. She wanted to know everything she could about things that affected her property.

She took a deep breath and dialed the first green number. "Hello. I'm calling for Mr. Clyde McMasters."

"Who the heck are you? And what do you want?" a gruff voice demanded.

"I'm Tammy Shields calling about your pacemaker."

"Now just a cotton pickin' minute. I paid that guy what he asked for. And it was a struggle. I don't have that kind of money lying around, especially after being sick. So, don't think you're getting another penny. Turn off the dern thing. I don't care anymore. And stop bothering me." The line went dead.

Jules dropped into her office chair. Well, that wasn't what she expected. She ran her finger across Mr. McMaster's row. Eight thousand dollars appeared in the far-right column.

On a whim, she dialed another green number, one with $10,000 in the last column.

"Hello," said a timid voice.

"Mrs. Grayson? Mrs. Georgie Grayson?"

"Yes. Do I know you?"

"No, Mrs. Grayson. I'm Tammy Shields. I'm calling about your pacemaker."

"Oh, dear." The woman began to sniffle. "Who are you? A man called last time."

"He's not available. I'm calling today." Jules tried to think of something else to say.

"I paid you once. And then my son found out. I can't get any more money. My son controls it now. You'll have to call him. Do you want his number?"

"Yeah, sure." Jules jotted the number with the North Carolina area code on the spreadsheet. "Thank you, Mrs. Grayson. I'll call your son."

What had she stepped into? Was Mr. Perkins extorting money from all these sick people? Preying on vulnerable people. Real nice, Mr. Perkins. The green numbers tallied up to over $2.5 million. She opened the other file with the bank records. The last bank entry was dated three weeks ago, and it was a wire transfer of $48,000. As of last week, there was $1.5 million in the account.

How was she going to tell the sheriff about what she found without sounding like she was butting into his investigation? The more she uncovered, the harder it was to tell the police she had been poking around in Mr. Perkins's world. He brought a lot of baggage on his fateful stay, and curiosity propelled her to get to the bottom of this. What was he doing to all those sick people?

Chapter Eight

Monday

The microwave dinged. Jules stirred her leftover baked spaghetti and returned to the planning calendar on her computer.

"Mmmm. Something smells good." Roxanne dumped a pile of files on her desk and reached down to pick up Bijou. "Hey, sweetie. You keeping Jules company today?" She kissed the top of the dog's head and set her down on the bed.

"Spaghetti. Did you eat lunch?"

"I snacked. I'm meeting some friends in town for sushi and drinks later."

Jules made a sour pickle face. "Have fun."

"All the bills are paid, and payroll's done. I'm going through our old accounting files. Purging what we don't need and scanning what we should keep. When I'm done, I should free up those filing cabinets."

"Good. Then we can get rid of them. We could use the space. I think Dad bought them at the Army-Navy outlet when I was a kid."

The bells on the door tinkled.

"I'll get it," Roxanne said.

A few minutes later, Roxanne stuck her head in the back. "Jules, there's a gentleman who needs to see you."

A man in jeans and a black dress shirt, who barely cleared the doorframe, followed Roxanne into the office. He had a military-style haircut and black boots. Bijou yipped several times from her bed and zipped over to the stranger.

"Ms. Keene, I'm Special Agent Will Stafford. I would like to talk to you about Ira Perkins." The FBI agent reached down and petted Bijou, who was sniffing his ankle.

"I've already talked to Sheriff Hobbs. I told him all that I know."

From behind the agent's back, Roxanne gave her a thumbs-up. She backed out the doorway and closed the door behind her.

"May I?" He took a seat at the round table near the kitchen area.

"Would you like something to drink?"

He shook his head as she sat in the seat across from him. He leaned over and patted the small dog.

"What can you tell me about Ira Perkins?"

"Not much. He was a long-term rental in one of my vintage trailers. He said he was here to finish his book."

"Anything suspicious about him?"

"Not really. He wanted to be left alone. He was adamant about that."

"Did he leave anything behind?"

She paused. "Personal stuff. Toiletries, clothing, stuff like that. I boxed everything, and the sheriff picked it up." Where was this going and why did he ask the same questions the sheriff did? Jules wanted to wrap this up.

"Anything else you can remember?"

It was odd Special Agent Stafford didn't write anything down. She stared at the agent, trying to see if he could fit the look of the guy with the truck in the video. "I'm sorry. Do you have any identification?"

He pulled out his shield and flipped it over to show her his ID. The photo and the guy in front of her matched. She handed it back to him, and he passed her a business card.

"Thank you," she said. "We've had a trespasser on the property several times since Mr. Perkins's death. And the trailer where he stayed has been ransacked twice."

"Did you report the break-ins?"

She nodded.

Agent Stafford leaned forward. "What did Mr. Perkins tell you about himself?"

"Not a lot. He said he was a writer."

The FBI agent stared at her as she talked, and Jules had to shake off the nerves.

"Anything else?"

"He didn't talk that much to me. He had an altercation with my part-time staffer Emily and my aunt about some other guests he felt were too noisy. I took care of the issue."

"How?" he asked.

"I moved the family with the three boys to the other side of the resort."

The agent continued to stare at her. "Then what?"

"Two of my guests tripped over a dead Ira Perkins in the woods."

Agent Stafford shifted in his chair. Jules thought he was about to leave until he said, "What do you know about MedPro?"

"Uh, MedPro?"

"MedPro." His stare bored into her. His deep brown eyes held her stare and his crooked nose looked like it had probably been broken more than once.

The butterflies in her stomach turned to bats. She had planned to turn over the contents of the encrypted file to the sheriff when she had some information. How was she going to explain what she had found? She looked at her hands.

"Let's just agree that we've both heard of MedPro." The special agent rose. "Call me if you think of anything else. I'm going to walk around the property, if you don't mind." He strode through the store and out the front doorway.

"Not a problem. Let me know if you need anything," she said to his back.

Roxanne swooped in the back office. "What did he want?"

"To know about Ira Perkins."

"That darn Ira Perkins won't go away. He's as annoying in death as he was when he was alive."

Jules smirked. It was true. Ira Perkins's actions lived on, and she wondered how long it would take to forget about him.

Jules grabbed her purse. "I've got to run into town for a little while. Will you be okay by yourself?"

"Yep. Bijou and I will have afternoon tea. Maybe that cute agent will come back, and we can have a nice chat."

"I'll be back as soon as I can. Don't chat too much with him. I got a weird vibe about him." Jules stopped to print the spreadsheet and notes.

Roxanne rolled her eyes and waved her off.

Jules drove to town and parked the silver Wrangler in front of the government offices. She slammed the Jeep's door and walked briskly to the front of the sheriff's office. It was now or never before she lost her nerve. She was tired of talking about her grumpy guest, and it was time to turn over the files to the authorities.

"Hey, Jules," said Ashley Sharpe from behind the glass reception area. "What can I do for you?"

"Hi. I'm here to see Sheriff Hobbs. Is Millie off today?"

Ashley nodded. "She's getting her hair done." The petite deputy picked up the phone and balanced the receiver in the crook of her neck. She turned to look at something in the office behind her. "Jules, he's out on a call. Deputy Dempsey is here. Can he help?"

"No, that's okay. Can you let the sheriff know I stopped by?"

"Sure will. How's Jake?"

"He's good. He's always busy. I'll tell him that you asked about him when I see him," Jules said.

Ashley beamed. "It's been a month of Sundays since I've seen him. You must be keeping him so busy at the resort. You need to let him out once in a while to have some fun."

Jules almost said something snarky, but she held her tongue. "Sure." Jules smirked, waved to Ashley, and wandered down the cement path to her Jeep. She'd have to let Jake know he had a fan in town.

She had a twinge of guilt about snooping around the contents of the encrypted file and not telling the police, but she dismissed it. Her inquisitiveness overpowered the guilty feeling and wrestled it to the ground. She had the right to know what Ira Perkins was up to in her trailer.

After a dinner of microwave popcorn, Jules curled up on her couch with the spreadsheet and the log of bank records. The totals still didn't match. But it was clear Mr. Perkins had access to a lot of money, hidden in an offshore account. Did he steal it? Was it his? Was he holding it for someone? So much for the story of him as a whistle-blower.

Jules stared at the numbers, hoping she would be able to divine some secrets or a hidden message. Something made a noise outside. Bijou ran to the front window to start a barkfest. After a few minutes there, the dog ran to another window on the other side of the door, barking the entire time.

"Shhh! Quiet!" Jules heard more noises that sounded like stomping. She peered out the window but didn't see any movement. Jules stood there for a while. Bijou returned to her bed. Jules relaxed for a minute. Then her imagination about something being out there caused her heart to beat faster again.

She saw a shadow move beside her house toward the woods. Staring into the darkness that lingered past the edge of what the porch light covered, she didn't see any other movement. After a few moments, she let out a heavy sigh. Relaxing a little, Jules still had an eerie feeling.

She chided herself for letting her thoughts run wild. It could have been Jake, Lester, or any of her guests, for that matter. They wandered around the grounds at all hours. Her heart rate felt like the rat-a-tat-tat of a snare drum. She took several calming breaths and convinced herself it was just someone on an innocent stroll. It was like any other night. But she checked to see that all the doors and windows were locked.

Chapter Nine

Wednesday

Jules pulled her sunglasses out of her curly hair and put them on to block the morning sun. She stuffed the Jeep with boxes and cartons of cleaning supplies, snacks, sunscreen, and paper products and slammed the back door. She spent more time and money in the store in Charlottesville than she had intended, but there were no chain or big box stores in Fern Valley.

At a stoplight, she spotted a green Chevy truck, like the one belonging to the resort's night visitor, fly past her in the opposite direction. Jules caught her breath and made a quick right at the light and followed. Mashing the accelerator to the floor, she had to switch lanes several times to keep him in sight. She pulled in behind the truck and verified it was a dark green truck with a white top, but the tailgate hung down, blocking the view of the license plate. Jules trailed the truck through Charlottesville to Ivy Road.

The driver of the truck ran a red light where Ivy turned into University Avenue by Mr. Jefferson's University, and Jules lost him. She cruised down another few blocks to Main Street, but the truck had vanished. Circling the downtown mall one last time, she gave up on the night visitor and headed back to the resort.

As she turned, the green truck flew by on a cross street. Jules signaled and turned in front of a small car, waving an apology to the blaring car horn and saying a silent thank you for all the foot traffic that allowed her to catch up to the truck that had stopped suddenly.

Hanging back a car length behind him, she followed him through town. He didn't seem to be in such a hurry until he hit Route 250 in Pantops, and then he floored it. Jules, taken by surprise by the sudden burst of speed, had to play catch up. He accelerated more as he approached the I-64 interchange and took the eastern exit to Richmond. Not ready for a road trip, Jules took the western exit. Where was the creepy night visitor headed?

She cranked up the radio and returned to the office. Thoughts of the mystery truck guy bounced around in her head. Why did he keep popping up in her life?

Jules punched in the code for the office's back door, and Bijou served as the welcome wagon. Voices in the store distracted her, so she put the dog on her bed and tiptoed up front.

Emily waved to a family. "Thanks for stopping by. Let us know if you need anything. Oh, hi, Jules. How are you? I didn't hear you come in."

"Good. How're things here?"

"Steady. Those were the Joneses. They checked in earlier and wanted information about area attractions. They're in the nineteen fifty-three Vagabond."

Jules smiled. That was one of the first trailers she and her father purchased and refurbished. They chose the famous Route 66 theme in honor of the trailer's era and the early travel craze. "I've got some research to do. You okay out here? When Roxanne gets back, I have supplies in the Jeep that need to be unpacked."

Jules revved up the coffee maker and settled in at her desk. She flipped through Mr. Perkins's spreadsheet again. He had taken a lot of money from a bunch of sick people. What had that man with the pacemaker said? She flipped through her notes and found Clyde McMasters. He had told her to turn off the appliance. *Ira Perkins, what were you doing? Why would you threaten to turn off someone's medical device?*

Her research so far on Mr. Perkins felt like a dead end. Jules had more questions than answers. Time to switch gears and look into the second nephew. Jules grabbed her laptop and searched for the reporter Kevin Bailey.

She scrolled through page after page of search results until she found his webpage with a "contact me" form. She filled in her name and email address and typed, "I need to talk to you about Ira Perkins." Maybe the reporter would bite.

Her cell phone rang, and Jules jumped. Butterflies flitted around her stomach. Was it Kevin Bailey already? She hadn't thought about what to say.

She looked at the caller ID–the sheriff's department. She took a deep breath and connected the call. "Hi, Sheriff. How are you?"

"Good. I'm up to my elbows in alligators. I'm getting through my messages. Everything okay there?"

"Fine." She tried to collect her thoughts.

"Any more night visitors?"

"No, not since last time. Any luck on the thumb drive?"

"They're looking at it now. It's a good thing they're whip-smart about computers."

"Good." She let out a breath she hadn't realized she was holding. If they were working on it, she didn't have to admit she'd been snooping. "I stopped in to check on the two people who showed up here, claiming to be Ira Perkins's nephews. I saw a similar green truck when I was in Charlottesville shopping. The driver got on I-64 toward Richmond."

"You followed him?"

"For a little while. I was a couple of cars behind him."

"Jules, that's police work."

"I know. I wouldn't do anything dangerous. I happened to see him, and I was curious about where he was going. How many old green trucks with a white top can be running around the area?"

The sheriff was silent a moment. "I dunno. I'll have one of my guys check it out. How 'bout you call us if you see him again. And no tailing him. Got it?"

"Will do. Did you find anything else about the other guy, Kevin Bailey?"

"He's a reporter."

Jules stayed silent a moment. "Speaking of reporters, did you see Jane's article yesterday?"

"U-huh. It was pretty tame and short. Hopefully, that's the last of her intrepid reporting. Anything else on your mind?"

"No, Sheriff. Thanks." She disconnected and set the phone on her desk. At least there was no lecture about poking around encrypted files. Jules felt like a kid who'd gotten caught with her hand in the cookie jar.

She busied herself with looking at email. Everything was ready to go for the scouts who would take over the meadow for almost a week. And, true to their creed, they were self-sufficient. No entertainment or meals. Easy guests.

Jules's next big event wasn't until the weeks around the Fourth of July. The town always celebrated with a parade, picnic, and fireworks, and she offered a hometown fourth package. Since the vintage trailer spots had sold out in a matter of weeks, she'd decided to open the meadow to campers. All the spots had been snapped up in a matter of days. Pleased she had advance payments for a family reunion in August and a writers' wine retreat in September, she thought about the winter holidays. Usually, Jules closed during the colder months, but she had an idea to extend the season. Maybe she could work out a package deal for her visitors with the nearby ski resort that offered a lot of snow fun.

Her cell phone rang. "Jules Keene."

"This is Kevin Bailey. I received your information from my website. What did you want to talk about?"

Her heartbeat increased, and the adrenaline surge made her jumpy. She took a long breath. "Why did you visit my resort looking for Ira Perkins?"

"I don't remember leaving my name. Are you some kind of reporter or investigator?"

"No. Just a curious business owner."

"Okay. If you'd like to talk, that's cool. What's your availability tomorrow?"

"The afternoon is better," she said.

"How about lunch then? I'm kinda fond of that diner in town. Let's say twelve-thirty."

"That will work. See you then at Pop's Diner."

Jules leaned back. It was curious he was interested enough to come back to town. At two and a half hours away, Washington, D. C., wasn't a hop and a skip to the Charlottesville area. Or maybe he had never left Fern Valley. *Mr. Perkins, what did you do that has so many people interested in you?*

Before she could ponder further about Kevin Bailey and Ira Perkins, the office phone rang. "Fern Valley Luxury Camping Resort. How can we make your getaway special?"

"Hi. This is Mollie Baxter, and I run an online crafting group and blog. I would like to talk to someone about planning a retreat."

"Hello, Mollie. This is Jules Keene. What type of event were you thinking about?"

She chatted with the blogger for about twenty minutes and jotted down her requirements and requests.

"Let me work up some accommodation and meal options. I'll get this to you, and we can make adjustments and then finalize the dates."

"Sounds great. I appreciate the help. We're looking forward to our session to learn new techniques and to hang out together."

"Thank you for thinking of us." Jules disconnected and fist pumped the air. This was what she needed to extend her season. She pulled up her catering menus and got lost in planning a girls' crafty getaway. Thoughts of Ira Perkins's murder and her lunch with the reporter got pushed aside, at least for the moment.

Chapter Ten

Thursday

Jules shut off her computer and pulled her purse out of the desk drawer. She checked her lipstick. "Bijou, be a good girl and hang out with Aunt Roxanne for a while. I promise we'll do a good walk this afternoon when I get back."

"Hey, Aunt Roxanne. I'll be back in a little while," Jules said, walking into the store.

"Okay. The scoutmaster called a few minutes ago, and we worked out the logistics for the event. They'll handle the campsite registrations. So, we're good to go."

The screen door opened. Bijou growled from the back office.

Agent Stafford stepped inside. "Ladies. How are you? Ms. Keene, do you have a few minutes?"

"A few. I'm heading to town in a little while for a lunch meeting."

"This won't take long. Is the trailer Ira Perkins stayed in available?"

"I took it out of rotation because it needs repair from the two ransackings."

Roxanne leaned over the counter and twirled the trailer key on her finger.

"May I look at it? I didn't get to see the inside when I was here last," he said.

"Sure. But I'll have to leave in fifteen minutes or so. I need to get to town for my appointment." She flipped her purse strap over her shoulder.

"It won't take but a few minutes."

She grabbed the key from Roxanne and followed him to the porch. Jules had to pick up her pace to keep up with his purposeful stride.

"It's over here." She pointed to the Robin Hood and handed him the key.

"Nice trailers. This doesn't look like the camping I did as a kid. We never had this much luxury. My dad believed in roughing it." Agent Stafford climbed inside. "Was anything else found here besides the thumb drive?"

"The normal, personal stuff. The sheriff picked up Mr. Perkins's belongings."

He poked around the camper for what seemed like an eternity. Then Agent Stafford stuck his head out the smallish door. "Thanks. I wanted to get a sense of where he'd been staying. Has anyone contacted you besides the two men you told the sheriff about?"

She shook her head.

"If you have any other inquiries, please let me know."

"Do you need to see anything else?"

"Not right now. Thanks for your time."

Jules locked the camper door. He never seemed to take any notes. And he stared too much. Jules was determined he wasn't going to unnerve her. Why was he so interested in the trailer where Ira Perkins stayed? The forensic team surely took enough photos on the day the body was found.

Jules brushed thoughts of him away and started her Jeep. She headed to town to see what Kevin Bailey had to say for himself.

Jules edged into a parking spot near the restaurant's front door. Pop's Diner, a fixture in Fern Valley since the 1950s, looked like the malt shop out of *Grease*. The current "Pop," the grandson of the founder, redecorated and expanded in the 1980s to draw on the fifties' nostalgia. Of all the novelty decorations, Jules's favorites were the life-sized black velvet painting of Elvis that hung in the hallway and the jukebox that played 45s from the early days of rock 'n roll.

Jules opened the door and got a whiff of French fries. That smell made her mouth water.

"Hey, Jules." A waitress with a light pink bouffant that matched her blouse and poodle skirt smiled.

"Hi, Marsha. How are you?"

"Good. Pick anywhere you want to sit. What can I get you to drink?" She tapped her black and white saddle Oxford on the tile floor.

"Thanks. I'm meeting someone here for lunch." Jules slid into a red vinyl booth near the lunch counter. "May I have a vanilla Coke?"

"Coming right up."

A few minutes later, Marsha, who looked like she stepped out of the *Happy Days* set, dropped off a Coke as Jules was perusing the menu. "Can I get you something while you wait?"

"I think I'll order when he gets here, if that's okay."

"Sure. New beau?"

"No, just a working lunch."

Marsha winked and retreated to the kitchen.

Jules had time to read the menu twice and check her email before she noticed a short guy with dark hair at the entrance who looked around for someone. Assuming he was Kevin Bailey, she waved, and he headed her way. The guy in jeans and a gray hoodie dropped into the booth opposite her. His sneakers squeaked on the black and white checkered tile floor.

"Sorry. I hope you haven't been waiting long. Traffic took longer than I expected. I came over from Charlottesville." He set his phone and keys on the table.

"Hi, I'm Jules Keene."

"Kevin Bailey. You weren't in when I stopped by your resort."

"Speaking of that…" She cocked her eyebrow.

"I'm doing a story on Ira Perkins, and I was curious to see if he had left anything at your place."

"Not that original of an idea. Another guy stopped in the same day with the same claim." Jules stared at the man across the table from her.

He looked sheepish. "Really? What did he look like?"

"I wasn't there. My aunt said he was tall and scruffy and was wearing a sweatshirt. So, what's your interest in Ira Perkins?" Jules wasn't ready to share what she knew about the other guy yet.

Before he could answer, Marsha returned to the table with a menu. "What can I get y'all?"

"I'll have a cheeseburger no onions or mayo, with onion rings," Jules said.

"I'll have the footlong hot dog with everything and onion rings. And a chocolate malt," Kevin Bailey said.

"Even the jalapenos on the dog?"

"Sure. Why not." Kevin pushed both menus toward the waitress.

Marsha moved on to another table.

"Okay. I'm up for a trade. I'll tell you what I was doing, but you have to fill me in on what you know about old Ira."

"Okay." Jules took a sip of her Coke. "But you first." Could she trust this guy? He had already lied about being Mr. Perkins's nephew. She would be cautious. Right now, he was her only new source of information.

He drew a deep breath that almost sounded like a sigh. "I'm working on a story, and Ira kept promising to provide some information. I got texts and emails from him and then nothing. He ghosted me several times. After his last disappearance, I tracked him down to your resort. He mentioned the Blue Ridge Mountains and Fern Valley in a rambling email, so I hung around town and spotted him at the sandwich shop."

"Mr. Perkins checked in a couple months ago. He told me he was here to finish his novel. I never saw him do much of anything."

Kevin squinted. "He's not a writer."

"That's what I figured. When we cleaned out his trailer, we didn't see anything that looked like a writer was in residence."

"What did he leave?"

"Mostly clothes and toiletries. My team had to do a lot of scouring. He wasn't the neatest guest."

"Did he hang out with anyone? Socialize much?"

"Some. My aunt said he talked about himself nonstop. He also said he was from Brooklyn and had recently come into some money. He didn't like kids or noise. And he complained a lot."

"I only talked to him on the phone a couple of times," Kevin said. "He kept promising me information, but then he'd seem to get cold feet. He'd say something intriguing, and then I wouldn't hear from him for weeks."

"Mr. Perkins rented my trailer for eight months and hinted he was going to extend his stay. Then he'd threaten to check out. I guess it depended on whatever mood he was in."

Marsha interrupted. "Here's lunch, y'all. I'll be back to check on drink refills in a little while. Sir, would you like a glass of water?"

Kevin shook his head. He had already started chomping on his hot dog.

Jules nibbled on her burger and waited. "How did you meet Ira Perkins?"

He wiped mustard and chili off his chin. "He contacted me through my website like you did. He wanted a secure way to chat about some information. He said he was a whistle-blower, and he needed my help to right a wrong."

"What kind of information?"

"He played his cards very close to his vest. He leaked one or two tidbits and then he clammed up."

Jules reached for the ketchup. "If I saw him around the property, he would wave or nod. He sat on the patio a lot. And he frequented town, usually for meals. He said he liked Fern Valley. He didn't seem like the 'go for a hike' kind of person. He wasn't there for the outdoor activities."

"He was an IT guy."

"I didn't see a laptop or a phone when I packed up what was left of his stuff."

Kevin polished off his hot dog. "He told me once that he started out as a network administrator, and he took classes when cybersecurity became a hot career. He worked at a company called MedPro."

Butterflies in Jules's stomach woke up and started fluttering, and her thoughts bounced around and collided with each other.

"Jules…"

"Uh, sorry. I'm listening."

"They make medical appliances like pacemakers and insulin pumps. The last thing he told me was he knew of something bad going on there, and he wanted me to do a story on it."

"Defective products?" she asked.

"He didn't say. He kept stressing it was big and bad and that it would make a great story. He was all excited about whistle-blowing, and then suddenly, he stopped the conversations. I was hoping to corner him here in town, but I got tied up in Northern Virginia with some things. When I got back, I found out he was dead."

"So, that's the end of the story you were working on?" Maybe if Kevin was still interested in Mr. Perkins's tale, then they could share information. She wanted to know what he had on her guest, but she didn't know if she should say anything about the thumb drive and the spreadsheets yet.

"No. I think there's still a story there." Kevin shoved half an onion ring in his mouth and paused. "Did you find the body?" He slurped his malt from the tall glass.

"No. I was doing rounds, and I heard a scream. Two senior bird-watchers were chasing a woodpecker, and one of them tripped over the body."

The reporter pulled out a small notebook from his pocket and started scribbling. "Do you know their names?"

"It was Mrs. Fillmore and Mrs. Greenbaum. Mrs. Fillmore said she tripped over a tree root and discovered the body."

Kevin looked up and smiled. "Anything else?"

She scrunched her nose and made a face. "He was shot and found wearing only a red satin thong."

Kevin stopped taking notes and looked at her again. She shrugged and caught a glimpse of a snicker.

"I'd be willing to share information as long as you don't talk to any other reporters."

"No offense, but I have no desire to do that. Jane Jenkins, the town's weekly's society reporter, has been looking for a scoop. I caught her sneaking around the office."

His forehead wrinkled, but he kept scribbling. "You talk to her?"

"No, but I think she overheard my staff talking. She did a short story in the weekly, but it was only about the murder, the first one in Fern Valley in years."

"Anything else you remember?"

"The trailer was ransacked twice after the murder."

"What?" Kevin stopped writing. "It wasn't me. Honest."

"The first time was right after the murder. Things were strewn around and a couple of pillows slashed. Then it happened again the next day. The trailer's front door was damaged, and the inside was trashed. Somebody was looking for something. It happened right after you and the other guy came by the resort."

She stared at him to see if he gave any indication he knew about the midnight visitor.

"Any idea why?" Kevin glared at her from across the table.

She tried to ignore him. "Who knows. I figured Ira Perkins wasn't who he said he was. I'd like to get to the bottom of it before it causes any more damage to my resort."

Pop wandered over to the table. "Jules, how are you? It's good to see you."

"Hi, Pop. It's good to see you, too." Jules hugged the man who resembled a professional wrestler in a white T-shirt and grease-stained apron. "This is Kevin Bailey."

"Nice to meet you." Pop shook the man's hand. "Hey, Jules, you going to the business council meeting this week?"

"I'll be there."

The older man smiled and patted her on the shoulder. "Good deal. Lots of your guests visit the diner, and I appreciate it. And you know the council elections are coming up. You really ought to consider running for office. It's right up your alley. Your energy is contagious."

"Thanks, Pop. Fern Valley is home, and I love sharing it with those who appreciate the mountains."

He smiled. "Spoken like a politician. You should think seriously about it. You've got my vote. Y'all enjoy lunch and come back soon."

The older man shuffled back to the kitchen.

Kevin finished the last of his onion rings. "I've got to head back home this afternoon. Call me if you find out anything else." He pushed his business card across the table.

Jules rummaged through her bag for a card for the reporter. "Will do." She waved Marsha over for their checks.

Jules followed Kevin outside and watched him climb into his Civic and drive away. She needed to find out more about her mysterious night visitors and why people were still so interested in Ira Perkins after his murder.

Chapter Eleven

Friday

Jules whistled. Bijou rocketed from behind the couch. The dog sat at her feet by the cabin door until Jules clicked her leash in place. "Come on, girl. Let's go check on the scouts." They strolled across the grounds and waved to the Riley family. The three boys zoomed around after each other in the grassy area.

"Here we are."

Bijou seemed more interested in a beetle. The terrier gave up on the bug and hopped in the golf cart for a short ride to the path through the woods to the meadow.

On the other side of the dirt path, the scouts had managed to turn the wooded area and field into a small town. It looked so different from last week's cruise-in. Tents stretched across every inch of open space, as far as the eye could see. Banners and flags flicked in the morning breeze. The boys and their leaders moved around in organized chaos. Everybody seemed to have a task. She drove down the asphalt path, taking in all the activity.

She stopped in front of a group of leaders wearing olive and tan uniforms. "Good morning, gentleman. I'm Jules Keene. I wanted to make sure everything was okay with your campsites."

"I see you have your assistant with you," said the man in the center with the graying buzz cut. "Everything's rolling along. Thanks for hosting us. We're having a great time."

"My pleasure. Let me know if you need anything."

The men returned to their conversation. One saluted with two fingers as she drove off. Jules and Bijou made a loop of the tent city and headed back to the office. It was nice to have the meadow filled with kids and lots of activity. Her dad would have been right in the middle of all the action. Fond memories from her childhood flooded her thoughts like a tidal wave.

Jules opened the back door, and a "Hey, there," drifted in from the store.

Bijou tore off to see Aunt Roxanne.

"Hey, yourself." She dropped Bijou's leash on her desk and walked toward her aunt's voice.

"Good. A little tired. I went to the art opening with Henry in Richmond. We had drinks on the rooftop of the Quirk Hotel. The sunset over downtown was gorgeous. The art show was a little weird, but, all in all, it was a nice evening out. Roxanne picked up Bijou for a snuggle.

"Sounds like fun." Jules straightened the flyers on the front counter.

"You need to get out more. You work too much."

"I'm done with dating for a while. Bijou and I have girls' night at home." The whole bad marriage to The Idiot had made her skittish about getting involved with anyone. And she didn't have time right now to date. The campground was her focus.

Her aunt frowned but refrained from commenting further.

Jules changed the subject. "I'm going to do some research and work on the proposal for a crafters weekend this fall."

"Your parents kept the resort open only in warm weather. It always made me sad at the end of summer. I'm glad you're staying open past the traditional season."

Jules missed her parents. Her mother died when Jules was a teenager. She cherished the time she and her dad spent restoring the vintage campers after her own divorce. She wanted the resort to succeed to honor their memories.

"We should plan some kind of holiday thing with lots of lights. That would be a big draw with people looking for things to do during the Christmas season," her aunt said.

"Sounds festive. Why don't you come with me to the next business council meeting?"

"I'm game, but I'm not volunteering to lead anything. I've done my time on church committees and PTAs. And I have enough to keep me busy. I'm done with herding volunteers and prodding them to get a move on. But it would be right up your alley." Roxanne winked at her niece.

"Are you conspiring with Pop? He said the same thing."

"Something to think about." Her aunt picked up a pile of papers and retreated to the front counter. "It'd be good for you."

"Maybe," Jules whispered to Bijou, who trotted after Roxanne "We'll have to see how busy we get here." It sounded interesting. Being president of the council would be something different. A challenge. Plus, it would be a way to unite the business owners to benefit everyone. Maybe it was worth pursuing.

Jules buried herself in MedPro research. She found a site that listed product reviews. Sixteen complaints. The screen names didn't match anyone on Ira Perkins's spreadsheet that she could recognize. She added the information to her growing pile of not related stuff. It didn't feel like she would ever be able to put some of these puzzle pieces together.

She spent the next hour reading product specification sheets for the items listed in the spreadsheet. "Hmmmm. That's interesting," she said aloud. "I wonder..." Jules called Pixel.

"Hey, girl. How are you?"

"Good. I was looking up the medical appliances in the list on that spreadsheet. And I'm looking for some common denominator. They all seem to have Bluetooth, like my phone."

"Yep. That's the IoT."

"Huh?"

"The Internet of Things. Stuff talks to you, to each other, and to the manufacturer. You'd be surprised what's connected to the net. And, in a few years, everything that plugs in will have the capability to talk to other things. And they won't always need the humans. It'll be wild."

"Scary," Jules said.

"Sometimes it is. Courts can get ahold of information from your car's

SmartTag or its black box. They can find out where you've been and how fast you got there. So, technically, your car can testify against you. New fridges can place orders when your food supplies are low. It's very Star Trekkie, but it's great for geeks in cybersecurity. They're always having to secure something or check for vulnerabilities. Anything on the great wild web can be hacked. If you can use it to lock your doors, someone else can use it to unlock them. The same with cameras. Technology is great, but sometimes, there are unintended consequences."

"Okay, I'm going to hide under my desk now." Jules was only half kidding.

"That's why people need to read their ULAs."

"English, please."

"The User License Agreement. You know that thing people click through when they're downloading software. It tells you what the company has access to and what they do with your data. People need to pay attention to what they're giving access to. Don't get me started. People click through it all the time. I'll get off my soapbox about people who put themselves at risk." She took a deep breath.

"Okay, so if it's on the internet, it has the potential to be hacked. If people have these Bluetooth medical devices, can they be hacked?" Jules asked.

"Definitely. When former Vice President Dick Cheney had a heart issue while in office, they turned off the wireless capabilities in his pacemaker so it couldn't be hacked. You wouldn't want someone controlling the VP's much-needed heart device. There was huge potential for blackmail or sinister deeds. Don't get me wrong. There's so much good technology can do. It can send metrics to the doctors, so they can catch anomalies before they become serious medical issues. But there's a dark side to everything too. Somebody will find a way to use things for other purposes."

"So, someone was blackmailing or threatening to turn off implanted devices, and Ira Perkins found out about it. And it probably led to his death…"

"Wow. That would explain the money in the Cayman Islands." Pixel tapped on her keyboard.

"Holy cow. What have we stumbled onto?" Jules asked.

Pixel stopped typing and let out a whistle. "Be careful who you talk to about this. You don't know how far the dead guy got into this."

"I'm gonna call the sheriff or that FBI agent and let them know what we've found. Someone's ransacked the trailer he stayed in twice, looking for something. I don't want anything else tragic to happen."

"Twice?"

"Yep. I'm sure it was for the info on the thumb drive. Thanks so much for your help. You're the best."

"Any time. Be careful." Pixel disconnected.

"Ira Perkins, what did you uncover? Crime is bad, but preying on sick people is despicable," she said to no one.

Bijou ran to the back of the office.

Jules needed a break from all the negativity of the MedPro stuff. She pulled up her file on the craft getaway and filled in some pricing for meals and snacks. She emailed Darlene Denunzio from On Pins and Needles and Rhonda Wilson and Kim Lacy from KnitWits to see if they would be interested in offering the crafters a deal on supplies. If this worked well, then maybe she could advertise crafting getaways throughout the year. There were enough local artisans who might be willing to teach workshops. She made some notes on her desk calendar.

Jules's stomach rumbled, reminding her it was past dinnertime.

"Come on, Bijou. Let's lock up here and see what we have to eat. Or maybe we could run into town and see what's happening on a Friday night."

The Jack Russell Terrier barked and zoomed around the office.

Jules parked her Jeep in the lot next to the Good Thyme Bistro, where she and Bijou found an outdoor table under a teal umbrella. The waitress brought Jules a menu and Bijou a bowl of water.

"Let me know what I can get you. Our specials today are a cheesy ravioli, a giant chopped salad, and a double fudge brownie cheesecake."

"Everything sounds good. I'll start with an unsweetened iced tea and the turkey club with a side of mac and cheese."

"Good choice. I'll be right back with your drink."

Jules checked email and posted a picture of Bijou on Instagram. A shadow crossed her table. She looked up.

Special Agent Will Stafford loomed across from her. Must be casual day for the FBI. Instead of a suit, he sported a white dress shirt with the sleeves rolled up and khaki trousers. All the better to see his holster and sidearm.

"Oh, hi."

"I stopped in for dinner and saw you over here." He leaned over and patted Bijou.

"Would you like to join us?"

The waitress swooped in to drop off Jules's utensils and drink. She gave Jules's companion the once-over. "What can I get you to drink? I'll bring you a menu in a minute."

"No need. I know what I want. I'd like a water with a lemon and your giant salad with the three protein scoops. I had it the last time I was here."

"I'll put your order in and be right back with your drink." The waitress gave a coy smile over her shoulder.

"Are you staying in the area?" Jules stared at the agent across from her. His deep brown eyes distracted Jules. Embarrassed, she looked at her plate.

"Charlottesville. For a few more days. I need to wrap up some interviews. Everything quiet at your place?" He might be dressed casually, but he was still in law enforcement mode. Did he ever have any fun?

"Pretty much, but I have a meadow full of Boy Scouts, so I doubt it's going to be all that quiet."

"You have a nice property. It's pretty country up here." He looked past Jules at the foot traffic on the sidewalk.

"Are you based out of Washington, D. C.?"

"Richmond."

"I don't detect a Virginia accent."

I'm originally from Lambertville, New Jersey. It's a small town, sort of like this." Will Stafford shifted in his chair. He watched as people strolled down the sidewalk. Was he on the lookout for someone or was this just a part of the job?

The waitress interrupted with the agent's drink and a basket of assorted breads and honey butter. "Your dinners will be out in a few minutes. Enjoy these. They're hot out of the oven." The waitress disappeared into the restaurant.

"How's the investigation going?" Jules asked.

"It's progressing. There are lots of little details I'm tracking down. Mostly legwork and interviews." The FBI agent reached for the bread basket.

Jules pushed the honey butter closer to him.

He broke open a roll and slathered it with the spread. "What do you know about MedPro? This time, you can tell me."

Jules took a deep breath and met his gaze as he looked her way. "It's a company Ira Perkins worked for at one time. I don't think he was a writer."

"Why?"

"I looked at the spreadsheet on the thumb drive before I gave it to the sheriff," she said in almost a whisper.

"How'd you get it open? It took our guys a few days to crack it." He raised one eyebrow and glared at her.

"My friend. She's a computer whiz."

He frowned slightly but settled into his seat "She must be. Maybe I should talk to her about joining us."

Jules laughed and relaxed into her seat. The couple sat in silence. Agent Stafford watched traffic on the street.

The waitress returned with their plates and another treat for Bijou, who had curled up at Jules's feet. Agent Stafford tore into his salad like he had missed lunch, while Jules poked her fork in the mac and cheese to release some steam.

She broke the silence. "I looked up the numbers in the spreadsheet. I know they're Bluetooth medical devices."

"And you called some of the numbers listed."

It was Jules's turn to frown. Of course, some of the victims' lines would be monitored if the FBI was involved in investigating the blackmail. She hadn't thought about that when she made the calls. That was why he kept asking about MedPro. "Yes. I wanted to see what the red, green, and black color coding meant."

"Figure it out?"

"Yes. The reds are wrong numbers, and the people on the green list have paid some sort of ransom."

He stabbed at an errant piece of lettuce. "So, what's your theory?"

"Someone was blackmailing people with serious medical conditions. I'm assuming it was someone who had access to account and product information. There was also a script on the drive. Ira Perkins may have been some sort of whistle-blower."

The agent squinted slightly but didn't comment.

"But he didn't act like he was hiding out. He spent a lot of time in town."

"Did he get many visitors?" Agent Stafford asked.

Jules squirmed in her seat. "Just the two guys claiming to be his nephews that I told you about. And he talked to some people at the campground."

"Call me if either show up again."

"I did talk to one of the nephew impersonators. His name is Kevin Bailey, and he's a reporter. He said Ira Perkins had contacted him about a big story."

Agent Stafford frowned and stared at her.

Jules was sure he was making mental notes of leads to follow.

The waitress swooped in and stood close to Agent Stafford. "Can I get you all any dessert or coffee this evening? Or maybe drinks?"

"Just the check," he said.

"Checks," Jules corrected.

"I've got this. It's work." Agent Stafford speared the last cucumber on his plate.

"Thank you for dinner." Jules rose. "Come on, Bijou, we need to check on our guests." Jules's imagination was getting the best of her. What she really wanted to do was contact Kevin Bailey to see if she could ferret out any more information.

Chapter Twelve

Monday

Jules slipped in the back door of the lodge.

Crystal pushed her blond bangs off her face as she closed the door to the industrial dishwasher. "There's still some coffee and cinnamon buns. I brought back those when I freshened up the dining room food tables." The younger woman pointed to the counter behind her.

"Thanks." Jules grabbed a plate and a mug of steaming coffee from the dispenser on the counter. She stirred in sugar and creamer and blew on the spoon. "Busy morning?"

"Word got around about Crystal's creations, and we had a pancake and cinnamon bun rush." Mel piped up from the back near the counter, where she diced fruit for tomorrow's breakfast smoothies.

Crystal beamed. "I'm almost done here. I'll prep the muffins in just a sec."

"Thanks for keeping everyone fed and happy." Jules took her things through the swinging doors to the eating area. "Hello, Holmes family. I hope you're enjoying your stay here."

The kids waved, and Mrs. Holmes smiled. "Most definitely. We're going to go for a hike today to the waterfall."

"Have fun." Jules slid into the seat across from Jake. "How's it going?"

"All quiet. That makes my job easier." Jake grinned his signature smile.

"No strangers wandering around?"

"Nope. Everybody here belongs here. And the scouts are having a good time." Jake took a bite of his gooey bun.

"Good news for a change. I like it when the campground is full."

Before he could respond, Aunt Roxanne dropped into the chair next to Jules and bumped her niece's elbow. She set her hot tea and a plate of cinnamon buns down. "What's shaking, you two?"

"Not much," Jules replied.

Jake smiled and ate the last bite of his cinnamon bun. "Crystal outdid herself today."

"Yummy." Roxanne used her fork to cut hers into tiny bites. She nibbled on one. "Something unusual happened last night. I got a call from an area code seven oh three number, but it didn't have a name on the caller ID. Anyway, it was a guy asking if the Robin Hood trailer was available. He hung up when I told him it wasn't."

"Do people usually specify what campers they want?" Jake asked.

"Some do. If they like one they saw on the website or if they've stayed in one before that they liked. But most people ask for one that will fit the number in their party," Roxanne said.

"That camper's seen a lot of action lately." Jake winked.

"Maybe I should rename it before I put it back in circulation." Jules stared out the bank of windows toward the woods.

"It's so cute as its namesake," Roxanne said. "Maybe you could change it to Sherwood Forest, or something related to the band of merry men."

"That reminds me. I need to call the cushion place. I ordered new throw pillows and curtains to go with the replacement cushions." Jules picked up her plate. "I'm going to get Bijou and make some phone calls. See y'all later."

Roxanne waved, and she and Jake continued to chat with their heads close. Jules wondered what they were conspiring about.

On their walk to the office, Bijou chased a butterfly and took off on a barking jag. She bounded up the steps and growled at Kevin Bailey, who sat in the wooden swing.

"Hi." He reached down to pet the terrier, who sniffed his cuffs. "And who are you?"

"That's Bijou. She runs the place."

Kevin Bailey grinned. "She's cute. I stopped by to see if you were in. I'm glad I caught you before you started your day. Let's take a walk. Nice place you have here," Kevin said.

"Thank you. My parents opened it in the seventies. I moved back here a few years ago, and my dad and I gave it a makeover."

"Clever idea. I like the idea that you've upcycled some outdated trailers. They look nice."

"We saved a bunch of them from the scrapyard. There's a lot of history in those campers. So, why are you really here, besides your love for vintage trailers?"

"Two FBI agents visited me recently at my townhouse and wanted to chat. I spent about four hours with them picking through everything I knew about Ira Perkins. I spent way more time than I wanted to with them."

They walked the perimeter of the campground and turned at the edge of the woods, near where she followed Mrs. Fillmore on that fateful morning. Jules shook off the sense of dread caused by the memory of that day. "We found him in the woods over there." She pointed to the tree line.

Kevin stopped suddenly. "Ira Perkins was into something that spiraled out of control, and it caught up with him."

"Do you have enough information without him to finish your article?"

Bijou sniffed a clump of dandelions.

"I'm almost there. I need some verifications and clarity on the whole blackmailing thing. I'm hoping to wrap it up with a few more interviews."

"So, is Mr. Perkins your hero or villain?" she asked.

"Not one hundred percent sure yet. Did you find anything in his things?"

"What are you looking for specifically?"

"Thumb drive, CD, laptop. Somewhere to hide information."

Jules hesitated and shook her head. "Maybe he used the cloud." She looked at her shoes, hoping he would change the subject.

Kevin Bailey broke the silence. "My hunch is Ira isn't the hero of the story."

"Why?"

"I'm close to breaking this thing wide open." He didn't elaborate, and they finished their loop around the vintage trailers and walked to the front of the parking lot. "If you learn anything else about our friend Ira, give me a call."

"Let me know when your article comes out," she shouted as he headed toward his Honda.

Jules shook off a sense of trepidation. She felt guilty about not sharing what she knew, but she wasn't sure she could trust Kevin. Her mind wandered with all kinds of scenarios about the odd reporter.

Jules and Bijou wandered back to the office. She settled in her chair and opened Ira Perkins's folder. Maybe it would shed some light on her grumpy guest who had brought a lot of secrets to Fern Valley. She flipped through the pages in the folder and then through the electronic files. Nothing stood out as important. She closed it and decided to work on her next newsletter. Mr. Perkins and his antics dominated too much of her time and thoughts lately. Maybe Kevin's article would bring some clarity to this chaos.

Chapter Thirteen

Tuesday

Jules's cell phone buzzed and lit up her dark bedroom. Bijou stirred. Jules grabbed the phone. No one called at one-twenty in the morning unless they were in the emergency room or jail. "Hello."

"It's me, Kevin."

"Kevin?" She didn't recognize the whispered voice.

"Kevin Bailey."

"Oh, hi." She sat up. "What's wrong?"

"I can't talk long. I've found something about Ira Perkins and the money. Can you meet me in Charlottesville at noon today? I'm interviewing some folks, and I have a meeting."

"Sure, I guess. Where?"

"By the tennis courts at Piedmont Virginia Community College. There's a parking lot there."

"Okay. I'll see you at noon…by the tennis courts."

He disconnected.

"That was strange," she said to Bijou. Why did they need a clandestine rendezvous point by the tennis courts? Why couldn't he just tell her over the phone? Why did he have to call so late? Jules rolled over, but she flipped and flopped for several hours before she fell into a restless sleep.

At eight, Bijou scampered across the grounds with Jules in tow. It was time to check on the office and get some work done before she had to leave to meet Kevin.

Jules turned on the lights in the store and made coffee. She tidied her desk and was well into her second cup before Roxanne bustled in and dropped her green Tory Burch purse and shopping bags on the other desk.

"You're in early," her aunt said.

"Checking reservations. I sent off a proposal for the craft event. I'm excited that the shop owners in town want to partner with us."

"Of course they'll help. They should be buying you roses. You bring in more business to this town than anyone I know. Don't underestimate what you've done here."

"A rising tide lifts all boats."

"You're too modest." Roxanne picked up Bijou and petted the wiggly Jack. "I'm almost done with the files back there. I'll call Jake later and have him take these behemoth filing cabinets out. Do you want to keep them?"

"I'm not sure we'll need them again. If they go in the barn, they may never leave. See if you can find a place that could use a donation. Any word from the sheriff or his team about Mr. Perkins?"

"I guess no news is good news. I haven't heard from Sheriff Hobbs or Bubba in a while. I guess I'm off their suspect list."

"I couldn't believe you were ever on the list," Jules said.

"It was that stupid fight with Ira. One of these days, I'll learn to keep my mouth shut."

Jules wondered if that would happen. Roxanne had always been the feisty one who wasn't afraid to speak out, whether politically correct or not.

"I'm going to run over to the meadow to see how scout life is going. Their little tent city seems to be running efficiently. Are you okay if I leave Bijou here?"

"Not a problem. We'll keep each other company."

Life was in full swing on the other side of the trees. The camp buzzed with scouts practicing archery or playing soccer. On the way back to the office, Jules rode by the barn, where Lester stood at the open door, tinkering with the tractor. She waved to the groundskeeper and made her rounds of the vintage campers.

Before noon, Jules pulled into the front gates of the community college. She followed the road through campus to the end near the tennis courts and arts center. She found a spot for visitor parking, facing the courts, where a couple swatted the ball back and forth. Jules rolled down the windows and enjoyed the warmness of the day. This time of year was her favorite.

Jules waited not so patiently for a half-hour with no sign of Kevin. She texted him but received no response.

Combing through her emails with still no word from the reporter, Jules dialed the number and waited while his voice mail played. "Kevin, this is Jules Keene. I'm here at the tennis courts. I don't see you anywhere. Give me a call and let me know what you're up to."

Jumping out of the Jeep, she did a lap around the courts, stopping to watch the couple lob the ball back and forth. She strolled over to the arts center and read the announcements of upcoming events.

"Well, Kevin, it looks like you stood me up and wasted my time." Jules slid gingerly into the Jeep, trying to avoid the hot seat. A gray Honda skidded into the spot next to her. Kevin jumped out and tapped on her side window.

"Sorry I'm late. I got tied up." He looked over his shoulder. "Let's take a walk."

Jules grabbed her keys and followed the reporter toward the tennis courts.

He approached the fencing. "Thanks for meeting me. I found some folks who worked with Ira Perkins at MedPro." He intertwined his fingers in the aluminum fencing.

"And?"

He looked back at their cars. "One was a guy who reported to Ira. He did nothing but bad-mouth him about his terrible management skills. He referred to him as a slob. The second guy I talked to was slightly more sympathetic. He asked a lot of questions about where Ira went and what happened to him. He said Ira didn't have many friends."

"He kept to himself a lot at the resort, too. He acted like he wasn't fond of people," she said.

"He'd bought the Corvette recently, paid off his credit cards, and sublet his apartment."

"Sounds like he came into some money. An inheritance?"

"Doubtful. I think he was more than a whistle-blower. And he ticked someone off. Let me know if you get any more inquiries about him."

"Are you done with your story?"

"Almost. I'm going to talk to Ira's coworker again. I sensed he was hiding something. I've got to get on the road. I'll call you later this week."

They walked back to where they left their cars.

"Be careful," she said.

The reporter climbed into the Honda and sped out of the lot.

That was an odd encounter, pointless even. Why did he want to have a clandestine meeting for that small amount of information?

Chapter Fourteen

Wednesday

Jules made an espresso as soon as she rolled out of bed. She tapped her calendar on her phone to see what else she had to do today besides the business council meeting.

Bijou bounded into the kitchen.

"Hey, baby. I've got to get a move on if I'm going to make it on time." Jules grabbed a yogurt and flipped through her email. She sent a text to Roxanne and Jake, reminding them she wouldn't be in until after the meeting.

After a quick shower, she rummaged through her closet for something that looked more professional than her normal T-shirt and jeans. She settled on a black pantsuit with a purple camisole. She twisted her hair in a clip and made a couple of swipes with the lipstick and mascara. It wasn't Aunt Roxanne's designer duds, but it would do.

"There." She patted Bijou. "I'm heading to town. You stay here and be on guard duty."

Jules entered the library's meeting room, already half packed with business owners. Her mood lightened when she saw so many friendly faces. Most people huddled around the two open boxes of doughnuts and the coffee maker that chugged and sputtered.

"Hi, Jules," said Kim Lacy from KnitWits. "It's good to see you. Thanks for including us in the craft event you're hosting."

"Yes," chimed in Darlene Denunzio. "Me, too. I love all your fun ideas."

"Thanks. I'm always up for trying things that will bring folks to Fern Valley," Jules said.

"Hey, who's in charge here?" J. P. Gross bellowed as he stood in front of his seat and waved his arm around. "It's about time to get this meeting started. We've got to get back to work."

Elaine James, current president and owner of the garden shop, Birds and Bees, frowned and stepped to the lectern. She cleared her throat. "Everyone. Everyone, please take your seats. I'd like to call the June meeting of the Fern Valley Business Council to order. Secretary Johnson, let's start with the minutes from the May meeting."

Cindy Johnson, co-owner of Johnson Motors rose. "The minutes were posted to our site for review prior to the meeting. And this includes the updated treasurer's report. Any additions or corrections?" Cindy scanned the audience.

Nobody replied.

"Do I have a motion to accept the May minutes?" Elaine James asked.

"So moved," J. P. Gross said. "Let's keep this going."

Pop, who was sitting in the back added, "Second."

"Then let the minutes stand." Cindy took her seat.

Elaine pushed her sleeves up. "Before we open the floor to new business, it's time to nominate our new slate of officers.

"I nominate Cindy Johnson for secretary, Marco Hooper for vice president, Margie Torres for treasurer, and Jules Keene for president," Pop said.

A flutter of excitement zinged through Jules. She could do this. But she wondered what her peers thought.

"Second." Roxanne slid into the seat next to Jules.

"And I nominate myself for president." J. P. Gross stood again.

Jules hoped she didn't scowl. She tried to get along with everyone in town, but J. P. Gross made that difficult with his coarseness and constant critical remarks. When he wasn't pointing his thick sausage finger at others, he was scheming to find ways to get out of paying for things.

"Can he do that?" someone in the crowd muttered.

"Any other nominations?" Elaine asked.

The room fell silent. She waited for what seemed like ten minutes.

When no one responded, she said, "Okay, then. I move we vote by a show of hands."

"Aye," said four or five members.

"Okay. Since three of the offices are unopposed, I move that Marco Hooper becomes vice president, Margie Torres becomes our treasurer, and Cindy Johnson remains as secretary." Elaine looked across each row for a response.

"Second," said a chorus of members from the first few rows.

"Then I suggest the two candidates for president come forward and tell us about themselves and their qualifications," Elaine said.

"Wait, wait," J. P. Gross yelled from the back of the room. "I move we have a special election meeting where each candidate can do a formal, prepared introduction and statement before the vote. This is too important to rush it."

"He wants to get more of his cronies here for the vote and to have time to campaign," Roxanne whispered.

Jules let out a breath. She hoped a delay wouldn't give J. P. more time to beat the bushes or literally twist arms for votes.

"Anyone second J. P.'s motion?" Elaine asked.

"Aye," said Ralph Teagle, owner of the junkyard on the outskirts of town.

"Okay," Elaine said. "The group has accepted the slate of officers. We will meet here Saturday morning at ten to hear the candidates and vote for president. And now for new business."

"Yes," Mitch Ford said. "I'd like to thank Jules Keene for all the guests her campground has brought to the area recently. My sales are up for this quarter, and I hope it continues for the rest of the summer."

"Whoo hoo," Roxanne yelled.

Jules's cheeks heated.

"Anything else?" Elaine asked.

"The Fourth of July Parade planning is going well," Cindy Johnson said. "We have two bands, three if you count the senior kazoo crew. We have eight floats, and we're still looking for volunteers and vendors. Let Elaine or me know if you're interested."

"And we're proud to be the major sponsor again this year for the fireworks. Our fundraisers and a couple of member donations made this possible. Any other items?" Elaine asked.

No one replied.

"Okay, then," she said. "There being no further business, I declare this meeting adjourned."

"Good," Roxanne said. "Now I can go send out emails and make calls about your candidacy. You'll be perfect for this. You have so much experience."

"And energy." Pop patted Jules on the shoulder. "This role was meant for you. You've single-handedly done more for this community than anyone in this room. You've got this in the bag."

"Thanks so much for your confidence in me, but there are folks here with years of business experience."

"That's part of the problem. We can't keep doing things the way we've always done them," Pop said.

Jules hoped the majority of the business owners felt this way. She wanted this position more than she was willing to admit, but she couldn't underestimate her opponent, who nominated himself. He had been a part of the good ol' boy network in the valley for years. And there were business folks around who didn't like change.

Jules shook hands with a few well-wishers. The stragglers had started talking about J. P. Gross and some of his antics, like hiring contractors, tradesmen, and caterers for different jobs and always finding fault with their work to avoid having to pay them. The conversation turned to some other of his antics that crossed ethical lines, and Jules snuck out the side door. She always tried to see the positive in people, but she was in no mood to have to explain or comment on anything J. P. Gross did.

Jules put the Jeep in gear and dodged other cars in the lot. On the main road, she heard an engine rev, and a large green and white truck zoomed toward her and almost hit her back bumper. Then he gunned the engine and swerved past her. He pulled in front of her and slammed on his brakes. She swerved and slid off the road. Dirt and rocks swirled, and she barely avoided rolling into the ditch. The Jeep came to a sudden stop and jerked once more. Jules bumped her lip on the steering wheel.

The driver of the truck took off like a shot. Jules inhaled deeply. Something tickled her lip. She wiped her mouth with her hand and noticed blood. Glancing in the rearview mirror, panic set in. But on closer inspection, the cut wasn't that deep. She would deal with it later. Right now, she needed to follow this guy. She mashed the gas pedal and zoomed after the truck.

Catching up to him, she repeated back his license plate several times to herself. The driver sped off and turned down a cut-through road that led to private property. She grabbed her lipstick from her purse and jotted the plate number on her window.

Jules pulled over. It wasn't a coincidence to see the same green and white truck again in town. And this time, he purposely cut her off. Was he waiting in town for her? He knew who she was. Pushing guilty feelings about not calling the sheriff or the FBI agent first and fears about her safety to the back of her mind, she flipped through her contacts and selected a number.

"Hey, Pixel. This is Jules."

"Great. What's up?"

"I need another favor. The driver of a green and white Chevy truck keeps popping up around town. He just tried to run me off the road. Can you look up a license plate for me?"

"No problem. Virginia plates?"

"Uh-huh." Jules looked at her lipstick scribbles and read off, "BXJ one nine four one."

"I'll text you what I find."

"You've been an amazing help with all of this. Call me when you have some time. Lunch is on me."

"Deal. I'll get you a name," Pixel said.

Jules knew she had to report the driver, but she wanted to see what Pixel could find first. This was personal, and Jules needed to see who this guy was and what he wanted. She could wait a little while, at least until she calmed down before she called Sheriff Hobbs with the new information.

Later that evening, Jules made veggie pizza and settled on the couch with Bijou to catch up on the recordings on her DVR. The plan was to binge-watch everything she had missed in the last few weeks. Her phone vibrated across the end table, interrupting her evening plans.

"Jules, it's me, Kevin. I have some news. Can you meet me tomorrow at the fruit stand on the edge of town? About three?" He sounded like he was out of breath.

"Sure. Tomorrow afternoon."

"At the fruit stand with the ice cream shop." He sounded distracted.

"You okay?"

After a few seconds of silence, he responded, "Yup. There's a lot of stuff going on. You'll like what I found. Gotta go. See you tomorrow."

This time the phone went dead.

She wanted to confront him about wasting her time at these clandestine meetings, but she didn't get the chance. Jules decided to address it tomorrow if he didn't truly have something for this meeting.

Chapter Fifteen

Thursday

Jules took her plate of French toast and fresh fruit and joined Jake at the table facing the windows.

"Hey," he said. "You've had a busy week so far."

She gave him a half-smile. "I'd kinda like it to get back to normal. I hope the sheriff and the task force get their guy soon."

Jake laughed. "I was talking about the business council nomination, but that, too." His face sobered.

"I have to work on my speech. I'm up against J. P. Gross. Not sure how formidable he'll be. I don't want to underestimate him."

He raised an eyebrow. "He's been around the block a time or two. And he's an expert on dirty tricks."

"I hope I can make a good showing. I want to see this area continue to grow. Too many little downtowns are boarded up. And I'm hoping the recent stuff with Mr. Perkins isn't going to taint that. Nobody wants to visit if they think there's a lot of crime."

Jake took another bite of his breakfast. "But statistically, we don't have a lot of crime. J. P. Gross and his buddies are the only ones spouting scare tactics."

"I hope you're right. I need to get back to the office."

"Speaking of work, I'm going to help Lester clean out the barn. The meadow looks good. We need to have scouts more often. They cleaned everything before they left. Oh, I have a new project."

"Did you find a trailer to refurb?"

"Nope, this is something totally different." Jake tapped on his phone. "Have you seen the tiny houses?"

"They're cute." She wondered where this was going.

"There's a show on HGTV, and it gave me an idea to do some more research. I can build one from a kit or from scratch for a few thousand dollars."

He pushed his phone toward her, and she watched a time-lapse video that showed the entire construction in a couple of minutes. The different models had varying square footage, but all could accommodate at least two adults.

"I like the cottage look," she said when the video ended.

"They usually have between one hundred and four hundred square feet of space. And they're portable."

"Are you going to live in it?"

"No. I'll probably sell it when I'm done. People have land around here. I think I can flip it pretty easily."

"What's it going to look like?"

"I'm going for a cottage look on the outside. That way, it could be sold as a kid's playhouse or a she-shed."

"An expensive playhouse."

"You'd be surprised what people spend their money on." Jake put his phone down and dug into his French toast.

"You know we still have the camper pads in the field on the other side of the fence. I let it go wild while we were focusing on the vintage trailers. There's space if you want to do a deal. I'd love to have a row of cottages that look like fairy tale homes."

"You'd be interested in a deal?" He looked up from his plate.

"Why not. I think people would want to stay in them. I don't know any place that has them. The vintage trailers are going well. Would they sit on the trailer pads?"

"Just like a trailer. And they could use the same utility hookups."

"I think you might be on to something." Jules pushed her plate back and reached for her coffee.

"It'll be a fun project. I've rebuilt cars and trailers. This would be a challenge. I've seen some plans online. There are a couple that look like gingerbread houses."

"Love it." Jules finished her coffee. "I've got to head back over to the office and get busy."

"You mean, Campaign Central?"

"Huh?"

"Roxanne and Emily are your new chairpersons. They're already making buttons and posters."

"I better scoot then. There's no telling how big of an enterprise they've got going." Jules hoped Roxanne wouldn't go crazy. She had probably contacted everyone in town by now.

Jules opened the door and found Emily engrossed in something on the front counter.

"Hi, Jules. Check these out. Roxanne has a button maker." She held up a "Jules for Prez" button. "Let me know if you have any other slogans you want me to use."

"Will do." Jules picked up one of the buttons and walked to the back.

"Bye, Elaine. We'll have lunch soon," Roxanne hung up the phone. "Hey, Jules. Where have you been?"

"Talking to Jake about a new project over breakfast. What's all this?"

"We're doing our part to get you elected. You have so much more to offer than that J. P. Gross."

"Thanks, but I don't want you all to go too crazy. It's a small election."

"It's a big deal around here. You and your dad have done a lot for this community. And I want to make sure all the members know it. Have you written your speech yet?"

"This afternoon if I get some time."

"We'll be your audience if you want to do a dry run."

Jules's phone vibrated. "Hi, Pixel. What's up?"

"Hey there. I traced that license plate. Sorry I didn't call you yesterday, but I had a night class, and I didn't get home until late."

"Were you able to find anything?"

"That plate belongs to a nineteen fifty-one Chevrolet C10. It's green and white."

"That's the one. We've caught it on camera a couple of times, and I've seen it around town and once in Charlottesville."

"It belongs to a Don Fisher, who lives in Northern Virginia," Pixel said. "And guess where he used to work?"

"MedPro?

"Winner. Winner. Chicken dinner. He's a computer programmer. It's probably not a far stretch to assume that he and Ira Perkins worked together at one point. Give me a few days, and I'll see what else I can find."

"You're the best. You name the date and place for lunch or dinner. I owe you big time."

"Nah. That's what friends are for." Pixel disconnected.

Jules put the phone on her desk and wrote down the truck owner's name on a sheet in Ira Perkins folder.

"Okay, Don Fisher. So, what were you doing on my property? And what's your connection to Mr. Perkins?" She fired off a quick email to the sheriff about yesterday's truck encounter and the plate of the truck that had visited her property several times.

After an hour of poking around the internet for more Don Fisher information, she got up, stretched, and prepared to trek over to her cabin to pick up Bijou.

"Jules," Aunt Roxanne yelled in a singsong voice. "Hey, Jules. There's someone here to see you."

Jules stepped through the Dutch door to find Roxanne leaning over the counter, talking to Special Agent Stafford. Jules thought she saw her aunt bat her eyes at the FBI agent.

"Hello. I was going to get Bijou."

"I'll get her," Roxanne said. "Keys?"

Jules flipped them to her, and her aunt winked as she headed for the door. "Bye, Agent Stafford." She passed the agent who towered over her.

"It's nice to see you again. Would you like a cup of coffee?"

"No thanks. It's a nice day. Can we talk on your porch?"

"Sure." Jules followed him out front. He lowered himself onto the swing, and she parked herself in one of the wooden rockers.

They sat for a long silence, that was punctuated by several bird caws and her squeaky rocker. "It's pleasant here. Quite peaceful."

"Thank you. I left for a while after college, but I'm glad I had the sense to come back. I missed the mountains and home."

"The sheriff called and gave me the plate on the truck. You're sure it's the same one?" he asked.

"It's a vintage green Chevy with a white top. How many nineteen fifties Chevys are tooling around the valley?"

His mouth twitched ever so slightly.

"Yes, I'm pretty sure. It's a tallish guy. When he showed up on our security feeds, he was in jeans and a hoodie. He also impersonated Mr. Perkins's nephew. Aunt Roxanne said he was tall and skinny. And there was that one video feed where he was with another guy, but I haven't seen him on the property since."

"The reporter?" he asked.

"No. Another guy."

"Where else have you seen the truck guy?"

"I was leaving Charlottesville one day, and I followed him through town until he got on I-64."

"And?" He paused and glared at her.

"Yesterday. I was leaving the business council meeting in town. He whizzed past me on the edge of town, where the road is all curvy. He slammed on his brakes, and I almost swerved off the road. Then he rocketed off and turned down one of the cut-thru roads."

"Interesting. You're sure it was the same green truck guy?"

"Without a doubt. He's popping up a lot lately."

"Do you know of any empty cabins or summer homes around here?" He glanced at the parking lot.

Jules wondered what that had to do with their conversation. "I'm sure there are a bunch in the area owned by folks who use them as rentals, especially near the ski resort. None that I can name offhand."

"Any foreclosed homes in the area that you know about?"

"There are a couple of houses for sale nearby. Not sure if they're empty. Why?"

"The truck guy is in town a lot, and I can't find any record of him staying nearby. He's either crashing with someone or using an assumed name. I'll check around to see what's vacant in the area." Agent Stafford stared toward the mountains. "With all these woods around, he could be camping somewhere off the beaten path. If you see him anywhere, call me or Sheriff Hobbs. He's dangerous. Stay away from him."

"Do you think he's the killer?"

"Don't know yet, but I'm going to find out. Call me if you see anything suspicious. Thanks for your time." He rose and scanned the horizon.

"Sure." Jules looked at the majestic mountains, too. She hoped Don Fisher was nowhere nearby.

As Agent Stafford trotted down the steps Jules looked over at the Robin Hood camper. "Mr. Perkins, what did you bring to Fern Valley?"

Jules pulled into the gravel lot of Honey's fruit stand a few minutes before three. Letting the dust settle, she climbed out of the Jeep. She looked up and down the lot but didn't see Kevin's car. She walked around the stalls, stacked tall with fruit and vegetables. Still no Kevin. She stepped inside the smallish store. Local honey, jams, and jellies lined most of the walls around the ice cream cooler. Jules picked up a jar of honey and a five-pound bag of roasted peanuts.

She waited behind an elderly couple with a sack of peaches. Finally, it was her turn to check out.

"Hi, Jules," the clerk said. "What brings you out this way?"

"Hi, Marie. I was out and about and stopped in for a few minutes. How are you?"

Marie West and her husband, Derek, had taken over the orchard and fruit stand when his mother, Honey, died.

"We're doing well. I'm finally retired, so I hang out more here. Hey, I heard you're running against J. P. Gross for council president. You have my vote."

Marie pushed her silver bangs out of her face and rang up Jules's purchases.

"Thanks. I appreciate it." Jules handed her cash to cover her purchase. "I can't wait to go home and make peanut butter and honey sandwiches. There's nothing like the fresh stuff."

"Enjoy it." Marie handed her the change. "And good luck with the election."

Jules smiled and stepped out into the bright sunshine. She held her hand up to shade her eyes. Still no sign of Kevin. She scanned both sides of the small parking lot.

Pulling out her cell, she dialed Kevin's number and left a message. "It's Jules. I've been at Honey's for close to twenty minutes. Where are you?"

She sat in the Jeep through three more songs and still no Kevin. She started the engine and drove to the office.

"Kevin, what is up with you and these clandestine meetings? Where are you? And what was so important we had to meet in person? And then you ghosted me," she said out loud to no one in particular.

Chapter Sixteen

Friday

Jules and Bijou cuddled on the couch watching *Stranger Things*. Her phone dinged with an incoming text that interrupted her show.

Sorry about missing U. Something came up. Can U meet now? Kevin Bailey asked.

Where? Great. She had changed into yoga pants and a long T-shirt and settled in for the evening.

Now, beside the library.

Fern Valley Library? She had no desire to trek to Charlottesville tonight. Going to town was bad enough.

After several minutes, her phone dinged with, **Yes.**

She replied with **OK** and gritted her teeth.

Jules grumbled and searched for her shoes and purse. Last time, he hadn't shown, and the time before that, he didn't have that much information to share. She thought about making him wait until daylight, but curiosity got the best of her. What if he did have something juicy? She didn't want to miss out, especially if it could help her business.

"This better be good. Bijou, stay here and guard the house. I'll be back in a little bit. Let's see what he found."

Twilight faded into night as Jules drove slowly through town, past the one stoplight to the government center. She pulled in front of the library, where the grassy area bumped against the nearby woods. Jules sat in her

Jeep for what seemed like hours. She turned off the car so she wouldn't kill the battery. **Where are you?** she texted Kevin Bailey.

Something caught her eye near the woods. Someone in dark clothing waved an arm at her. Or was it a tree branch? She grabbed her phone and keys and walked down the sidewalk toward the tree line. A figure sat by one of the trees. Was he the waving guy?

"Hey," she yelled. "Hey, Kevin."

A few night frogs broke the silence. The person next to the tree didn't move or answer her. He seemed to be slumped over. Jules's heart pounded in her ears. She turned on her flashlight app and stepped closer.

The blood rushed out of her head and arms. She felt woozy. It was Kevin, and he had a large dark spot on the front of his hoodie. She grabbed his wrist. No pulse. Her hands felt damp. She wiped her hands on her jeans. Dark streaks covered both thighs. She stifled a scream and backtracked to the Jeep. Once safely locked inside, she called Sheriff Hobbs.

"Hello," he said after a few rings.

"Sheriff, this is Jules. I'm at the library. I need help. There's a body near the woods."

"Slow down. A body by the library?"

"Yes."

"Are you in a safe place?"

"Safe as I can be. I'm locked in my Jeep."

"Stay there. I need to hang up to call dispatch but call me back if you see anything. I'll be there in a few."

Jules felt dizzy. She put her head on the steering wheel and took several deep breaths. Once the swimmy headed feeling abated, Jules looked toward the woods. Kevin's body sat by the tree, where she had left him. What had he planned to tell her? She would never know.

About ten minutes later, Sheriff Hobbs pulled up. The blue lights from his cruiser bounced around the interior of her Jeep. A state police car arrived next. She rolled down the window as the two men approached.

"What brings you to the library after hours?"

"Kevin Bailey, the reporter." She pointed toward the trees. "We were to meet yesterday, but he stood me up. He texted me around eight-thirty tonight and said he needed to talk. He said it was important." She paused and tried to swallow a sob. "When I arrived, there was a person waving near the woods. When I got closer, I saw someone slumped by a tree." She took a deep breath. "It's Kevin, and he's dead."

"You've got some blood on you." The sheriff indicated spots on her shirt.

"Oh." Jules pulled on the hem. Smeared blood streaked her T-shirt, jeans, and hands.

"Step out of the car for me. When forensics gets here, we'll get them to assist," Sheriff Hobbs said.

Her heart pounded again. She took several deep, calming breaths and reminded herself to relax. There was a reasonable explanation for this. She was a Good Samaritan. The sheriff couldn't think she had something to do with Kevin's murder. She hoped she didn't need Roxanne's lawyer friend.

Deputy Dempsey and the forensic van arrived a short time later and cordoned off the edge of the woods and the parking area. One of the techs took blood samples from Jules's T-shirt and wiped her hands for residue.

"Jules, we're going to need to search your vehicle in order to discount you as a suspect," the sheriff said. "Anything in the car we should know about?"

She paused and then shook her head. "Go ahead. There's a tire iron and my toolbox in the back."

"Any other weapons? Guns or knives?"

"Uh, no. There's a metal thing in the door that can break a window if you go off a bridge. I think that has a blade on it to cut the seat belt with, but no guns or knives."

"You can sit in my car until Trooper Hughes finishes his search."

Jules sat in the back seat of his cruiser with the door open and her feet on the pavement. She watched the trooper methodically search her Wrangler.

A bright flash startled Jules. She spotted Jane Jenkins scurrying back to her car. Great. Jane the Pain snapped a picture of her sitting in the back of a squad car.

Jules tried not to think about the reporter. She focused on Deputy Dempsey, who stood sentry nearby while the two technicians moved portable lights and a generator to the area near the tree. None of the police paid much attention to the reporter, who jumped in her dark-colored Beetle and sputtered away. A funeral home van arrived a few minutes later, and Sheriff Hobbs waved the driver across the grass near the woods.

Time creeped as the trooper finished with Jules's Jeep. The only things he left with were the samples that he handed over to the forensic team. She hoped she wasn't on the suspect list. What would this do for business if campers didn't feel safe at her place or in Fern Valley? And would the paper really let Jane run the picture of her in the police car? She could probably kiss the business council presidency goodbye.

Jules jumped when Sheriff Hobbs opened the driver's door of his patrol car. She must have dozed off.

"Sorry. I didn't mean to startle you." He tossed a black bag in the front seat.

"It's been a long day." Jules climbed out of the cruiser.

"Forensics is done. And they're taking the body to the morgue for more tests. I know it's late, but I want to go over my notes one more time. Do you mind stopping by the station before you go home?"

"No." She rubbed her eyes. "Can I follow you?"

"Yep," he said.

She grabbed her purse and shut the back door. Hopefully, this meant she wasn't about to be arrested.

After a short ride that would have been a walk during daylight, Jules pulled into the visitor lot at the police station. She followed the sheriff through a side door that he held open for her.

"Coffee?"

"Yes, please."

"Have a seat in my office. I'll be there in a minute."

Jules tried to get comfortable in the wooden chair. The sheriff's office looked like it had the last time she was here. Piles of files littered his desk.

"Here." He handed her a mug of coffee. "If you need more cream or sugar, let me know."

"This is fine." She blew on the steaming mug.

"Okay. Kevin Bailey called you both times?"

"No. He called and asked me to meet him at Honey's fruit stand yesterday, but he never showed. Then tonight, I got a text. He wanted to meet near the library."

"That normal for him?" The sheriff picked up a pen and twirled it while he talked.

"I don't know. I've only talked to him a couple of times. Every time we meet, it's in a very public place."

"Did he ever want to meet at night?"

She shook her head. "No. We always met during the day."

"What did he want to tell you?"

"He said it was about Ira Perkins."

"And, of course, you went." The sheriff's brow furrowed and concern flooded his face.

"I wanted to see what he found out. I would have told you if it was pertinent to your investigation."

The sheriff scowled. "So, you have no idea what this was about?"

"Nope."

"He didn't have any notes on him or a cell phone, which was odd. You saw someone else other than the body when you arrived?"

"I think so. When I pulled up, I saw someone in a dark shirt waving. I locked the Jeep and walked toward the woods. When I got there, there was only one person leaning against a tree. When I called his name, he didn't respond."

"So, you saw two people?" he asked again.

"Maybe. It was dark, and I was expecting only Kevin. I didn't see anyone run away."

"Could they have slipped back into the woods?" the sheriff asked.

"Possibly. I wasn't paying that much attention. I wasn't looking for two people."

"Did you hear anything?"

"No. It was quiet, except for the normal night noises. There wasn't any traffic. Did you search his car?"

"The only car nearby was yours. My guys are canvassing the area. Anything else stand out?"

Jules paused and then shook her head.

"That's enough for tonight."

What did he find in the woods? Evidence of two people? Did Kevin bring somebody with him?

Jules was too tired to think about this anymore. She slid into the Jeep and started the engine. The radio clock let her know it was after one-thirty. And now her reporter contact had died before she found out what he knew. What happened to his phone and his car? And what was going to happen to his big story?

Chapter Seventeen

Saturday

Jules's alarm buzzed. Rolling over, she smacked the clock. It felt like she had just fallen asleep. Bijou stirred in her bed. Jules almost drifted back to sleep, but she realized today was the business council election at the library.

Needing a jolt of caffeine to shake off the gloomy pall that Mr. Perkins's and Kevin's deaths created, she padded to the kitchen to get the coffee maker going.

After a mug laden with caffeine and sugar and a shower, she felt more human. Flipping through her closet, she wanted to find an outfit to project confidence and credibility, without the dragon-lady look. Finally settling on a royal blue skirt and jacket with a cream blouse, she found her Fern Valley Business Council pin and attached it to the jacket's collar. Jules put on more makeup than usual to cover the dark circles. Hopefully, no one in the audience would notice.

"There," she said to Bijou. "Almost ready. Wish me luck this morning. I have to take on J. P. Gross and his good old boys. I want this. I really want this." She patted the dog on the head.

Bijou snarfled and headed for the couch.

Jules could make a difference on the business council. She had lots of ideas and wanted improvements that would benefit everyone. Her smarmy opponent was just out to pad his bottom line and help his good buddies.

Fingers crossed that today's vote went in her favor.

She fumbled in the Jeep's console for her sunglasses. It was a quick ride to town, but traffic came to a complete standstill at the government center. Deputy Dempsey directed cars to the courthouse's lot as overflow parking for the library.

The car tracks across the grass to the woods were the only sign of last night's investigation. She shook off the eerie feeling about the dead reporter and what he wanted to tell her and tried to get her thoughts to focus on what she was going to say about the election. *Keep it positive and highlight economic developments*. She dropped her keys in her bag and fumbled for her well-worn notes. She clutched her speech and walked toward the meeting room. Jules wiped her sweaty palms on the side of her skirt.

Jules stepped inside the library's conference room, and Roxanne and Kim Lacy swooped in and shooed her over to the corner.

"You look good. Now don't be nervous." Roxanne pinned a "Jules for Prez" button on her other lapel. "You've got this."

"Yes, you do." Kim, a tall brunette with ringlet curls outlining her heart-shaped face, patted Jules's arm. "We're counting on you."

"Go get 'em, tiger." Roxanne nudged her niece toward the front row.

Jules took her seat in front of the lectern next to Mitch Ford. Kim and Roxanne returned to passing out Jules's buttons as more business owners filed in.

"Hi, Mitch. How are things?" Jules settled into the hard, plastic seat.

"Good. I'm curious to see what J. P. has to say. I think this is a shoo-in for you. The majority of the people here are sporting your button."

Before she could comment, Roxanne and Kim slipped into seats behind Jules. Her aunt squeezed Jules's shoulder.

Elaine James made her way to the front of the room, "May I have your attention, please." Elaine tapped the microphone. "Excuse me. Order!" She hammered a wooden gavel on the lectern. "Thank you." The crowd noise subsided. "I hereby call the special election meeting for the Fern Valley Business Council to order. Today, we will hear from both candidates and elect our new president. We will flip a coin to see which candidate goes first.

"That's not necessary," J. P. Gross said from the other side of the room. "My opponent can go first as long as she addresses the fact that her business attracts some undesirable characters." His smile looked more like a sneer that complimented his slicked-back black hair and piercing blue eyes. He adjusted the sleeves on his charcoal gray suit.

"Very well," Elaine said. "First, we have Jules Keene, owner of the Fern Valley Luxury Camping Resort."

"Thank you, Elaine." Jules stepped toward the lectern, ignoring her opponent's snarky attack. He was not going to rattle her. She took a deep breath and scanned the standing-room-only crowd. Quite a few people in the crowd displayed her button. "Good morning, Fern Valley Business Council. I am happy to be here to talk with you about our future and opportunities for all of us. The valley has undergone a resurgence over the last few years, and it has been profitable to our community. As the council president, I want to continue to promote this economic growth and create more opportunities for tourism dollars. The people of our town are special. We've been given a variety of resources and talents. Together, we can continue the prosperity and put us on a great footing for the future."

The crowd burst into applause. The noise faded.

"Thank you. As president, I want to work with all the business owners to plan events and projects to attract visitors to our beautiful valley year-round. We have an amazing amount of creativity and energy when we work together, and I look forward to the partnerships that we'll forge to benefit our community."

The audience interrupted her again with a round of applause.

"Thank you. I am Jules Keene, and I would be honored to earn your vote for president of the Fern Valley Business Council. And I promise to do my best to promote the area and our resources and to find opportunities for all of our futures."

Applause echoed in the library's conference room, and most of the crowd stood as Jules returned to her seat.

Elaine James returned to the lectern. "Thank you, Jules. And now we have our second candidate, J. P. Gross. He is the owner of several properties in town and Gross and Sons Landscaping."

The man who resembled a bear in size and girth plowed to the front of the room. He clutched several manila folders. Papers hung at all angles. He slapped his papers on the wooden lectern. The microphone squealed. After retrieving his reading glasses from his jacket pocket, he flipped open the top folder.

"Good morning." He cleared his throat. "I am J. P. Gross, and I am the only viable candidate for this office." He flipped through his folder and pulled out a photograph. "My opponent," he pointed at Jules with his beefy finger, "has been involved in two, not one, but two murders in our town recently." He held up a picture of a surprised Jules in Sheriff Hobbs's cruiser.

Jules's face burned. She wanted to respond but bit her tongue. Some in the audience murmured.

"She's too busy lately being smack dab in the middle of these heinous crimes. Is this what we want for our council and our town?" J. P. Gross asked.

Some man in the back yelled, "No."

J. P. Gross cleared his throat again. "No. Of course not. We haven't had a murder here in the past ten years. Sure, we have prosperity now, but her kind of prosperity means bringing crime and the big city evils to our little part of the mountains. She has that campground full of all sorts of people every weekend. Do you know who's coming to your town? I say that's not right for us."

Jules heard whispers in the room behind her.

"We need to go back to our roots and our traditions. Maybe we don't need to grow so fast. We have to know where we came from. Our heritage. And if you agree, then I'm your candidate for the presidency. Return to our roots with J. P. Gross."

A guy in a T-shirt and jeans near the door yelled, "Yeah. Go, J. P.! You tell 'em."

J. P. gathered up his folders. Loud whispers followed him to his seat on the other side of the room.

"Thank you, candidates," Elaine James said. "And now, for the voting. The board members are at a table in the back of the room. They'll give each member a ballot. Mark your ballot and place it in the box. When everyone has had a chance, we'll count the votes."

"Wait," Mitch Ford said. "I think Jules should have the opportunity to respond."

"Quickly," Elaine replied.

Jules took another deep breath and stepped behind the lectern. "Thank you. Yes, Mr. Gross. I am involved with the recent murders, but through no fault of my own. I am entangled because a murder occurred in the woods on my property."

"It's because your place attracts all kinds of undesirables," J. P. bellowed.

"I take offense to that, Mr. Gross." Jules stood taller by the lectern. "I own a family establishment. I want to bring prosperity to our valley."

The room erupted in applause. Jules returned to her seat.

Elaine adjusted the microphone. "Mr. Gross, do you have anything else?"

He shook his head.

Elaine said, "Very well then. Let the voting begin."

Time crawled as Jules and the crowd filed to the back to cast their votes. She smiled and talked to those who came by to wish her well. Finally, the three officers brought the box to the lectern. Marco and Cindy dragged a table to the front, and they began the count.

Bats bounced around Jules's stomach. She hoped the murders and J. P.'s speech didn't sway the voters. Elaine and the other officers put their heads together and whispered. Then, Elaine stood and banged the gavel again. "Attention, attention, everyone. We have a new president."

Jules held her breath as the room grew suddenly quiet. The ticking of the clock on the back wall permeated the room.

"I am pleased to announce that our new council president is Jules Keene."

The audience exploded in cheers and applause. Heat flooded Jules's face. Roxanne, Mitch, and Kim congratulated her, and she made her way to the front.

"Thank you, everyone. I appreciate all the support. I want to make our council and town the best that they can be. Thank you again, and I look forward to serving you this year."

J. P.'s supporters and the candidate slunk out the door. So much for being a gracious loser.

"Wrap it up." Roxanne blew into the back office. "I want to take you to dinner to celebrate. Whatever you're working on can wait until Monday."

"Thanks so much, but I was going to head home for a quiet dinner with Bijou."

"She won't mind it if you hang with me tonight. Come on. It's just dinner. I'll have you back before you turn into a pumpkin."

"Okay. Let me take Bijou home, and I'll meet you at your car in a few minutes."

After securing Bijou at the cabin, Jules hopped into the passenger seat of Roxanne's Mercedes. She barely got the door shut before her aunt sped out of the parking space and floored it down the access road.

"What's the hurry?" Jules asked.

"I'm hungry," She gave a slight smile.

Jules adjusted her seat belt and settled down in the soft leather seat.

Roxanne made it to town in record time. It was a good thing Bubba didn't have his speed trap set.

She pulled into the side lot of Pop's. "I feel like burgers. I hope that's okay. My treat."

"Sure. Pop's is always good." The mention of the diner reminded Jules of her last visit there with Kevin Bailey. A twang of sadness overcame her.

Roxanne held the door for her niece, who lagged behind.

Marsha, decked out in her pink bouffant, was perched on a stool by the cash register. "Hi, Jules. Hi, Roxanne. Follow me, ladies. I have a table all set for you."

Jules followed the waitress around the corner.

"Surprise!" echoed from the side room. Two long tables full of friends waved and cheered, and balloons and a "Congratulations, Jules" banner decorated the wall.

"Just a quick, quiet dinner?" Jules was flattered that her friends would go to all this trouble to celebrate her election to the business council.

"I don't know what you're talking about. We wanted to get together for dinner, and Pop graciously offered us his back room. Pull up a chair and figure out what you want to eat." Roxanne cocked her eyebrow.

Jake and Lester entered with a vase full of a dozen red roses. The chatter in the room stopped, and all eyes were on her handsome maintenance guy.

"Congratulations, Jules." Jake handed her the vase and brushed her hand in the exchange. A tingle of excitement zinged through her.

"Thank you. These are lovely. You all went to way too much effort," Jules said.

After dinner and Pop's best desserts, the celebration started to wind down. Jules picked up her purse and the flowers. Roxanne tapped her on the shoulder and tilted her head toward the door. Special Agent Will Stafford, in jeans and a casual black shirt, leaned against the doorframe. His sudden appearance surprised Jules.

"Hi, Agent Stafford. Why don't you join us?"

"Looks like the party's wrapping up. I came over to offer my congratulations."

"Thank you. It's definitely going to be an adventure."

"I'm headed out, too. Have a good evening." He turned and disappeared as quickly as he arrived.

Jules almost asked about the investigation and whether they knew any more about Kevin's death but stifled the urge. There would be plenty of time tomorrow to check into it.

Jules followed Roxanne to the parking lot. She barely got the car door closed before Roxanne sped off. She kept the accelerator floored until she reached the access road to the resort and stopped sharply in front of Jules's cabin. "Home again, jiggedy jig. I told you I'd get you back all safe and sound. Why don't you park in the garage?"

"Sometimes I leave the Jeep outside. It's easier when I'm in a hurry. Thanks for everything tonight. I had a wonderful time."

"You deserve some fun." Her aunt kissed the top of Jules's head. "I'm proud of you and all you've done, but I want you to live a little, too. This council role will be good for you."

"See you Monday." Jules let herself out and watched as Roxanne hightailed it down the access road.

Jules cracked her door open and whistled. Bijou ran straight into her and bounced off her knees.

She tightened her grip on the vase of roses. "Hey, baby. Missed you. Let's go outside." She set everything on the side table by the door.

While Bijou explored the perimeter of the cabin, she checked her phone. Pixel texted, **Found more on the truck guy. I'll send you an email.** Jules responded with a happy emoji and slid the phone into her pocket.

Bijou sniffed the flower beds and the corner of the house. The dog was nowhere in sight. Jules whistled. Still no dog.

"Bijou!" She whistled again.

The dog trotted around the corner. "Where'd you go? It's time for bed."

The dog's ears perked up as she bounded into the house.

Something caught Jules's eye out the front window. She stared as whatever it was moved toward the woods. She chided herself for being jumpy, but something looked odd. She flipped off the floodlights. A shadow, too tall for a deer, moved across the access road between the light posts. She slipped out the door and pulled it shut behind her. A lanky, dark figure moved into the woods. Jules caught her breath. She followed at a brisk pace. Her heart pounded in her ears. Jules knew it was careless, but she had to find out who was skulking around her cabin. Maybe it was just a guest out for a late evening stroll.

Hugging the tree line, Jules watched for any movement. She heard footsteps ahead of her. Twigs cracked and leaves crunched. She paused for a moment, and the footsteps sounded farther and farther away and slowly disappeared. An engine roared to life. She was left with the creepy night noises in the woods. Jules flipped on her cell phone's flashlight and retraced her steps. She quickened her pace, and, in her haste, she almost ran into Jake and his golf cart on the access road.

"Hey, Boss. What are you doing out here so late?"

"I heard something over by the woods."

"What was it?"

"Somebody walking around. I saw something move, and I followed it to the woods. I heard an engine, so I think he's gone."

"You going to check the cameras tonight?"

"Nah. It can wait until morning. I've had enough tonight."

"I'll hang here until you get inside. If you decide to go walking in the woods again at night, call me."

Jake waited nearby as Jules headed up the sidewalk. She grabbed the doorknob and twisted, but it didn't move. Her heart sank. In her hurry to follow the mystery guy, she had locked herself out of the cabin. Bijou ran from window to window, barking.

"You okay?" Jake walked up behind her.

"Not really. I locked myself out," she said sheepishly.

"Do you have an emergency key?"

"I thought about it, but nope."

"Let me take a look."

Bijou bounced from window to window, trying to see what was going on.

Jake pulled out a credit card and took several swipes at the lock.

After one good try, Jules heard a click.

"There," he said.

"Thanks. And now I'm slightly freaked out about how easy it was to get into my house." She opened the door, and Bijou rushed out and jumped on Jake.

"Something I learned from an army buddy." He picked up Bijou and patted her on the head.

"I guess it's good to have skills. Thank you. You saved me from having to break a window. See you tomorrow."

He handed her Bijou. "Night."

She closed the door. "Come on, Bijou. It's bedtime. We'll worry about the green-truck guy tomorrow after we call a locksmith to put in some deadbolts. And get a spare key."

Chapter Eighteen

Sunday

Sliding her phone and keys in her jeans' pocket, Jules slipped out the side door before Bijou realized she remained behind. Jules wanted to see what Mel and Crystal had created for Sunday brunch.

She saw her Jeep and gasped. The front tire sat flat on the ground like a deflated beachball. Everything from the glove compartment and center console lay strewn around the driveway.

"Enough! What else is going to happen around here?" She pulled out her phone and snapped a couple of pictures. Then she punched in the number for the sheriff.

"What's got you up at the crack of dawn on a Sunday?"

"Hello, Sheriff. I'm sorry to bother you so early. Someone broke into my Jeep and flattened my tire."

"Any idea who?"

"I can guess. Somebody was sneaking around last night. I haven't checked the security cameras yet. But that's next on my list after breakfast."

"I'll be over in a few minutes."

"Thanks, Sheriff. I'll be here, waiting."

Twenty minutes later, Sheriff Hobbs's cruiser pulled up in front of Jules's cabin. He opened the trunk and pulled out a bag and set it on the ground. "Hey, Jules."

"Hi, Sheriff. I can't believe I had to call you again. It's not that I don't like to see you, but this is getting old." She smirked. "And you're up early on a Sunday, too."

"I do some weekends so my deputies can have the time off." He snapped on a pair of rubber gloves and pulled out a camera.

She sat down on the steps and watched Sheriff Hobbs document the scene.

Jake walked over as the sheriff photographed everything and dusted the Jeep for prints.

"Morning, Sheriff. Boss. More trouble?" Jake sat next to Jules, their legs almost touching.

"Yep. I was headed over to brunch, and I found a flattened tire and all my stuff strewn across the driveway."

"I'm about done here. You're gonna want to wipe this down to get the powder and residue off," Sheriff Hobbs said.

"Thank you, Sheriff. Would you like to come over and get some breakfast?"

"No thanks. I'm headed back to the station. Let me know if you find anything on the video cameras or if any of your stuff is missing."

"Sure. I'll check as soon as I grab some coffee. Jake, have you eaten?" Jules picked up the items on the ground and returned them to the glove box.

"I'll be over in a little while."

They parted ways in Jules's driveway, and she was left with her thoughts of why the truck guy kept prowling around her resort. This had to stop. There was nothing left at the campground related to Ira Perkins.

Jules grabbed breakfast and headed to the office to pour over the security feeds. She walked by her cabin. The Jeep's tire had been changed, and Jake was nowhere in sight. She'd have to find a way to pay him back.

She opened the door and whistled for Bijou. The dog bounded out the door and waited by the Jeep. Jules snapped on her leash. "Come on, baby. Let's go to work."

Jules punched the numbers on the security pad at the back door. When she unclicked the leash, Bijou ran through the store and the office looking for Roxanne. Not finding anyone, she decided to see what Jules brought with her in the plastic to-go container.

Jules settled in her office chair to go through hours and hours of security camera footage. Bijou stood on her hind legs, sniffing at the bacon. "How about a taste of bacon when I'm done?" Bijou stared intently as Jules ate her chocolate-chip pancakes.

About nine-thirty last night, according to the time stamp, Jules saw the familiar old truck pull off the main entrance road. A guy in a dark shirt got out and hiked through the woods. This time he had on a dark ballcap. She crawled through the feed, frame by frame, but didn't see him return to his truck until after three-thirty this morning. She shivered and made a note to hire additional security. Then her thoughts flitted to Pixel and her text from yesterday.

Jules opened her email and scrolled to find what Pixel had sent. "Aha," she said to Bijou, who jumped on her chair. "Here's the bacon I promised."

The dog wolfed it down and looked around for more.

"Pixel said our creepy night stalker is an IT guy from MedPro." She read further to find out he had been on medical leave since May. That would explain all the free time he had for skulking around her property. "So, Don Fisher. Were you extorting money from very sick people, or was that Ira Perkins? And what do you think he left on my property?"

"Huh?" Jake came in the back door and stomped his feet.

Bijou barked and ran over for a proper greeting. Jake reached down and patted her on the head.

"Thanks so much for changing my flat tire. You didn't have to."

"I know. But I didn't know if you needed to go somewhere today. If you give me your keys, I'll give it a quick wash and wipe down to get rid of all the fingerprint dust the sheriff left."

"I can't ask you to do that."

"It's no big deal. I don't mind. I was going to wash my Mustang later anyway. Find anything on the cameras?"

"Same guy. Same stuff. He parked and walked through the woods. He didn't leave until the wee hours of the morning." She clicked a few times to save the camera footage and sent a copy to the sheriff.

He slid a mug under the coffee machine. "Keys?"

"At least let me pay you for your time. You're technically off today."

"Don't worry about it. It won't take but a few minutes."

"What else do you have planned for your Sunday?" She flipped him her car keys.

"I found some good designs for the tiny houses, and I've started the frame for the first one. If you get a minute, come out to the barn, and I'll show you. It's got a cottage flair to it."

"Bijou and I'd love to see it. I'm fascinated by the whole tiny house craze. I'm amazed people can get their whole lives in those small spaces. I think this will be a neat addition to the campground. We'll have to come up with a clever name for our tiny house community."

"I'm building these from blueprints, not a kit. I think I can finish the first one for about five thousand dollars, not including the interior decorating."

"Do you want to sell them outright to me, or do you want to work up a rental agreement?"

"I think I like the partnership idea. Your expertise is the decorating. I need your help with choosing colors and stuff. We make a good team."

"Come on, Bijou. Time for a walk. Let's go see what Jake's been up to in the barn."

Bijou's ears perked up, and she danced around Jules's feet until her leash clicked into place.

They trekked across the campground, where some of the guests milled around after breakfast. One couple relaxed in the double hammock. Bijou rushed ahead, trying to smell everything between the office and the barn.

Jake opened the doors to the big red barn. One creaked, and Bijou jumped back on high alert. When it looked safe, she darted into the darkened structure. Jake flipped on the overhead lights, and they popped and buzzed, slowly illuminating the space.

Behind the tractors and lawn equipment, Jake had cleared an area in the back corner where he had framed a two-story tiny house.

"Wow, you've got a good start already. Is it easier to build here and then move, or would it be better to construct it on the pads on the other side of the service road?"

"I think with the summer heat fast approaching, it would be cooler to work inside here. Plus, I can continue construction on rainy days or evenings. It doesn't take much to move these. All I need is a flatbed and a couple of guys. They're meant to be transported. People build these and move them around all over the country. This one has a little over five hundred square feet of space. You can see enough of what it's going to look like. The front door opens to the main room for living and dining with a loft for a bedroom. There is another bedroom and bathroom on the other side."

"Right now, I have too much stuff. It would be a lifestyle change to do this permanently, but I'm intrigued by the tiny spaces. And I think it will be a cool addition to the campground. People would like to use these as getaways. Now, are the doors and windows big enough to bring in beds and furniture after you finish?"

"I'm going to put a sliding glass door or a double door on the back, so that should work for moving things in and out. Otherwise, you have to move the big stuff in before you finish the construction, and that affects portability."

"So, we could get a queen and a double in this one? I guess we could put a fold-out couch or a futon in the living area for some extra sleep space. For the kitchens, I'd like to do it like the trailers. Is there space for a dishwasher and microwave?"

"Yep. I'll put in cabinets where the stove and oven would go. I'll anchor them like the trailers, and we can do the electrical and water hookups the same way."

"Do you have a picture on the plans of what the completed house looks like?"

"Here," he handed her a color printout. "I was thinking about putting gingerbread molding on the trim. Think about the colors you want. We have a little while before we paint."

"We need a theme for these, like literary row or fairy tale row. So, as folks drive up to the classic campground, we'll have a little village of tiny themed houses. I want fun and whimsical, but not really like amusement park kitschy. I think this'll be a big draw for families with kids. Let's go with cottage whimsy. You sure you're up for this? I kinda hijacked your project and magnified it into a tiny village."

"It'll be fun." Jake grinned. "I was thinking about building these to sell, but it would be good to have some models done, so people could see or even stay in before they invested. You come up with the themes and let me know. I should be able to incorporate them into the trim and finishing designs."

"This is what that part of the field needed. It's gone to seed since we revamped the campground. Let me know when you're ready to start specking it out, and I'll get Lester to tame the tall grass and find the old cement pads. When you have a few minutes, we can sit down and hash out the partnership agreement and the money."

"How about you take a first crack at the contract terms?"

"I'll start a draft when I get back to the office. Come on, Bijou. We need to wrap up things at work and do fun stuff like laundry."

The dog turned her head and sniffed.

"I agree, but we need to get our chores done. Say goodbye to Jake."

The Jack Russell danced around his feet until he picked her up and she licked his nose.

Bijou followed Jules back to the office. The contract for the little houses shouldn't be that hard. They would agree on the terms, and then she could send it to the lawyer for his review.

Her thoughts kept bouncing back from the fun, tiny houses to Don Fisher and his all-too-frequent visits to her campground. Why did he keep nosing around? And what was the attraction? Down deep, she knew law enforcement had it under control. But there was that nagging feeling that she needed to get to the bottom of this before something else happened that could damage her only source of income.

Chapter Nineteen

Monday

The store door creaked open. Bijou raised her head from the middle of her puffy bed.

"Hey, Jules. You here?" Roxanne asked.

"Back here." Jules stepped into the store and shut the bottom of the Dutch door.

"What in the devil happened here?" Roxanne stood on the porch wither her arms outstretched.

Jules frowned and walked outside. Broken eggs covered the wooden decking, sidewalk, and rocking chairs. She sighed at the sight of the mess. "I can't tell you how many times I've called the sheriff's office in the last week or so. This is just one more thing." Her shoulders sagged. "We came in through the back door. I had no idea this was out here." The frustration built up inside of Jules.

"Here. I'll call the sheriff. And you check the cameras," her aunt said.

Jules sighed again and headed toward the coffee maker. While it was brewing, she opened the camera application.

It didn't take long to spot the culprits. About one-thirty in the morning, a large red truck with a Teagle's Junkyard logo pulled into the front lot. Three guys stumbled out and pelted the front of the store with eggs. They seemed to be having a good time. When they ran out of eggs, they threw the empty cartons in the truck bed and drove off.

"Did you solve the mystery of the splattered eggs, Nancy Drew?" Roxanne started her own coffee.

"Yep. Ralph Teagle and a couple of his cronies. Not sure what caused him to bombard my front porch."

"General meanness. The sheriff said to leave it as is, and he'll be over in a while," Roxanne said.

"I feel bad that I keep having to call him. The police have been out here way too much lately."

"Teagle and his bunch are sore losers. I can't believe they'd do something this dumb, especially in a world with security cameras. J. P. Gross probably put them up to it."

"From their antics, it looks like they had some liquid courage before they dreamed up this stunt. They stumbled and bumbled around until they hightailed it out of here in Ralph's truck."

"Not the sharpest tools in the shed. The sheriff should have fun with this one." Roxanne winked.

About twenty minutes later, a car door slammed out front. Bijou ran to the dividing door and waited patiently for someone with thumbs to open it.

"Hi, Sheriff," Roxanne said from the store. "How are you this morning?"

"Fine. I see you all had some more visitors last night."

Jules stuck her head out of the office. "Hi, Sheriff. I pulled the camera footage."

He took his hat off and opened the half-door to the back office. "What'd ya find?"

"This was kind of surprising. I've been thinking about the green-truck guy and his adventures all week. I didn't expect to see this." She clicked on the viewer on her laptop.

Ralph Teagle's truck rolled into the picture, and the band of merry men jumped out and began their egg rampage.

"Make me a copy of this, please. These three should have known better. I'm going to have a chat with them about the way they treat others' property. If it doesn't cause any harm, leave the mess for a little while. I think Ralph and his buddies may have a change of heart."

"I'd like to get it cleaned up before my guests see it." Jules scrunched her nose.

"Trust me on this one. Leave it there until I get back."

"Okay. But the longer it stays out there, the harder it'll be to clean it off," Jules said.

"Then they'll just have to scrub with a little muscle." He walked toward his cruiser.

"Hey, Roxanne. I'm going to run home for a sandwich." Jules yelled from the back office. "Do you want me to bring you anything?"

"Nope. I'm good. But you may want to come out here and see this."

Jules and Roxanne joined Lester, Jake, and Crystal in front of the building, where Ralph Teagle, Donnie Titus, and Boogie Jones scrubbed the front porch under Sheriff Hobbs's watchful eye. Roxanne whipped out her phone and videoed the scene of the three large men in coveralls scraping dried egg off the rocking chairs and steps.

"Hello, Jules. I stopped by Ralph's place, and he and his friends wanted to come over and right a wrong. Right, Ralph?" Sheriff Hobbs asked.

"Yes, Sheriff. Jules, I'm sorry for what happened here out front. We had a little too much fun last night, and I think we got a little out of hand. I want you to know it won't happen again."

The sheriff cleared his throat.

"And congratulations on being the new business council president."

"Thank you." Jules stared at the three men, who didn't look as menacing when they were on their hands and knees, cleaning her front porch.

"Jules, it's up to you if you want to press charges. And you don't have to decide today. You've got about thirty days to make up your mind."

"Thanks, Sheriff. I'm glad the mess is gone. It wasn't a pretty sight for my guests."

"We're about done here." Ralph stood and wiped his hands on his coveralls.

The three men walked with their buckets and their slumped shoulders back to Ralph's truck. It didn't take long for them to zoom down the driveway.

After they watched the truck's taillights disappear, Sheriff Hobbs said, "I don't think you're going to hear from that bunch again. But if you do, call me. I'll slap enough charges on them they'll have to stay in jail at least overnight."

"Thanks, Sheriff. I thought this was part of the Ira Perkins's thing when I first saw it. Any news?"

"Nope. We're still looking for your night visitor. I'm sure it's a matter of time before we bring him in and find out why he's so fascinated with slinking around your property in the wee hours."

"I'd like to know that, too," Jules said.

The mail carrier parked in front of the office. He climbed out and handed Jules a stack of rubber-banded items.

"Thanks, Tom," she said. "How are you?"

"Couldn't be better. I love this weather." The letter carrier climbed back in his truck and sped off as quickly as he arrived.

"I better be heading out, too. Let me know if anything out of the ordinary happens," Sheriff Hobbs said.

"I have you on speed dial." Jules hoped she didn't have to call him anytime soon.

Heading back inside, she sorted the mail as she walked. A small brown envelope addressed to her from Kevin Bailey made her pause. Butterflies fluttered around her stomach. She took a deep breath and ripped open the padded envelope, postmarked last Friday from Charlottesville. A small copper key and a piece of white paper fell out. On the paper, Kevin had scrawled, "In case something happens to me, I want you to have my notes. They're at the post office on East Main Street in downtown Charlottesville."

Jules's heart did a flip-flop. Kevin must have been suspicious about something.

"Roxanne. I changed my mind. I'm going to run to Charlottesville for a little while. Can you watch Bijou?"

"Not a problem. We'll hang out and watch my video go viral."

"What?"

"I posted my video of the cleanup of the egg massacre to Facebook, and I made sure to send Jane the Pain a link. Maybe ol' Ralph and his buddies will make Tuesday's paper."

Jules grinned and raced out the doorway.

She drove with purpose to the Charlottesville downtown business district. It felt like it took forever for the elevator to reach the third level of the parking deck. Jules gave up and took the stairs down to the pedestrian mall.

Standing outside near the post office and the government offices, she dug through her purse for Kevin's key.

Inside, Jules looked at the wall of post office boxes and located the match to her key stamped with a "B-150." The key clicked in the lock.

She held her breath as she opened the small brass door.

Inside, a manila mailing envelope sat alone in the metal cubicle. She retrieved it, took a picture of the key and the metal mailbox, and left the key in the lock.

On second thought, Jules pocketed the key and shut the door. Knowing Sheriff Hobbs, he would want to search everything, and he probably wouldn't be too pleased she retrieved the contents without telling him first. She assuaged her guilt by reminding herself the package had been addressed to her. It could have been a present that had nothing to do with the police.

She pushed thoughts of the sheriff and his investigation aside and zipped back to her Jeep. She locked the doors, slid her nail under the flap, and tore open the envelope.

Inside was a small black notebook. She wanted to dive into it and see what Kevin had left her, but she would have more time to read it in the comfort of her home instead of a public parking lot.

The butterflies in her stomach were awake and dancing. She had to know what was in Kevin's notes. He'd said he was almost ready to publish his story. Did Don Fisher know about this or was he on her property looking for something else?

She sped back to the resort and headed to the office. Jules walked through the empty store, unusual for the afternoon. Several shrill whistles emanated from outside, and someone called Bijou.

Pocketing her phone and keys, she locked her purse with Kevin's notebook in the desk drawer and headed outside toward the noise. Spotting Lester and Roxanne at the edge of the woods, she hustled over.

"What's up?" She stepped closer.

"Oh, Jules. I'm so sorry. Bijou slipped out of the office behind me. A couple had the store door open. There was a cat or a squirrel or something, and she tore off near the woods. We've been looking all over for her." Roxanne wiped the tears that flowed down her cheek with her hand. "Jake's in the woods searching for her."

"It's okay. We'll find her. We have to find her." Jules said a prayer for her missing dog. "I'm going to go get the treat box. If she's within range, she always responds to a whistle or her treats. I'll be right back."

Jules jogged home and let herself in her cabin. Grabbing the cardboard box of treats, she hoped this would work. She couldn't imagine life without that little dog.

Jules, Lester, and Roxanne trekked the perimeter of the campground. With no sign of the terrier, they ventured toward the woods.

"Hey," said Lester. "I'm going over to the meadow. She might be exploring over there. I'll let you know what I find."

The women walked under the dark canopy of the trees, and the temperature immediately dropped ten degrees. Jules worried about her aunt turning an ankle in her heels. "Why don't you head back to the office and be our communication center? You're not dressed for a hike in the woods."

"Jules, I feel so bad about this. This is all my fault. We've got to find Bijou."

"We will. She's okay. She's a spunky little dog. Head back to the office, and we'll holler as soon as we find her. Plus, our guests may need something in the meantime."

Roxanne hung her head as she made her way over roots and unlevel ground.

Jules turned and whistled. About every ten yards, she shook the treat box. She hiked for what seemed like miles. Her stomach rumbled, and she ignored the hungry growls. She had to find Bijou. Tears welled up in her eyes. "Stop it," she said to herself. "You will find her. This is not how this ends." She wiped her eyes and continued on. "Bijou! Bijou, where are you?"

Twenty minutes later, she sat down at the base of a large tree. She fought back the tears. Hunger, exhaustion, and fear were creeping in and taking over. She sniffed and wiped her eyes with the back of her hand. Sitting in the coolness of the woods for a while, she tried to convince herself that things would be okay.

Jules heard a rustling in the distance. She sniffed again and stood. The noise got louder. It sounded like someone stomping through the underbrush.

She hid behind the tree. They'd had bear and coyote sightings here before, but it usually wasn't something they worried too much about. She was more concerned about two-legged predators like Don Fisher.

The noise got louder and closer. Jules held her breath.

Then she heard a yip. "Bijou!" she yelled without thinking.

"Hey, wait a minute." And several more barks broke the silence of the woods.

Jules peeked around the trunk of the large tree. Jake held a wiggly Jack Russell Terrier.

"Bijou! Oh, Jake, you found her!"

Bijou jumped from his arms and ran to Jules. She scooped up the dog, and the lickfest was on.

"Oh, baby. You had us all scared. Jake, where did you find her?"

"She was way back in the woods. I found her at a campsite near old Crosby Road. That's got to be a mile or so from here."

"Bijou, what were you doing?"

"I think she chased something into the woods and kept going. I found her eating scraps at the campsite," he said.

"Anyone there?" Jules asked.

"No. It was back in the woods. There was a tent and the remnants of a campfire. Leftover food was out. Bijou helped herself to what was left of a can of pork and beans. I'm not sure who's camping there, but it's not too smart to leave all that trash around. I hope she doesn't have an upset stomach later."

"Thank you so much for finding her. I don't know what I would have done if she were gone for good." Jules hugged Bijou and Jake. "I'm so relieved."

She grabbed her phone and called Roxanne. "Jake found her. She was deep in the woods. And it looks like we have some squatters back in the woods again."

"Oh, thank goodness he found her," her aunt sighed. "I was so worried."

"Could you let Lester know? Also, I'm starving. Could you order some pizzas and drinks for everybody?"

"Sure. Y'all come on back to the office. And I'll let the others know."

The trio made their way to the campground. When Bijou got heavy, Jake took her from Jules. The hike back seemed like an eternity. The dog seemed to be content to be carried through the dark woods to the office after her adventure and snack.

"Bijou!" Roxanne ran over and grabbed the dog and squeezed her until she wiggled. "I have never been so glad to see you in my life. You scared me to death." The dog answered with several face licks. Roxanne hugged Jules and Jake, too.

Lester plopped down at the table, and Emily rushed over to Roxanne. "Oh, Bijou. I was so worried." The teen hugged the squirmy dog.

"Help yourself to the pizzas. They should still be hot." Roxanne dealt paper plates to the group like they were playing cards.

Everyone grabbed slices and drinks and found places to sit in the back office. Bijou danced around and enjoyed being the center of attention. And more than one person slipped her some pepperoni.

The party broke up about seven-thirty. Roxanne cleaned up plates and cups while Jake pulled the garbage bag out of the can and collected the pizza boxes.

Jules grabbed her purse and attached the leash to Bijou's collar. "See you all tomorrow. I'll let the sheriff know there are some campers in the woods. I hope it's just temporary. Thanks again for jumping in to find our little wanderer. I think we've all had enough excitement for one day."

Roxanne patted Bijou on the head again and kissed her. "Hey, girl. Let's not have any more solo adventures. I don't think my heart can take it."

Jules and Bijou followed Jake out the back doorway. "Good night. And thanks again for all you did. I don't know what I would have done if this had turned out differently."

His grin showed off his deep dimples, and, for a minute, he reminded Jules of the teenaged Jake. "I'm glad I found her. I'm curious about that campsite, though. It looked fresh, not something left over from last season. And there was food lying around."

"The FBI agent asked about abandoned properties. I'll text him about what you found. Maybe they can send Charles or someone over to check it out."

"It could attract unwanted predators," he said.

Or provide shelter for them.

Chapter Twenty

Tuesday

Jules woke up from a dead sleep with a start. In the darkness of her bedroom, she wasn't sure if Bijou stirred or if she heard something outside. She lay in bed on high alert for a few minutes. Nothing sounded out of place, so she rolled over. Then she remembered that in all this afternoon's excitement, she hadn't looked at Kevin's notebook.

She jumped up, and Bijou followed her to the kitchen. Jules flipped on the lights and rummaged through her purse for the envelope. After pouring a glass of milk, she settled in at the table to read what he had sent her. The first section contained notes about meetings with Ira Perkins. She wondered where his article draft was.

A dog-eared page started a section with notes on Don Fisher, the infamous green-truck guy. According to Kevin, Fisher worked as an application developer at MedPro. He had created a database and application for the company to track customers who purchased medical devices. Ira Perkins claimed Fisher had put backdoor code in the application to collect secure data over time. Perkins told Kevin he had found the suspicious code and he was going to turn Fisher in. Then Perkins disappeared from Northern Virginia.

On the next page, Kevin had jotted random facts about Fisher. He lived outside of Arlington, Virginia, in a rented room in a house with three other boarders. He wasn't well-liked at work, and he had been written up several times for not following MedPro's security policies. In red ink, Kevin noted that Fisher didn't exhibit any signs of having money, but Perkins did. He bought a Corvette and an expensive watch. Kevin listed several trips and computer gadgets that Perkins had purchased in the last eight months.

Jules thought about what she had read. It didn't make sense if Perkins were the good guy in the story. Where did all this quick money come from? And Perkins wasn't worried about hiding it. Why did he disappear when he was going to blow the whistle on Fisher?

The last few pages of the journal were notes from coworkers at MedPro. None of the people listed had anything good to say about either man. Ira Perkins left the company suddenly about two weeks before he had checked into her resort. His coworkers were surprised that he left, but they had moved on and Perkins was all but forgotten. From the notes, it looked like Fisher still worked for MedPro, but he was on medical leave of absence. That jived with what Pixel had found out.

Jules flipped through the notebook again and spotted a note in pencil in the margin on the page with the coworker interviews. She didn't remember seeing this before. Kevin had jotted, "Interview with Don Fisher" with an arrow to his notes. Interesting. It looked like the reporter had talked to Don Fisher before Perkins started revealing his secrets. Was Kevin verifying a lead or checking on Perkins's story?

Jules photographed all of the pages and slipped the notebook and the post office key in the envelope. She made coffee and fixed a quick breakfast.

After a shower and Bijou's walk, Jules popped into the office to scribble a note for Roxanne.

Envelope in hand, she headed to town a little bit before eight. She zipped into a front row parking space at the sheriff's office.

Minutes later, she approached the reception desk, where Ashley Sharpe, a petite blond, held down Millie's usual spot. "Hey, Ashley. How are you? Is Sheriff Hobbs in yet?"

"Hey, gal. Long time no see. He's here and working on his second cup of coffee. But he's on the line right now. Do you want to wait? I'll let him know you're here."

"Thanks. Millie off again?"

"She's having a me day. I think she went shopping in town."

Jules dropped into the first plastic chair. The décor was definitely 1970s public building, complete with that sour antiseptic smell. She scrolled through her email and pictures on Instagram.

Several people came and went from the reception desk.

Ashley said, "Hey, Jules. I didn't get to the sheriff fast enough. He hung up the phone and hightailed it out of the office. Do you want to leave a message? I'm not sure when he'll be back."

"No. That's okay. I'll call him later."

"Sorry about that. It's not my day to watch him. Tell Jake I said hello." Ashley's face lit up with a smile that spanned ear to ear.

"Will do." Jules flipped her purse strap over her shoulder.

The mountain air and the gentle breeze caused her to slow her pace. She had the urge to get Bijou and head up to the mountains, but the campground and the unfinished marketing ideas drew her home. As she sat in the Jeep, she changed her mind about Kevin's envelope and retraced her steps back to the reception area.

"Ashley, I changed my mind. Do you have a piece of paper for me to leave a note for Sheriff Hobbs?"

The younger woman handed her a sheet of copy paper and an inter-office mailer. Jules returned to a seat and scrawled a note about the package that had arrived in the mail. She also added a P. S. about the odd campsite in the woods. She dropped Kevin's envelope inside and sealed it.

"Thanks, Ashley. I appreciate it. This is evidence he'll want to see."

"Good deal. I'm sure he'll call you if he has any questions. I'll make sure he gets it."

Jules drove back with the windows down in the Jeep. Thoughts of Kevin and his notes kept creeping into her mind. Hopefully, someone would be able to publish his story. She would hate to think he died for an article that never saw the light of day.

She opened her cabin door, and Bijou greeted her with her usual Jack Russell bounce. "Hey, kiddo. Let's go see what's going on in the office."

The terrier pranced around and sniffed everything in the flower beds in front of the office. Bijou was in no hurry to go inside.

A black Suburban sped up the entrance and stopped in front of the fence. Special Agent Will Stafford stepped out and clicked the lock on his key fob. "Good morning." The agent, in jeans and a dark shirt, closed the distance between them in a couple of steps.

"What brings you here so early?"

"I looked through what you left the sheriff this morning, and I have a few questions." Agent Stafford bent over and patted Bijou.

Jules was surprised she hadn't barked.

"When did you get the package?" he asked.

"The key and the note arrived in the mail yesterday. Kevin Bailey said he was trying to tie up a few loose ends on his Ira Perkins's story."

"Why didn't you call us before retrieving the item?"

"The key and the note were mailed to me. I wanted to see what he wanted me to have. It could have been a birthday present."

"Is it your birthday?"

Jules stared back at him and slowly shook her head.

"Where was the package?"

"The post office near the downtown mall in Charlottesville."

"Do you have his article?"

"No. He didn't say where he stored it."

Jake walked by and slowed his pace. He waved and sauntered toward the office's back door.

"Do you have anything else that belonged to the reporter?" the FBI agent asked.

"No." She looked him in the eye, determined he wasn't going to intimidate her. "It was addressed to me. If this is an interview, why don't you ever write anything down?"

"Don't need to."

"I have to get back to work."

"If anything else appears, call me."

"Uh, did the sheriff mention the campsite we found back in the woods?"

"No. What campsite?"

"Yesterday, Bijou got loose from Aunt Roxanne. Jake found her at a fresh campsite near Crosby Road. There was no trace of a camper. We haven't had squatters here in a while."

"How do I get there from here?"

"Go out to the main entrance. Hang a right and go about two miles. There's a big yellow farmhouse on the left. Then turn right at the stop sign." Jules pointed down the tree-lined road to the entrance.

"Do you think Jake can find it again?" the agent asked.

"You can ask him. He just went in the office."

A few seconds later, Jake opened the screen door and stepped on the porch. He saw the agent and frowned.

"Jake. This is Special Agent Stafford of the FBI. He wanted to talk to you about the campsite you found in the woods. Do you think you could find it again?"

"Probably. It was about a mile or so through the woods," Jake said.

"Could you show me from the road?"

"Yeah, sure," Jake replied cautiously. "Jules, I was going to check on the nineteen fifty-nine Air Stream. One of the guests reported a broken bed. The mattress keeps slipping." He turned back toward Stafford. "Can you wait a minute so I can check it out?"

Agent Stafford nodded. "I'm parked over there." He nodded his head in the direction of the dark SUV.

"I'll be there as soon as I see about the bed."

"Would you like coffee while you wait? Or breakfast?" Jules shaded her eyes with her hand.

"Breakfast sounds good," Agent Stafford said.

"Jake, we'll meet you over at the lodge. Let me know how bad the damage is."

Jake nodded and jumped in the golf cart. He jammed it in gear and sped off toward the vintage trailers.

"I need to put Bijou in the back," she said to Agent Stafford. "I'll be back in a minute."

Bijou followed her inside. The dog ran through the office, looking for Roxanne, and found her in the back.

"Hey there. I'm going over for breakfast. Do you want anything?" Jules asked.

"No. I'm good. Have fun with your FBI agent." Roxanne winked.

Jules smirked and slid out the back door before Bijou noticed.

"Beds get broken often?" Agent Stafford asked as they walked to the lodge.

"Stuff breaks occasionally. Jake and Lester are pretty good with the repairs. Most of our guests are professionals or young families. We don't have spring break issues or wild parties, like other resorts have."

Agent Stafford held the oak door for her.

"It looks like Crystal and Mel have quiche and assorted pastries today. Help yourself. We have coffee, tea, and juices over there."

Jules and Agent Stafford chose fruit, quiche, and coffee and settled in at a table by the wall of windows.

"What a view." Agent Stafford tore into his breakfast.

"My dad had the architect incorporate the mountains in his design. He wanted it to be the focal point of this building."

"The food is good, too. How much do I owe you?"

"My treat. You picked up the last tab for dinner."

"How long have you lived here?" he asked between bites.

"All my life. My parents bought the campground before I was born. I left for college and returned later when my dad fell ill. I'm glad I did. This is home, and I missed it."

"I move around a lot. When I retire, I'd like to find a place near water to build a cabin. I want to stay in one place for a while. I like to travel, but not like I do now. I'm never home for more than two or three days."

"I like it here. It's a place to put down roots." Jules gazed out at the mountains. "It beats city life any day." She took a bite of her quiche.

They had finished breakfast and started second cups of coffee by the time Jake wandered in. He grabbed a muffin and a to-go cup.

"How bad was it? Do we have to move the guests?" she asked.

"It wasn't much. The box springs shifted, and the mattress slid down on one side. They were sleeping on an incline. I tacked up a support board and put everything back. The guests were out, so I left a note. Everything's good as new."

"Thanks," she said. "I'm glad we don't have to replace the furniture."

"You about ready to leave?" Jake finished off his muffin in several bites.

"Sure. I want to check out that campsite. It may be nothing," Agent Stafford said.

"Sometimes, hikers stay for a day or so on their way to somewhere else." Jules picked up her plate and mug.

The men cleared their areas, and Jules topped off her coffee. They parted ways as the guys trekked over to the Suburban.

Roxanne and Bijou greeted Jules when she stepped inside. Her aunt flipped through folders at her desk, while Bijou was snuggled in the chair beside her.

"So, how's your FBI agent? Anything new? Why is he here so early this morning?"

"He stopped by to ask about what I dropped off for Sheriff Hobbs," Jules said.

"Which was?"

"A key the reporter mailed to me," Jules said.

"The dead reporter? You didn't tell me about that. Hidden fortune? A treasure map? Spill the beans." Her aunt rested her chin in her folded hands.

"It was a post office box key. Inside was a notebook. He had notes on Ira Perkins and Don Fisher. They worked together."

"Go on," Roxanne said.

"There wasn't much more. He had notes from some interviews he did with Perkins's coworkers. He interviewed Don Fisher about Perkins. Too bad there was no article."

"It's still interesting. The police and FBI stood up and took notice."

"He also wanted to see the campsite where Jake found Bijou. We'll see what that means." She turned on her laptop and perused email.

About an hour later, Jake came in the back door and wiped his feet on the mat.

"Was the campsite still there?" Jules looked up from her newsletter draft.

"Yep. It took me a little while to find it from the roadside. Nobody was there. I couldn't tell if anyone had been back since Bijou's visit. Agent Stafford marked the trees closest to the entrance, so I guess he's going to send someone back to check it out."

"It's odd that someone would abandon all that gear," Jules said.

"The stuff is relatively new, so it hasn't been there for a long time. I'll keep a lookout to see if we have any trespassers."

"Hey, you all," Roxanne swooped in the back office. "Mail call." She dropped several envelopes and a manila folder on Jules's desk.

"I'm headed back to the barn. Call me if you need me," Jake said.

"Could you or Lester check on the amphitheater this afternoon? One of the guests said she spotted a snake in the grass. I'm sure it's long gone, but I want to make sure the grass isn't too tall," Roxanne said.

"I'll send Lester and the mower over." Jake pulled the back door shut behind him.

"It's been fairly quiet here. We have a whole new crop of weekend check-ins on Thursday and Friday. All of the vintage trailers have guests this weekend," Roxanne said.

"I'm working on the newsletter and a referral promotion. Hopefully, we'll get some repeat visitors and their friends."

Jules picked up the envelope in the pile of bills and ripped open the flap. A thumb drive fell out onto her desk. She tipped the envelope over, and a yellow sticky note lay scrunched in the bottom. The scratchy scrawl read, "Jules, here's a copy. I'm sending it to you for backup. Kevin." She studied the envelope. It had the same postmark as the package with the key. Why had he sent them separately?

A twinge of sadness washed over Jules as she flipped the thumb drive over in her hand. She popped off the plastic cap and plugged it in the side of her computer. There were two files. One was a detailed article about his clandestine rendezvous with Ira Perkins and his whistle-blowing claims. The second was an article about the whistle-blower gone bad. Kevin's take was Ira Perkins figured out what his colleague was doing, and he wormed in on the action. Instead of righting the wrong, he went after the money. Had Kevin filed the stories? If not, what prompted him to send her his notes and his article separately? Both envelopes were postmarked from Charlottesville the day he was killed. She took a deep breath and copied all the files to a folder on her laptop. Then she photographed everything for her Ira Perkins file.

She let out a heavy sigh and reached for her cell phone. She disconnected when she heard the sheriff's voice mail message. Jules tried another number, and, after a couple of rings, she connected with Special Agent Stafford. "Hi, Agent Stafford. This is Jules Keene. I received a package today that you and the sheriff are going to be interested in."

"I'm in downtown Charlottesville right now. I can be back in Fern Valley in about an hour. Can you meet for lunch?"

"Where?"

"How about that fifties diner?"

"Okay, I'll see you at Pop's."

She took another deep breath. First Perkins and then Kevin. And Kevin was concerned enough right before his death to send her his notes and story. What happened on that day he stood her up at the fruit stand?

Jules shook off the creepy feeling and wrapped up a few tasks on her desk.

About twenty minutes later, she said, "Hey, Roxanne. I'm going to run into town. Do you need me to bring you anything back?"

Jules put the envelope from Kevin and its contents in a larger white envelope with the resort's logo on it.

"Nope. I'm good. I have dinner plans, so I need to leave about four-thirty."

"I'll be back in plenty of time to get Bijou."

She cranked up the radio and opened all the windows in the Jeep. Cruising through town, she drove by the library. At the sight of the woods, she thought about Kevin. She caught her breath. There was nothing there that indicated it had been the site of a murder. Everything looked normal. She changed the radio station to something with a peppier beat to shake off the feeling of melancholy.

Jules rounded the corner and pulled into the packed parking lot at Pop's.

Too hot to wait in the car, Jules stepped inside and soaked up the coolness of the restaurant.

Sitting on the vinyl bench in the lobby, she waited for her table and Agent Stafford. The lobby walls in this section sported Pop's wall-to-wall Coca-Cola collection. He had every red and white gadget, toy, or marketing gimmick imaginable from the soft drink company.

During her wait, she had enough time to check her email and the campground's Facebook feed. Something distracted her from her phone. She looked up as Special Agent Stafford strode through the doorway with the art deco doors with round glass windows, trimmed in shiny silver.

A ponytailed young woman in a pink poodle skirt showed them to a booth in a corner decked out in Buddy Holly, the Big Bopper, and Richie Valens memorabilia. Jules looked through the menu and set it down.

Agent Stafford flipped through his as Marsha in her pink bouffant hairdo approached. Today she sported a shiny pink jacket over a white blouse with a Peter Pan collar. She had little black velvet bows in her bouffant do. "Hi, Jules. Who's your friend?"

"This is Will Stafford," she replied.

He looked over his menu and didn't say anything.

"What can I get for you on this fine day?" Marsha pulled a pencil out of her cotton candy hair.

"I'll have the cobb salad and a vanilla Coke," Jules said.

"I'll have the footlong Coney dog with mustard and relish, with a side of onion rings and a vanilla shake."

"Sounds good. I'll be back in a flash." Marsha winked at Jules.

"So, what did you find out about the campsite in the woods?" Jules asked.

"Not much. We're watching it until it proves not to be anything. What did you get in the mail?"

"It came today from Kevin Bailey. It's a thumb drive."

"Containing?"

"Two articles that he was working on," she said.

"Why did he send you two packages?"

"I have no idea. I don't know why he sent them to me in the first place.

There were no instructions for me to contact anyone like an editor or publisher. Maybe it was just a backup?"

"How well did you know him?"

"I didn't. He showed up at the campground after Ira Perkins was killed. He told my aunt he was his nephew. After I contacted him, we met here. We sat over there." Jules pointed to the next dining room. "He said he was doing a story and Perkins was his source."

"Anything else?"

"He wanted me to meet him at the tennis courts at a community college. Then he said to meet him at a fruit stand. He didn't show for that appointment." Her voice trailed off as she thought of the late reporter.

"And then what?"

"I got a text from him on the night we found him in the woods by the library."

Marsha interrupted and dropped off their drinks. She sashayed back to the kitchen.

Jules continued, "At the tennis courts, he seemed kind of jumpy, but I didn't know if that was normal for him. Here's the second package."

Agent Stafford reached across the table and took the white envelope. "What did he say in his last communication?"

"To meet near the library. He had some important information."

Marsha returned with their meals. "Let me know if you need anything else. Y'all save room for our homemade pies today."

Agent Stafford poured ketchup on his onion rings and started on his hotdog, which was disappearing bite by bite.

"So, what's next?" She got a whiff of his onion rings.

"Our computer forensic team will look over this and all the other items to try to draw some connections. And we have a manhunt going on for Don Fisher. If you see him, call us immediately. Don't chase him or detain him. Or follow or talk to him. Got it?"

"Yes." She rolled her eyes. "You think he's the killer?"

"I didn't say that. He's a person of interest."

"Okay, tell me about MedPro." She speared a slice of boiled egg.

"What do you want to know? Do you want one of these?" He pointed to the onion rings.

"Sure." She reached across the table for one of the golden rings. "At first, I thought Ira Perkins was the whistle-blower, but the more I read of Kevin's files, I don't get the sense that he's the good guy in the story."

"How so?"

"He's come into a lot of money lately, and he's made no secret of flashing it around. He told my aunt he inherited it."

"You want my unofficial two cents' worth?"

"Uh, huh." It surprised her he was being so candid.

"I think Perkins convinced himself he was the good guy in the story. I suspect his hands were pretty dirty."

Jules finished off the croutons in her salad.

Marsha sauntered over. "Who saved room for apple pie?"

Jules shook her head and Agent Stafford said, "Just the tab."

Marsha placed the bill on the table. "Let me know if y'all need anything else."

Agent Stafford reached for it. "This was good, but I'm going to have to run an extra few miles tonight to work it off."

"Pop's has the best diner food around. When I want a cheeseburger, this is where I come."

He dropped two twenties in the tray. "This should cover it. Keep the change."

"Thanks. See you two soon." Marsha checked out the tall FBI agent who tipped generously.

Jules followed Agent Stafford to the parking lot. She sat in her Jeep long after he and his black Suburban disappeared around the corner. Ira Perkins had been in semi-hiding, but not because of being a whistle-blower. He had something Don Fisher wanted. And Don Fisher was still looking for whatever it was. That thought made her shudder.

Chapter Twenty-One

Wednesday

After breakfast and an espresso, Jules opened Ira Perkins's spreadsheet again. The color-coded amounts in the bank account in the Cayman Islands didn't reconcile and that bothered her. She was convinced this wasn't an inheritance he was hiding in an offshore account. Either he bilked all those sick people, or he swiped the money from the person who did. And what did Don Fisher want so badly?

"Hey, there. What's going on?" Roxanne walked through the store to the office.

Bijou met Roxane at the Dutch door.

"Sweetie pie." Roxanne picked up the wiggly dog. "Hey, Jules."

"Good morning. Has anyone been in the Robin Hood since the last ransacking?"

"I'm fine. And no, I don't think so. We're waiting for the new cushions to come in. Jake fixed the door, but you knew about that."

"I want to check on something. I'll be back in a little while. I have my phone if you need me." Jules rummaged through the closet for a flashlight and a small toolkit. She grabbed the key out of the lockbox. And what would it hurt to spend a few minutes poking around the trailer? The murder happened on her property, and she felt compelled to figure out why.

Jules spent the rest of the morning combing through every inch of the Robin Hood trailer. She pulled out drawers and emptied cabinets. Looking under beds, mattresses, and cushions, she searched every out-of-the-way spot. Not having any luck on the inside, she walked the perimeter and looked under the camper.

Unscrewing the metal plates on the outside storage area that had been sealed, Jules swung the flashlight around inside. The light bounced off something odd. She reached in and pulled out what looked like three bricks, each wrapped in black plastic like a garbage bag.

She unwrapped one and caught her breath. A stack of crisp $100 bills.

Someone tapped her shoulder. "Whatcha doing, Boss?"

Her heart leapt into her throat. She pushed the bricks behind her back.

Jules relaxed when she saw Jake. She let out the breath she didn't realize she was holding. "Just making sure everything is in tip-top shape. When the cushions come back in, I'm going to put this one back in the rental rotation. What are you doing sneaking up on people?"

"Sorry. I couldn't resist. You looked like you were totally focused on the storage area. I thought you were about to crawl inside."

"I've gone over every inch of this trailer. It looks fine to me." She screwed the metal plate to the storage area back in place.

"Here, let me help you." He took the screwdriver and reattached the metal plate. He handed her back the screwdriver when he was done.

"What am I missing?"

"Nothing. As long as our vandal doesn't return, it should be good to go."

Jules stood and dusted her hands on her jeans. She locked the door and picked up her find and her tools. "I need to check on the office."

"I'm headed into town to pick up some stuff. And I'm getting Roxanne's lunch. Do you want anything from Lula Belle's? You've got your hands full. Do you want me to carry something?"

"I'm good. But could you bring me a ham and Swiss sandwich box? Let me go get some money." Little did he know she had thousands in her hand in the wrapped bricks of cash.

"We'll settle up when I get back. I know you're good for it. See ya in a few."

By the time Jules opened the back door to the office, she heard the roar of Jake's Mustang.

"Did you find anything in the trailer?" her aunt asked.

"Huh? I was checking to see if it was ready to go back in rotation."

"If you say so. I'll call Van at the upholstery shop and see when we can expect the cushions. Did you want to rename the camper?"

"Think we need to?"

Roxanne shrugged her shoulders. "I don't know. Robin Hood seems to be jinxed lately. New name, new vibe?"

"I'll think of something. Maybe we should have a new image and new photos when we put it back in circulation."

Jules retreated to her desk and slid the load of cash in her desk drawer. This had to be Mr. Perkins's. There was no way it came with the trailer. They would have found it when they did the renovations and sealed the storage areas. Jules was antsy all afternoon, and she could hardly finish her boxed lunch. She wrapped up the sandwich and grabbed her purse and the three bricks of cash. "I'm headed home. Call me if you need me. Come on, Bijou."

She and the dog jogged across the back lawn to her cabin. After closing the blinds and double-checking the locks on the doors, she sat on the bed to count all that loot.

She whistled. Four hundred thousand dollars in $100 bills covered her bedspread. Resisting the urge to toss loose bills around, she rewrapped everything as it had been and took it out to the cabin's living room/kitchen area. Jules slid the package into the freezer for safekeeping.

Hang on to it for a few days or call the sheriff? She toyed with both ideas for a few moments and daydreamed about all the cool things she could do with the found money. But then she remembered all those sick people. It was nice to dream, but the money needed to be returned. She fished through her purse for her phone. This was the best way to get the money back to the rightful owners.

Jules punched in the sheriff's number and waited for his voice mail to finish. "Sheriff Hobbs, this is Jules Keene. I found something in the trailer you should take a look at sooner than later."

Had the police searched the storage area? They must have missed it because if they had opened it, they would have seen the wrapped bricks of cash.

Her phone dinged a few minutes later with a text. **We'll be over soon. Where are you?**

I'm at my cabin, she tapped into the phone. She sat on the couch and willed her blood pressure to stabilize. Her heart pounded in her temples. Jules hated this jumpy feeling. Ira Perkins wouldn't get out of her life. If she had known he was going to be this much trouble, she would never have accepted his reservation.

She turned on the TV, but nothing held her interest. Bijou, on the other hand, had no trouble relaxing. She curled up in the side chair and snored softly.

A knock on the door shook Jules from her thoughts and Bijou from her nap. She crossed the room and looked out the window. Sheriff Hobbs and Special Agent Stafford stood on the small stoop. The FBI agent followed the sheriff into her living room. Jules looked around outside and locked the door behind them.

"Thank you for coming over. Have a seat."

Both men stood in the living room.

"After Agent Stafford and I talked yesterday, I went through Mr. Perkins's trailer one last time. I even looked in the outside storage compartments we had sealed shut. I found something interesting."

"How interesting?" Sheriff Hobbs asked.

"Four hundred thousand worth of interesting." She got up and retrieved the package from the freezer. "Sorry it's cold. I couldn't think of anywhere else to hide it."

Agent Stafford smiled, and Sheriff Hobbs put on a pair of rubber gloves and took the bag from her. "You counted it?"

"Yes."

"Did you wear gloves?" the sheriff asked.

"No. That wasn't my first thought when I found a pile of money on my property. Sorry." She gave her best sheepish look.

"You'll need to come down to the station so I can fingerprint you. We want to isolate your prints from the mix."

"Sure, okay. Today?"

"That would work. I'm headed back after we leave here," the sheriff said.

"Did you find anything else?" Agent Stafford asked.

"No. This was today's surprise."

"If you uncover anything else, let us know. Did you tell anyone about this?" Special Agent Stafford asked.

"No. I was shocked when I found it. I didn't know what I had."

"Here's a receipt for the evidence," Sheriff Hobbs said. "Please sign here on this copy. I wouldn't talk too much about this."

She scribbled her name on the paper. The sheriff picked it up, along with the money. Jules grabbed her purse and followed the two men to the door.

Jules shut and locked the door behind them and let out a breath she didn't realize she was holding. Maybe she found what Don Fisher was looking for. Could there be more?

Jules pulled open the sheriff's office door. Frigid air and an antiseptic smell enveloped her. She had been here lots of times over her lifetime, but this time, the police station's empty front room made her think of a scene from a horror movie. It looked like the perfect setting for a zombie attack.

Ashley drifted in from the back work area with an armful of folders that she dropped on the desk. "Oh, hi, Jules. I hope you haven't been waiting long. What's up?"

Jules shook off the eerie feeling. "No. I just got here. Sheriff Hobbs asked me to come in and get fingerprinted, so he can exclude my prints from those found at the resort."

"Okay. I'll get someone to help you." She punched a few buttons on her phone. "Hey, Mike. Could you do some fingerprinting for the sheriff? Okay. Yep. She's in the lobby." Ashley hung up. "Someone will be right up to help you."

Before Jules could get comfortable in the plastic chair, the door opened.

Mike Cooley, who had been a couple of years behind her in school, stuck his head out. "Hey, Jules. The sheriff needs your prints?"

"Yep. I touched a lot of stuff at the resort that he's investigating."

"Come on back. It shouldn't take long."

She followed him down the cinder-blocked hall to what looked like a spartan closet. The narrow room, with walls painted an institutional yellow, contained a counter with equipment and a couple of cabinets from the era of pet rocks and disco balls.

"Sorry. Most people who visit here are under arrest. It wasn't built for comfort. Stand here, and I'll be done lickety-split."

Jules stood on one side of a counter with the cracked vinyl top.

"Uh oh," Mike Cooley said.

"Problems?"

"The Live Scan machine is down. I'm gonna have to do this the old-fashioned way." Mike Cooley slipped around the other side and pulled out a white card and a black box. He took her right hand and inked each finger. He rolled each in boxes on the top row of the card. He repeated the process and filled the remaining boxes on the card.

"There. Quick and painless. You're all done." He handed her a wipe.

She scrubbed the ink off her fingers. The black smudges turned a light gray.

"When everything is working, we scan them digitally. It's a lot faster."

"And neater. See you around." Jules retraced her steps to the lobby, where she found Ashley buried in a stack of folders.

"Tell Jake not to be a stranger. I haven't seen him in town in ages. He used to be a regular at Red's for karaoke night." Ashley smiled and returned to her stack of folders.

Jake and karaoke night? That seemed out of character for him. Maybe there was another side of him she didn't see at work. He used to be fun-loving and full of practical jokes when he was younger. So had she. Before she ended up with a lot of responsibilities.

At the curb, Special Agent Stafford climbed out of his SUV and walked toward her Jeep.

"All printed?" The FBI agent took off his aviator sunglasses to reveal his deep chocolate eyes.

Jules looked away, to keep from getting distracted by his gaze. "Yep. Hope this stuff comes off." She splayed her fingers for him to see.

"What, you don't like the badge of shame? Try baby oil or hand sanitizer."

"Thanks. It kind of makes me look dodgy." Jules turned and opened the door to her Jeep. A movement in the woods caught her attention. Right near the same spot where she had found Kevin Bailey.

"Hey, Agent Stafford," she called. "Does that look odd?" She pointed toward the spot.

He turned. They watched a tall man run along the edge of the tree line and then disappear into the woods. They stood for a few minutes, and the guy came out of the woods a few yards closer to the street. He jogged across the grass and climbed into a green and white truck parked against the curb a block away. He revved it and took off.

Jules gasped. Don Fisher.

"Stay here." Agent Stafford jumped in his SUV. The big engine roared to life as he zoomed out after the truck.

Jules pretended she hadn't heard him and slid in her Jeep to tag along.

Agent Stafford gunned his engine and blew through town. He swerved around a bicyclist and turned onto a side road. Jules had to floor it to keep up with the two other vehicles. Watching the truck and the SUV get smaller and smaller, she mashed the Jeep's accelerator to catch up, even though she knew better. She didn't want to miss out on where Don Fisher was leading them.

She caught up to the SUV about two miles down the road. The green and white truck sat with two tires on the embankment. The driver's door hung open, and the engine was still running.

Jules parked the Jeep a few yards behind the black SUV. Agent Stafford approached the truck with his gun drawn. He searched the inside and the bed and turned the truck off. He scanned the wooded area, but there was no sign of Don Fisher. Agent Stafford pulled out his phone and punched in a number. He glared at Jules and walked to his vehicle.

She put the Jeep in reverse as he walked toward her.

"I thought I told you to stay put! I've got backup and a state police K9 unit on the way. Go home. I'll call you later."

"Be careful," she whispered as she pulled around the parked vehicles.

On the drive home, a state police helicopter buzzed low over the road. A few minutes later, two deputy cars and a blue and gray state police cruiser, with lights flashing, shot past her in the opposite direction.

Jules did a U-turn and retraced her route. She knew she should go back to the resort, but this was too good to resist. Pulling off the road, she parked near where she had stopped before. The helicopter's rotors thumped overhead as it buzzed the woods. Five flavors of law enforcement vehicles lined the side of the road, and two deputies blocked the traffic in both directions up ahead.

There was no sign of law enforcement, except for the two deputies who redirected cars because of the road closure. A tow truck drove slowly by her, and one of the deputies pointed to where the green and white truck sat on the side of the road. The driver hooked up his wench and, within minutes, Fisher's truck was ready for a tow.

Watching got boring. Jules turned the Jeep around and headed home. They had his vehicle now. Maybe it was just a matter of time before they found him.

Jules slid into her desk chair. Bijou jumped in her lap with puppy-kiss greetings.

"Okay, girl. I love you, too."

"Where've you been?" Roxanne asked. "You missed all the action. Lester ran in here about thirty minutes ago with news from his police scanner. Someone got carjacked outside of town. Can you believe it? In Fern Valley? And then there was some kind of manhunt out on Route 10. Lester said the state police and several other jurisdictions were called in to assist. We're having a regular crime wave around here."

Something else for J. P. Gross and his bunch to blame her for.

"I went to see the sheriff," Jules said.

"You spend a lot of time down there lately. Are you going down there to flirt with that FBI agent?" Roxanne flipped through a manila folder.

Jules glared at her aunt, who never looked up from her papers. "I found something in the Robin Hood trailer, and I didn't wear gloves when I handled it. Sheriff Hobbs wanted me to get fingerprinted to eliminate me from the suspect pool."

"What did you find this time? More of Ira's things?"

"Possibly. Don't say anything to anyone. I found a stash of money in the trailer's storage area."

Roxanne's eyes widened. "The old goat really had money. I thought he was just being a puffed-up bantam rooster. That little so-and-so caused a lot of problems around here. I'll be glad when we're not talking about him anymore." Her aunt ran her fingers through her platinum blond hair. "How much?"

"About four hundred thousand."

Roxanne whistled, "Maybe some of Ira's claims were true? Who'd leave that much money in a storage area?"

"I know it wasn't there when we refurbished the camper."

"Dirty money. Ira's drama goes on and on. I hope J. P. Gross and his cronies don't make a big deal about all the police activity lately. It's been on all our local news. And Ira's murder was on the cable news for a day or so."

"Just because the dead guy stayed here, doesn't mean Fern Valley's got big city problems. But knowing him, J. P. will probably try to use it to his advantage. He wants things the way they were forty years ago." Jules sighed. "But I've got other things to attend to. I looked at our numbers, and all the commotion around here hasn't affected our reservations. Actually, our numbers are up from last summer. I need to work on some more marketing ideas to keep the visitors coming."

"You should do some kind of romantic retreat for Valentine's Day. I'm sure you could partner up with some of the businesses to offer some nice amenities."

Jules got lost in her brainstorming for special events and pushed thoughts of Mr. Perkins and the manhunt out of her head.

Her phone rang and jolted her back to reality. "Hello, Agent Stafford."

"We combed through the woods for hours with no sign of Don Fisher. The forensic unit is going over his truck. But, meanwhile, he's still out there. He's cornered and dangerous." Agent Stafford paused. "I mean it. No following, no talking to, no anything. Call the police. Call even if you think you see him. He's running out of options."

"Gotcha. Anything else?"

"No. Just call in anything that's suspicious or if you find anything else." The line went dead.

She dropped the phone on her desk and fumed. Jules would be glad when they captured Don Fisher. She wanted to get back to running her resort. One side of her wanted to get the word out about the money she had turned over to the police, so the Perkins thing would finally be over. But the more she thought about it, she didn't want to give people the idea there could be more hidden money. The last thing she needed was added interest in a secret fortune and a bunch of amateur treasure hunters. She decided to keep quiet for now. Hopefully, he would flee the area. But for now, she would keep looking over her shoulder.

Chapter Twenty-Two

Saturday

Jules sat at her desk and reviewed the check-in report. She, Emily, and Roxanne registered twenty-four families in the last two days. Jules celebrated the news that the two murders didn't cause a decline in reservations.

She jotted a to-do list and doodled for a minute. Bijou snored not so quietly in her bed. If she could keep the resort this busy through the fall, they would have an exceptional year. And she was excited about the addition of the tiny houses to their offerings. Next year could be even bigger.

Jules rinsed out her mug and put it in the sink. "Hey, puppy. You about ready to head home and see what we have for dinner? Movie night?"

The dog raised her head and stretched. Jules checked that the door was locked. The sun slid behind the mountain, and the sky was a swirl of pinks, purples, and oranges.

In her kitchen, Jules poked through the freezer and pantry for dinner. She settled on microwave popcorn, and she and Bijou curled up on the couch to stream a series of 80s classic movies.

She woke up with a jolt. Bijou growled. She heard sirens in the distance. Before she could figure out what was going on, someone pounded on the door.

Bijou jumped into guard dog mode with a growl and a barking jag. Jules glanced at the clock on her DVR and padded to the door. It was almost midnight.

Jules pulled open the door, and Jake stood there in mid-knock. "Hey, Boss. I'm sorry to bother you. You didn't answer my texts, and I thought you'd want to know about this."

The breeze moved her hair, and she got a whiff of burning leaves.

"What's up?"

"Look over there." Jake stepped off the porch and pointed to the wooded area. Off in the distance, they could see an orange glow through the trees. The smell of smoke grew heavier by the minute. "It's on the other side of the woods, but we could still be in its path. I think it's over near Crosby Road. I walked a few yards into the woods, but I didn't want to go too far in case the wind changed."

"I'm going to call the sheriff's office to see if we should start waking and evacuating our guests." She stepped back into the living room, slid on her shoes, and grabbed her phone.

She clicked on Sheriff Hobbs's contact as she followed Jake out into the yard. They heard sirens. "Hi, Sheriff. This is Jules. I can see the fire across the woods near Crosby Road. Should I go ahead and start rousing people and getting them to move out of the area?"

"We have several units on it, and there are another couple on their way from Charlottesville. Let me check with the emergency center. I'll call you right back."

Jules and Jake stood in the cool evening air, laden with smoke and ash.

Lester joined them. "I heard it on the scanner. They've got crews on the scene. They think they'll have the fire under control in a little while. Lots of stuff going on around here lately."

"Do you think there's any danger to the resort?" Jules asked.

"No, not unless the wind picks up and spreads sparks. It's at least a half-mile away," the groundskeeper replied.

Jules's phone buzzed. "Hi, Sheriff."

"The fire chief said the blaze is basically under control. He thinks your property is out of range. You may get the smoky smell, but the fire should be out soon."

"I appreciate it." Jules disconnected. "Sheriff Hobbs said they've got it under control."

Lester's head bobbed as he nodded vigorously. He lived for an active police scanner. Lester shifted his weight from foot to foot. "You think it's related to the two murders?"

"A lot of weird happenings and not a lot of explanations," Jake said.

Jules shrugged her shoulders. She didn't mention the cash she found.

They watched in silence as the orange and yellow glow died off and the thick smoke dissipated.

"I'm headed back home. It's way past my bedtime." Lester turned and headed off into the darkness.

"I think I'm going to head back inside, too," Jules said.

When Jules opened the door, Bijou jumped off the couch and greeted her. "The fire's out. Time for bed." She had dodged a bullet tonight. It would have been terrible to have had to rouse her guests to evacuate in the early morning hours. That wasn't the kind of vacation she wanted her guests to remember.

She pulled out her charger and plugged her phone in as it binged. Special Agent Stafford texted, **Meet me for lunch tomorrow? I want to talk to you.**

Where?

The Good Thyme Bistro 12:30.

Okay, Jules texted. What did he want?

Her thoughts drifted to Agent Stafford. Did he want to share information or ply her for what she knew? She liked spending time with him, but the little voice in the back of her head kept reminding her he wasn't that interested in her. He was just doing his job. She really wasn't ready to date anyone anyway.

She pushed notions of romance and the FBI agent aside. But the investigation kept jumping to the front of her thoughts. Could there be a connection between the fire, Ira Perkins, Kevin Bailey, and Don Fisher?

Chapter Twenty-Three

Sunday

Jules finished her French toast with raspberries as Jake slid into the seat across from her in the lodge. She got a whiff of his cologne, and his hair was still damp from a recent shower. Her maintenance guy looked relaxed in jeans and a red T-shirt. He was still as cute as he was when he was a teen. Embarrassed that he caught her staring, she looked at her plate. Heat crept across her cheeks. At least he didn't tease her as much these days.

"Are you in a rush this morning?" he asked.

"No. What's up?"

"I found something in the woods on my rounds." Jake took a bite of his bagel and wiped the excess cream cheese off of his stubbled chin.

She sighed and hoped he didn't hear her. "Since when do your rounds include the woods?"

"Since there was a suspicious fire. I was curious, so I took a little walk in the woods. If you have some time, I'll show you." Jake finished his breakfast in a couple of bites.

"Hear any comments from anyone about the fire?" she asked.

"Nope. Everything seems normal around here." Jake wiped his chin with the napkin and put it and his utensils on his plate.

Jules cleared her dishes "Let's see what you found."

He wiped his hands on his jeans and followed her out the door.

"Where are we going?"

"Almost the same place where I found Bijou the other day."

Jules was glad she wore sneakers this morning. The abandoned campsite was a pretty good hike through the woods. "At that campsite?"

"Nearby."

They crossed the tree line. An odd smoky, earthy scent wafted up and tickled Jules's nose. Under the canopy of leaves, the coolness of the loamy forest surrounded them. As her eyes adjusted to the darkness, she trailed Jake deeper into the woods, watching the ground for uneven spots and stray roots.

They followed a freshly trampled path to the other side of the woods and the empty campsite. The abandoned tent still stood, surrounded by trash. The unzipped tent flap fluttered in the breeze. Jules peeked inside. A balled-up sleeping bag and several blankets took up most of the floor space. Dirty clothes, heaped in the corner, stood sentry by the opening. Empty beer bottles and open food cans littered the outside.

"Nothing's changed here. The interesting thing is over there." Jake pointed and led her out of the woods. They walked along the grass until they spotted the charred area. The burnt smell hung in the air. Jules had to cover her nose with her sleeve. All the nearby trees were reduced to partially blackened trunks, with a few scraggly branches jutting out. Ashes covered the ground like dirty snow.

Jake stared at what was left of a small car a few yards away. The scorched remains sat in the soot. Jules couldn't tell what color the car used to be. The rubber tires were gone. A seared Mazda logo hung askew on the grill.

Jake and Jules circled the car. The car's interior looked more like a huge plastic blob next to a singed metal frame.

"I don't think this is random," she said. "Why did someone torch a car in the woods near a suspicious campsite?"

Before Jake could answer, they heard a car engine and then a door slam. Jules looked over her shoulder.

Deputy Dempsey picked his way across the grassy field toward them. "Hey, Jules. Hey, Jake. Sheriff sent me over to make sure the site was secure until they can get this car towed. The firefighters were here pretty late putting out the hot spots. I'm afraid I'm gonna have to ask you to leave the area."

"Sure, Charles. We saw the fire early this morning and wanted to see how bad it was. I'm relieved we didn't have to evacuate our guests." Jules stepped gingerly over the blackened grass and sticks. Jake followed her back to the woods.

When they were out of Charles's earshot, Jake put his hand on Jules's shoulder. "Know anyone who owns a Mazda?"

"Nope."

"Think anyone was in the car?" He ran his fingers through his longish brown hair.

"Probably not, or we'd see more police action. But I do wonder what's in the trunk. And what's so important to hide that you have to torch the car?"

"Wait here. Bubba may want to chat if he's bored." Jake turned and made his way back to the tree line.

Jules moved closer and found a big tree to hide behind to eavesdrop.

"Hey, Charles," Jake said. "Do you need anything while you're waiting?"

"I'm good. Hopefully, I won't be out here too long. I'm waiting on the tow truck." Charles fished his phone out of his shirt pocket. "The fire guys cleared the site just a bit ago. I'm supposed to be on the lookout for flare-ups."

"It looks like a total loss. I hope they'll be able to find out some stuff from what's left," Jake said.

"Yup. Definitely arson."

"Any idea who owned the car?"

"Sawyer Kelley over off Route 250. He got carjacked yesterday. Sheriff had to tell him the bad news. I think he was traumatized when the guy took his car. And now, there's no chance he'll get it back."

"A carjacking in Fern Valley?"

"Probably our first one." Deputy Dempsey hiked up his pants. "Sawyer said he was loading dirty clothes in the trunk for a trip to the laundromat when this guy approached. He threatened him and then hightailed it with his car and a couple of loads of dirty laundry."

The carjacking happened on the same day Jules and Agent Stafford saw Don Fisher run into the woods. Was this his campsite? She shuddered at the idea he was so close to her campground. It made sense he was hanging around to find what Ira Perkins had hidden.

Jake shook hands with Deputy Dempsey and wandered back toward Jules. "So, did you hear what Bubba said?"

"I did. And I'm pretty certain Sawyer Kelley was carjacked by Don Fisher."

"He would have needed a car. His option pool is narrowing." They retraced their path back through the trees.

Jules dodged a large root and picked her way through the woods. "But why torch the car if you don't have transportation? This doesn't make sense."

A shiver went down Jules's spine. No transportation meant he was within walking distance of her resort. Would she ever be rid of Ira Perkins and Don Fisher?

"Bubba didn't act like it was all that urgent. He's just out here standing guard. Hey, I know a way to find out more info. Follow me." Jake quickened his pace.

They trudged to the field toward the cabins. Jake keyed his radio. "Lester, you there?"

"Ten-four. Whatcha need?"

"Warm up your police scanner. Jules and I will be there in a minute."

"Roger that."

Lester had lived on the property as the groundskeeper since Jules was in elementary school. He had lived alone in the smaller cabin since his wife died about twelve years ago.

Jake knocked on the cabin's front door and a "Come in," echoed from inside.

"Hey, Lester," Jake opened the oak door. "Sorry to barge in on you, but we wanted to see what you've heard on the scanner."

"Not much. There hasn't been too much chatter lately. Deputy Dempsey checked in at the site of the fire a little while ago. Come on in and sit down."

The cabin's interior was sparsely decorated, except for an olive-colored couch and well-worn, orange recliner facing the outdated TV in the corner. Jules hadn't seen a TV that wasn't a flat screen in a long time. An oak kitchen table and four chairs divided the den and kitchen areas. The table, covered in piles of paper, didn't appear to have been used for meals in a while.

They found a spot on the couch. Lester sat at a large rolltop desk in the corner, facing Jake and Jules. A police scanner and a shortwave radio took up most of the workspace.

"It took 'em a while to declare the fire out. They knew it was Sawyer Kelley's car last night. That's about it. Earlier today, they dispatched an officer and a tow truck to pull Emma Hopkins out of the ditch, and there's a BOLO out for Darla Huggins's big orange cat. It hasn't been home in three days, and she's worried sick about it."

"Thanks, Lester. If you hear anything else interesting, let us know." Jake stood.

Jules followed him. "Thanks, Lester. Enjoy your day off."

The older man put his oversized headphones back on and listened intently to his radio.

"I have an appointment with the FBI agent in town later." Jules walked down the path with Jake. "I'll see what he has to say."

Jake's smile faded, and he hesitated. "Let me know if you find out anything."

Curious to see what the FBI agent wanted to talk about, Jules hoped the meeting wasn't for him to scold her again. She pushed thoughts of the investigation out of her head as she headed home to take a shower to get the smoky smell out of her hair.

A little after twelve-thirty, Jules stood in front of the Good Thyme Bistro. Her hair and flowered sundress fluttered in the breeze. She didn't see Agent Stafford inside or on the patio. She inched toward the hostess stand. "Hi, there. May I get a table for two outside?"

The brightly colored umbrellas blocked the sun, and the gentle wind made it a perfect afternoon for dining alfresco.

"Sure." The young woman grabbed two menus and utensils. "This way, please."

She led Jules to the table closest to the sidewalk with a good view of the street.

By the time the waitress with the sleeve tattoos dropped off her iced tea,

Jules saw Agent Stafford, who seemed to dominate every space, making his way toward the table. Today, he wore black jeans and a white dress shirt with the sleeves rolled up to his elbows.

"Sorry I'm late." Agent Stafford pulled out the black metal chair. "Been waiting long?"

"No. Are you working today?"

"Not right now."

The waitress swooped in and stood close to the FBI agent. "What can I get y'all?" She stared at Agent Stafford.

Jules interrupted their moment. "Hi. I'll have the chicken Caesar salad."

"I'll have a cheeseburger with everything and fries." He handed the waitress the menu. "With an iced tea."

The waitress brushed his hand as she reached for the menus. "Sweet?" She winked.

"Unsweetened is fine." He turned to Jules. "How have you been?"

"Fine. Except the fire last night. The sirens woke me up."

"How close was it to your place?"

"On the other side of the woods. We could see and smell it. It took them a while to contain it."

"It's still under investigation."

"Do you think it's linked to the murders?" Jules asked.

"I'm not ruling out anything. It was awfully close to that campsite your guy found in the woods."

Jules waited for him to continue, but he seemed distracted by something. He stared at people walking along the sidewalk for quite a while.

Jules turned her head. A blondish guy stopped on the sidewalk to tie his shoe. It took him longer than normal. He eventually straightened up, looked over his shoulder, and hustled across the street. Another guy stood in the doorway of the insurance company across the street for a few minutes until he wandered off. Jules wasn't sure what distracted Agent Stafford.

The waitress arrived with their lunches and broke the silence. "Can I get you anything else?" She looked at the FBI agent.

"We're fine." Agent Stafford reached for the ketchup. He waited for the waitress to leave before speaking again. "The carjacking was the same day Don Fisher took off after abandoning his truck. There's a good chance the campsite could belong to Fisher." He took a bite of his gourmet burger.

Jules cut the chicken into smaller bites and dug into her salad. "What did you want to see me about?"

"We've got the campsite and other areas under surveillance. Our suspect is feeling like we're closing in. He's desperate and dangerous. If you see him again, call the police. Immediately. We've got a lot of assets out there looking for him. And you always seem to be in the middle of things. No following. No chasing. No talking to him. Call the authorities. Understand?" He took another bite of his giant cheeseburger and wiped the grease from his chin on his napkin.

"Got it. I'm hoping he's done visiting my resort and we can get back to normal."

"I mean it this time. He's killed two people and carjacked another. You do not need to interfere." He furrowed his brow.

"Got it." She stabbed a stray crouton and a piece of lettuce with her fork and avoided eye contact.

The butterflies in her stomach woke up. Obviously, Agent Stafford was concerned enough about the suspect to warn her again.

The waitress wandered up, breaking the tension. "How are you all doing on this fine day? While y'all are finishing your lunches, can I put in an order for dessert?"

"No, we're good." Agent Stafford looked at Jules, who nodded in agreement.

"More tea?" the waitress asked.

"No. Just the check next time you're by," he said.

The waitress pulled a plastic folder from the pocket of her apron and set it in front of Agent Stafford. This time, Jules didn't offer to pay half.

The FBI agent slipped his credit card in the folder and the waitress exited. "You know Fisher is looking for the money."

Chapter Twenty-Four

Monday

As Jules stared at her notes on Ira Perkins, Bijou ran to the Dutch door and let out a low growl that quickly grew into a full-fledged barking jag.

"Okay, girl. Settle down." She peered into the store.

A young man in an olive-colored canvas jacket and jeans stood behind a couple that Roxanne was assisting at the main desk.

Jules slipped out and walked up to the man. "May I help you?"

"Uh, yeah. I'm looking for the owner. My name is Tom Hamilton. I'm a reporter from D. C." Under the jacket, he wore a white, wrinkled dress shirt and stained blue tie. He sported a patchy, stubbled beard and a noticeable scar under his left eye.

"You've found her. I'm Jules Keene. What can I do for you?"

"Is there a place we can talk?" His gaze flitted around the store. "You know, in private."

"We can sit on the front porch if you like." Jules pointed toward the front door.

"Nah, inside's fine." He stepped toward her.

She opened the bottom half of the door. Bijou darted for his feet and started barking again.

She picked up the dog and gestured toward a guest chair next to her desk. The dog calmed down but let out an occasional growl as a warning in the man's direction.

"Mr. Hamilton, what can I do for you?"

The man looked around the office like he was casing the place. After a long pause, he finally settled in the guest chair.

"I'm a reporter covering the death of Ira Perkins, and I was hoping you could give me some details." His gaze continued to dart around the office. He didn't seem to focus on anything.

"About what, specifically?" Jules closed the folder on her desk.

Bijou stirred in her lap.

"I'd like to know about any interactions you had with him and who found him. Any information you can share would be helpful."

Jules had a funny feeling about this guy. It was odd he would show up out of the blue so long after the murder. "Okay. He came here a few months ago and paid in advance for an extended stay. He told my team he was writing a book. He seemed very nice, and we didn't have much interaction with him. And then I found out from the sheriff that Mr. Perkins was dead. It was a terrible tragedy, and my staff took it hard. Have you been into town yet?"

"I drove through it. I didn't stop to visit."

"I think you should go see Sheriff Hobbs. He'd be a good person to give you some details for your story. He's leading the investigative team."

"That sounds like a plan. Do you have a minute or two to show me around the property?"

"Follow me." Jules put Bijou on her bed. The terrier didn't stay put long. She followed them to the door and tried several times to nip at Tom Hamilton's ankles. Jules apologized and scooted Bijou back into the office.

"This way, Mr. Hamilton."

Roxanne gave her a strange look, but Jules waved the reporter toward the door. They lingered on the long porch for a minute.

"You have a lovely place here. I can see why Mr. Perkins would want to stay here for an extended period. Did he give you or your staff any indication he wasn't a writer?"

"He wasn't a writer?" She stopped so suddenly on the steps that the reporter almost bumped into her.

"Uh, well. I have reason to think he was in hiding. That's what my story's about."

"Oh, my goodness, no. All he talked about was his book. We were all looking forward to him finishing it. We even talked about having a book signing in town. We were going to have a big party to celebrate." Jules led the way to the vintage campers. She stopped again to face the reporter.

"I like it here. I'm going to have to come back for a vacation." His gaze darted around like he was looking for someone.

"You should. The mountains are beautiful, and there are lots of things to do."

"Where did Ira stay?" he asked.

That was odd. He suddenly became very informal with the deceased. And what reporter didn't take notes or record the interview?

"This way. I'll show you. Oh, wait. I don't have the keys. Just a minute. I'll be right back." She left him standing in front of the security camera as she ran inside. She returned a few minutes later, breathless. "This way, please. Have you ever seen the inside of a vintage trailer?"

"My parents had a pop-up in the nineties."

Jules tried not to be snarky in her reply. "We refurbished all of these. They're classics, but we modernized them for today's guests, who like amenities." She led him up the sidewalk to the salmon and white topped 1959 Sunliner Caravan. The smallish camper, shaped like a jellybean, sat next to the infamous Robin Hood, the one where Mr. Perkins stayed. Jules had given this one a Barbie theme, in honor of the classic doll's debut the same year. It wasn't quite Barbie's Malibu Camper, but it was a plush pink and white trailer that appealed to doll collectors, pink fanatics, and little girls everywhere. One young lady spent her eighth birthday here and nicknamed it the "Princess Camper."

She unlocked its pink door and stepped inside.

Tom Hamilton followed her. "Ira Perkins stayed here?" He curled his lip.

"He liked it. He said it reminded him of New York and his mother. Pink was her signature color. He said it helped him get in the mood to write. He told me his mother was in the New York fashion industry." Jules grinned at

Tom Hamilton.

"Oh." He looked around the tiny camper that had been refurbished to hold a queen-sized bed with a faux white fur spread over a pink-striped bedspread. Lots of pink, white, and black pillows nestled against the headboard.

"Would you like to look around further? The police took everything that belonged to Mr. Perkins. I hope his family was able to claim his things. Have you talked to his nephew, Don Fisher?"

Tom Hamilton made a coughing sound and turned to face her. "No. I didn't realize he had a nephew."

"Oh, yes. He stopped by after Mr. Perkins's death and talked to my aunt."

Tom Hamilton seemed to recover from his start, stuck his head in the kitchen area, and opened the stainless-steel microwave. "Thanks. It was nice to get a look at where Ira stayed. I'm still surprised he chose this camper. It doesn't look like his style."

"Alrighty then. If I can answer any more questions, let me know."

"Un, no. Not right now. I think I have a good picture of Ira's last days here. Did he let you read any of his novel?" Tom Hamilton opened and closed several of the cabinets.

"Oh, no." Jules stepped out onto the patio. "It was secret! He was very protective of his work. He said it would be a surprise for us when the book came out."

"Did he ask you to hold anything for him?"

Jules mustered her best puzzled look. "Why would he do that? He was an extended stay guest."

"So, he didn't ask you to keep anything for him or someone else?"

"No. He was very private. He had very few requests for my team. The perfect guest." She gave a Cheshire Cat smile.

"I see." He followed Jules outside. "Well, thank you. I may be back if I have more questions."

"Call me if I can help with anything else. Here's my card with my name. You know, for the correct spelling for your article. I was hoping to get mentioned in Mr. Perkins's book. But I guess that won't happen now." She sighed and tried to look disappointed.

"Uh, I guess not." He pocketed her business card and surveyed the grounds. "Well, I'm going into town to talk to the sheriff."

"Tell him I said hello." Jules waved and walked back to the general store. She watched as Tom Hamilton walked down the entrance road.

Jules dashed inside. The odd conversation left her wondering about who Tom Hamilton really was and why he walked to her resort.

"What was that all about?" Roxanne looked up from her magazine.

"I'm not sure. But I want to make sure I got him on camera." Jules advanced through the last hour's camera feeds until she found the point when Tom Hamilton walked into the store. She checked the other feeds to see if he parked away from the resort, but the camera only caught him walking out the main gates to Baker Road. She copied the footage of Hamilton and sent it to Sheriff Hobbs with a quick note about the weird encounter with a reporter who was overdressed for a summer day.

"Who was that?" Roxanne patted Bijou.

"He said he was Tom Hamilton, a reporter. But his story was a little fishy. So far, I can't find him anywhere on the big wide web."

"The sheriff or that cute FBI agent might be interested." Roxanne leaned over to give Bijou a tummy rub.

"I sent the footage to them. The whole conversation with Hamilton was weird, and I didn't get the sense he was leveling with me."

"Is that why you showed him the wrong trailer?"

"I wanted to see his reaction. He acted surprised Ira Perkins would have stayed there."

"Ira wouldn't have stayed there. Pink's not his color," Roxanne said.

"I wish Ira Perkins hadn't found our resort at all."

The terrier woofed in agreement and circled the bed for a good napping spot.

After an hour of searching online for Tom Hamilton with no results, she logged off, stood, and stretched. "Come on, Bijou. Let's go for a walk and see what we have in the fridge for dinner. Hey, Roxanne. Do you need me to do anything before I leave?"

"Nope. Everyone's checked in. I'm meeting friends in town for dinner, so

I'll be packing it in, too, in a little while. You have big plans?"

"Nope. Bijou and I are going to hang out."

"You need to get out more." Her aunt scowled.

"I go out, but I like my home, too. I need to recharge sometimes."

Her aunt frowned. "If you say so." Roxanne returned to straightening the flyers on the front counter. "I think you need to go out with friends your age. You're all work lately."

Bijou and Jules made their way across the grass. Empty spots dominated the parking lot. She hoped her guests were out having fun. Maybe Roxanne was right about her needing a break. Jules couldn't remember her last day off. Maybe a change of scenery was in order.

The terrier finished sniffing the flower beds. Jules led her to the cabin. Nothing in the pantry or freezer looked like it would be an interesting dinner. On an impulse, she decided to go into town. She changed into a gauzy white top and swapped her tennis shoes for a pair of snappy red sandals. She fluffed her hair and did a couple of swipes with lipstick and mascara. Maybe a trip into town would change things up.

It took her longer to find a parking space in town than the drive over. Jules pulled into a spot next to the curb on a side street when the previous occupant vacated it. She walked toward Between the Covers, the town's independent bookstore.

Pushing open the glass door, Jules spotted Elizabeth Rhoney, the proprietor, at the front counter. Elizabeth wore her long silver locks in a twisted up-do, and her silver bangle bracelets jangled when she moved. "Hi there. Congrats on your victory over J. P. Gross. I'm excited I get to work with you on the council."

Her fluffy gray cat Bronte sat on a pile of books, purring contentedly. His tail flicked as he surveyed the store from his perch.

"Thank you. I'm excited about all the opportunities. Hi, Bronte." Jules scratched the cat's neck.

He purred and inched closer to Jules.

"I've been a part of that council for the ten years I've been in business. It's refreshing to focus on new ways of doing things. There's a contingent there who want things to stay the way they've always been. Enough of that. It's a new era. What can I help you with today?"

"I'm browsing, but I'm always drawn to your mystery section, so maybe that's where I should start." Jules headed to the back of the store where wall-to-wall mysteries were shelved next to a cozy, reading nook.

"Holler if you need anything. We'll be up here."

Jules got lost in the stacks. She loved the rolling bookshelf ladder for the taller shelves. That, and the overstuffed chairs in the reading nook, reminded her of a dream library. She browsed through the shelves and the specials on the nearby tables before settling on books by Lee Child, Nevada Barr, Rhys Bowen, and Michael Connelly.

"These look good. They'll keep me busy for a while." Jules put her finds on the counter.

Bronte looked up from his napping spot and yawned.

"All great choices." Elizabeth stacked the books in a large shopping bag adorned with literary quotes. "I added a copy of our events calendar. We're having Mysterypalooza in October. I'm hoping to have at least ten mystery authors for the event."

"I'll save the date. Send me the details, and I'll put it in my newsletter. See you soon. Bye, Bronte."

The majestic gray cat lifted his head. Not interested in the conversation, he returned to his nap.

Jules headed out the doorway and up the sidewalk. Scents from the nearby restaurants competed for her attention. She decided on Nacho Mama on the corner. It was time for dinner.

The hostess seated Jules at a wrought iron table near the patio's fencing. "Here's our menu and our specials this evening." She placed the menu on the table. "What can I get you to drink? We have giant margaritas for happy hour."

"I'll have an unsweetened iced tea and the shrimp tacos meal," Jules said.

"*Gracias*." The waitress picked up the menu.

Jules pulled out one of the books from her bag and started reading.

A steady stream of folks walked up and down the sidewalk. She liked to see people out supporting local businesses. A shadow crossed her table. She looked up to see Special Agent Stafford standing behind the empty chair across from her.

"Oh, hi. Are you off again tonight?"

"I'm always on call, but I decided to stop in for some dinner, and I saw you over here. Do you want company?"

"Have a seat. I stopped by the bookstore on the way over here." She slid her book into her shopping bag.

"It's a nice place to browse," he sat down. "I like the history section."

The waitress returned with a menu. "Hola. What can I get you to drink?"

"Iced tea is fine. And I'll have the shrimp fajitas."

"Good choice. I'll be back with your drink and more chips." The waitress picked up the menu.

"Any news on the manhunt?" Jules asked.

"It's going." He paused. "I saw the video you sent over to the sheriff this afternoon. You wanna tell me more about this new guy?"

"He walked in this afternoon. He had a wrinkled dress shirt and tie on under a canvas-like jacket. Too hot for a summer afternoon. He came into the store and said he was a reporter from Washington, D. C., and wanted to talk about Ira Perkins's death."

"Did he show any credentials?"

"No. And he didn't offer a business card. Usually that's the first thing the press hands out."

"Did you get a license plate?"

"No. He walked up the main entrance and out to the road. Maybe someone dropped him off?"

"What did he want to know?"

"About Mr. Perkins's stay. He told me the story he was working on was about him not being a writer, but he didn't go into any other details. Then he wanted to see the trailer where he stayed. He also asked if Mr. Perkins wanted me to hold anything for him."

The FBI agent pursed his lips, but, before he could speak, the waitress brought their plates. Agent Stafford's sizzled and filled the table with scents of peppers, onions, and shrimp.

"Looks good." Jules hadn't realized how hungry she was. She dug into her shrimp tacos and Spanish rice.

The FBI agent didn't waste any time assembling and biting into his first fajita.

Jules people-watched while they ate.

Will Stafford jarred her back from her daydream. "I have no idea who this new guy is, but chances are, he's not a reporter."

"He was kind of pale with freckles, and he had light, sandy hair in a buzz cut. I guess he was about thirty. He used Mr. Perkins's first name a lot in his questioning, almost like he knew him. And he acted nervous. Most other reporters I've encountered have a list of things they want to ask. And he didn't write anything down." She looked at the FBI agent.

Jules polished off her second taco and put her utensils on her plate. Will Stafford seemed preoccupied with assembling another fajita.

She waited for a reply, but none came. "Have you located Don Fisher yet?"

"No. He's still on the run. Forensics has gone over his truck and the burned-out car."

"Why burn it? The poor guy lost his car and a bunch of his clothes. That didn't make any sense. Why wouldn't he leave it on the side of the road somewhere when he was done with it?"

"He probably panicked. We have his truck, and we know who he is. He couldn't drive the carjacked vehicle around, and he can't go back to his old life or his job. He's dangerous and unpredictable. If you see him, don't engage in any way."

"I know. You've reminded me before. I don't plan to get near him. I'm hoping he's done poking around the resort. But we're on high alert, in case he comes back."

He put his fork down and pushed his plate forward. The tall agent leaned back in his chair.

The waitress swooped in. "Looks like you're done here. Anybody save room for dessert or coffee?"

"What's good?"

"We have Mexican cookies, a banana split, and cheesecake with fruit."

"You wanna split a dessert?" He looked at Jules.

"I might have a bite of something, but I'm pretty full."

"We'll have the cheesecake with two forks."

"Good choice." The waitress retreated to the kitchen with the pile of dishes.

"So, what do you do for fun when you're not investigating? Every time I see you, you're working." Jules stared at him, looking for a reaction.

"I could say the same for you."

Before she could retort, she took a deep breath. He was the second person to say something about her working too much. Jules put in long hours, but it was for the resort.

"I like to ski in the winter. And I like to fish," he said.

Jules wrinkled her nose and hoped he didn't notice. "My dad liked to fish, but he never seemed to have the time. He worked so hard to get the campground going. It's his legacy, so I want it to be successful. I guess it doesn't help that I live where I work."

Before she could continue, the waitress put the dessert and the two forks in the middle of the table.

"I travel a lot. I live in hotels mostly. I don't even keep house plants. They die while I'm on assignment. And I never keep food in my fridge. I never know when I'll be called out for an extended time. No one wants to clean out spoiled milk or fuzzy yogurt after being away for two months."

Jules smiled and took the pointed end of the cheesecake, along with a couple of raspberries. He cut off a large hunk of the dessert. She grabbed one more bite and put her fork down. "You eat the rest."

He finished the dessert in a couple of bites. Interrupted by his phone, he checked the screen. He sent a reply. "Sorry about that. I've got to go." He waved the waitress over and pulled out his credit card. "Could I get the check, please?" He handed her the card.

"Thank you for dinner."

He signed the restaurant copy. "Have a good evening." Agent Stafford stood and pushed his chair under the table. "The state police may have a lead on Fisher. Call me if you see anything strange."

Jules rose and grabbed her purse and shopping bag. The tall FBI agent scooted around the wrought iron fencing and jogged toward his SUV. For a couple who weren't dating, they seemed to eat out a lot together, even if it wasn't planned. It was almost like he knew where she would be.

Chapter Twenty-Five

Tuesday

A young mother dropped bandages, salve, sunscreen, and lip balm on the counter. Jules bagged the items, and the woman handed her cash. "I hope everything is okay, Mrs. Stephens."

"We're having fun. Probably too much. We've had two skinned knees and a touch of sunburn. But they're having a great time. We're never outdoors this much, so it's all new and exciting for my kiddos."

"I hope the boo-boos aren't too bad." Jules handed the woman her purchases.

"They'll be fine. They're excited about hiking in the mountains today."

"Enjoy." Jules closed the register drawer.

A hike to the waterfall today sounded fun, but Jules had things to do at the resort. And the whole second reporter thing bothered her. She had a hunch he knew Mr. Perkins from somewhere. She scanned MedPro's website, but they didn't display any employee pictures. On a hunch, she checked the company's LinkedIn and Facebook sites but had no success there either. She picked up the phone and called the MedPro number.

After several rounds of automated menus, Jules pressed zero in hopes of getting a live person.

After a transfer and another short commercial, she heard, "Hello. Welcome to MedPro. How may I direct your call?"

"May I speak to Tom Hamilton, please?"

"I'm sorry. We don't have any Hamiltons in our directory. Could someone else help you?"

"I thought he said his name was Tom Hamilton. He's a young guy with short reddish-blond hair."

"MedPro has thousands of employees in several locations across the country. Let me switch you to Customer Service." The phone clicked.

Jules disconnected and returned to the internet.

Roxanne breezed in an hour later. She dropped her oversized Dooney and Bourke purse and an insulated lunch bag on the other desk.

"How was dinner?" Jules asked.

"It was fun to catch up. How about you? I heard you had dinner with the FBI agent again. Is this a thing you want to tell me about?"

Fern Valley's gossip grapevine was alive and well.

"No. It's not a thing. I went to the bookstore last night and stopped for dinner. He happened to be there, and we shared a table. It was nothing."

"If you say so."

Jules glared at her, but Roxanne didn't seem to notice. She put her purse away and leaned over to pet Bijou.

"It was just dinner."

"Bijou. I think she protests too much."

"I'm going to pick up the cushions for the Robin Hood trailer. Do we need anything else while I'm out?" Jules asked.

"I don't think so. The supplies look pretty good."

Jules retrieved her purse and sunglasses. "Be back soon." She drove through town and east toward Charlottesville. The mountain view and the summer smells of grass and clean air reminded her why she didn't want to live anywhere else.

After picking up the repaired cushions and a new set of matching pillows and curtains, she loaded everything in the back of the Jeep. Her stomach rumbled, so she took a side street toward the downtown mall. Surprised to find street parking, she decided it was her lucky day.

She ordered a sandwich and a glass of water from an outdoor café and sat under the trees to enjoy lunch and the sunny day. Jules watched shoppers and their dogs stroll up and down the street. Not in any hurry to get back, she wandered down the mall. The pet boutique on the corner caught her eye. She browsed through the people and pet gifts and settled on a blue dog paw scarf and several pet charms for Bijou's collar.

Across the plaza, she spied a travel agency. The big posters of tropical beaches drew her inside, but the coolness of the office made her shiver. She glanced over the racks of colorful brochures of exotic beach vacations and themed tours. She got lost for a few minutes in the wonderful sites and a bucket list of places to visit.

After a brief chat with the travel agent with the bright pink hair, Jules stuffed flyers and a catalog into her purse. It felt odd planning a vacation for one, but a getaway would be nice.

She headed back to the mall and to her Jeep. Time to get back and check on Roxanne and Bijou.

She blasted the air-conditioning to counteract the summer heat. Cranking up the radio, she rummaged around for her sunglasses. On the way back to the valley, she spotted a guy walking along the side of the road ahead of her. From the back, he looked like Tom Hamilton in his olive-green jacket. But what was he doing this far from Fern Valley on foot? A gray sedan sped toward her, away from Fern Valley. Before the car passed the guy in the olive jacket, it stopped suddenly. The guy jogged toward the car. Tom Hamilton leaned inside the driver's window. Then he ran around and hopped in the passenger side. The car sped off toward town.

Ignoring Will Stafford's voice in her head about not engaging, she did a U-turn and followed the gray Honda back into Charlottesville. She would call the FBI agent as soon as she knew where the guy was headed. The car zigzagged down a warren of streets and alleys and finally pulled into a McDonald's. Tom Hamilton jumped out and slammed the car door. Don Fisher followed him inside the restaurant. Jules snapped a picture of the car's license plate. She pulled around to the side parking lot, where she could watch the car and the door without being too conspicuous.

Jules grabbed her phone to alert the authorities, but she hesitated. *It would be better to know what they are up to before I call the sheriff.* While she rationalized with herself about the right thing to do, the two men returned to the car, clutching several paper bags. She barely had time to start the engine before they sped back through town. Jules dodged a truck in the parking lot and managed to get two car lengths behind the speeding Honda Civic. She tailed them through a series of side streets but lost them near the University of Virginia. She circled the block with no luck and pulled to the curb. Not wanting another lecture from the sheriff or the FBI agent, she decided to send the picture via text instead of calling. She typed, **Saw Fisher and Hamilton in C-ville in this car** and added, **just minutes ago** for good measure.

Jules dropped her phone in her purse and headed back to the resort. At least now she knew what happened to Kevin Bailey's car.

Jules grabbed the key to the Robin Hood and returned to her Jeep to get her purchases. Balancing the seat cushions, throw pillows, and curtains, she walked across the grass, where she spotted Lester and Jake staring at the 1959 Sunliner Caravan.

"Hey, Boss. We were about to call you. It looks like a family of gophers took up residence here." Lester stared at the ground.

Jake caught two of the cushions as they teetered.

Jules peeked around the remaining stack. Someone had dug at least twenty holes around the patio and both sides of the vintage trailer. "What in the world?"

Jake said, "It looks like we had another night visitor looking for something."

"Like buried treasure," Lester added.

"What else is going to happen around here? Did anyone see anything?" If Lester only knew that his guess wasn't too far off.

"No. I came through on my last patrol about ten-thirty, and everything was normal," Jake said.

"I noticed this mess this morning when I came by with the weedwhacker," Lester wiped his forehead with the back of his hand.

Pulling out her phone, Jules dialed Sheriff Hobbs.

"Hobbs, here."

"Hi, Sheriff. This is Jules. We've had another night visitor. I think someone from your team should take a look at it."

"How bad is it?"

"Someone dug about twenty holes around one of my campers."

He made a hrumping sound and tapped something. There was a long pause. "Okay. Sit tight. I'll get someone out there."

Jules disconnected and pocketed her phone. "Someone will be here in a little bit. And how can you dig quietly without waking anyone? I'm going to put these in the trailer. I'll be back."

Jake followed her to the neighboring trailer with two of the cushions. They spent the next half hour putting everything in place.

"Thanks for your help. There. This looks better. I can put this trailer back in circulation now," Jules said.

Jake flashed a smile that showed his dimples and reminded her of the guy she knew twenty years ago. They stood facing each other for a few seconds in the smallish kitchen. After a quiet pause, he backed out of the trailer, and she followed.

"Why do you think they'd dig all those holes around the Barbie camper?" he asked.

"I think that's my fault. This guy came by the other day, claiming to be a reporter. He was acting weird, so when he asked to see Ira Perkins's trailer, I showed him that one."

"Hey, you all," Lester yelled. There are holes around the back of this camper, too." He pointed to the back of the Robin Hood.

Jules followed Jake around the back.

"Watch where you step," Lester said. "You don't want to turn your ankle. Somebody was on a mission."

Jules snapped a few pictures and walked around to the front of the Barbie camper to wait on the patio for the sheriff. Jake settled down in the chair beside her, with his legs outstretched.

"I'm gonna head back over to the barn. Let me know when it's okay, and I'll fill in the holes," Lester said.

"So, how is the tiny house coming?" She tapped her foot on the cement pad.

"Pretty good. I have walls, doors, and windows. It's wired for electrical. I need to do the plumbing. Then I need to finish the inside and do the gingerbread trim on the outside."

"You're doing all of it?"

"Yep. Between the plans and YouTube videos, I'm set. I'm guessing it will be another few weeks before it can be painted and moved."

"I can't wait to see it."

"Come by the barn later. I think you'll be surprised."

Jules heard a motor, and she shielded her eyes with her hand.

The sheriff's car pulled into the front lot. He slammed the door, adjusted his gunbelt, and walked toward them. "Hey, Jules. Hey, Jake. How are you? Still finding interesting stuff?"

"We didn't find anything this time," she said. "Except all these holes, and I don't think we have a gopher problem."

"Somebody's definitely looking for something. Anything missing?" The sheriff poked at one of the holes with a pen.

"Actually, I didn't go inside this one. We returned the cushions to that one, the one Ira Perkins stayed in," she said.

"I'll go get the key while you two look around." Jake trotted off toward the office.

"I can guess what they were after." The sheriff snapped pictures from all angles.

By the time they returned to the patio, Jake appeared with the key. He opened the aluminum door and stepped inside.

Jules followed close behind him. They inched past each other awkwardly in the galley kitchen.

"Everything looks fine in here," she said. She retreated to the patio, and Jake stopped to lock the door.

"What's on your camera feed?" Sheriff Hobbs asked.

"Come on over, and we'll see if we caught anything."

"I'm going to get Lester, and we'll fill in these holes if you're done," Jake said.

"Yep, go ahead." Sheriff Hobbs followed Jules to the office.

Once inside, her eyes adjusted to the dimmer, inside lighting. Jules turned her laptop so he could see and opened the camera application. She backed up the recording to ten last night and started moving slowly forward on the main gate feed. When that didn't pan out, she repeated the process on the other cameras.

"No luck," she said. "They either walked up or came across the resort from the woods. Jake said he did his last round about ten-thirty and didn't see anything."

"Call me if you notice anything else. Any idea why it was mostly around the other camper?"

"That's my fault," she said sheepishly. "That second reporter came by asking about Mr. Perkins. When he wanted to see the camper, I showed him the Sunliner Caravan. Obviously, he or somebody thought Ira Perkins had left something important."

"Let me know if either of those guys come back."

"Did you get the text I sent you?"

He nodded.

"I saw the second guy, Tom Hamilton, with Don Fisher in downtown Charlottesville today. And I'm pretty sure he was driving Kevin Bailey's car."

"It was Bailey's. The tags matched. I'll add the mysterious digging to our report of incidents at your resort." The sheriff retreated to the store area.

"Thanks, Sheriff." Jules let out a heavy sigh.

They had called the police more this summer than any other time in the campground's history. She wanted to ask the guests in the nearby trailers if they heard any noise last night, but she changed her mind when she thought it might cause unnecessary panic.

Roxanne's singsong voice from the general store interrupted her thoughts. "Bye, Sheriff."

Jules sent a text to the security company, asking for overnight patrols of the resort until further notice. Her phone binged a few minutes later with a text from Mark O'Rourke. **Not a problem. I'll send a guy starting tonight for 10 P to 7 A.**

Jules felt better knowing there was extra security on duty with Don Fisher and Tom Hamilton determined to find the hidden money.

Chapter Twenty-Six

Wednesday

Jules's phone chimed. When she didn't respond, it chimed again a few seconds later. Rolling over, she glanced at the clock and grabbed her cell. Bijou was now on high alert at the end of the bed. Two in the morning was too early for a perky Jack Russell.

Something's not right with security. Meet me at the office? Jake texted.

OK. Be there in a few, she tapped in her phone.

She sat on the side of the bed and shook off the fog that left her brain somewhere between reality and a dreamworld. Jules slid on a pair of jeans and a sweatshirt. She managed to find socks and her tennis shoes. A ponytail and no makeup would have to do for this early hour.

Jules grabbed her keys and phone and hiked over to the office. No sign of the golf cart. She stood on the back stoop and hugged herself to ward off the early morning chill. She fidgeted and danced around to get warm just as Jake drove across the grass at top speed for a cart. He skidded to an abrupt stop in front of her.

"Sorry to wake you. I gave the new guard a tour of the premises. We drove around all of the property this side of the meadow. And I gave him one of the walkie-talkies. About thirty minutes ago, he came on the radio and said that something looked fishy over near the trailers and the fence line. Then I couldn't raise him."

"What'd you find?"

"Nothing. It's weird. And I have no idea where he is. It's like he vanished."

"Let me call the dispatch at his company." Jules thumbed through her contacts for Mark O'Rourke. After a couple of rings, she cleared her throat. "Good evening. Or morning. I'm Jules Keene at the Fern Valley Luxury Camping Resort. We can't reach one of your guards who was patrolling our grounds. Do you have a way of contacting him?"

"Let me try his radio. And if that doesn't work, I'll call his cell. Hold, please."

After what seemed like too many musical versions of seventies songs, the operator returned. "Ms. Keene, I'm not able to make contact with the guard either. I'm sending another unit to assist you."

"Thank you." She disconnected. "They can't reach him either. Do you think he went in the woods?"

"That's my guess."

"I dread calling the sheriff again. They've been out here more times than I can count." She slid in the passenger seat next to Jake, who looked too awake and in charge for this hour in the morning. "How about we do one more loop around the perimeter? Where's the radio?"

He tossed the radio to her as he put the golf cart in reverse.

She pressed the button. "Security. Come in security." After no response, she sank back in her seat.

Jake drove slowly down the tree line behind Jules's cabin toward the barn. They passed Jake and Lester's cabins and made the turn that led to the meadow.

A few minutes later, Jake retraced their route. "Did you see anything?"

"No." She hit the squawk button on the radio several times.

Jules dialed the sheriff's office, and when the dispatcher answered, she gave a short version of what had happened. The dispatcher promised to send a car over.

"I'm going to check the camera feeds."

"I'll stay outside in case he comes back or security or the sheriff's office arrive." Jake parked the cart so he could watch the edge of the woods.

Jules punched in the security code and turned the lights on. She rummaged through the container for the strongest coffee she could find. While the water heated up, she scanned all of the camera feeds. She caught Jake and the guard patrolling the perimeter in the cart. About thirty minutes later, other cameras showed them completing the circuit near the office.

Stepping outside, she handed Jake a steaming mug. "Here. This should warm you up a bit."

"Thanks. I still can't raise him on the radio."

"Where's his vehicle?"

"The front lot," he pointed. "It hasn't moved."

Jules jogged over to the black sedan that said "O'Rourke Security" in big letters with an oversized gold star on both side doors. Jules walked around the car and peeked inside and checked out the surroundings. Nothing looked out of place.

"I wanted to make sure he wasn't napping in the car." Jules slid into the cart seat next to Jake.

A few minutes later, a car door slammed. Mark O'Rourke stepped out of his car and scanned the parking lot. Jules waved, and he headed toward the golf cart.

"Good morning, Mark. Sorry to get you out of bed at this hour."

"No problem." The tall man wore jeans and a leather jacket. "It's part of the job. So, what happened?"

Jake set his empty mug on the cart's dashboard. "I gave your guy a tour of the property a little after ten. I left him and headed to the barn. About one-thirty, I heard him on our radio. He said something looked unusual, and he was going to check it out."

"He didn't say where he was?"

"No. We haven't been able to reach him. And nothing except their first patrol showed up on the cameras," Jules said.

"I haven't been able to get ahold of him either. That's unlike Anthony. He's one of my best guys. He doesn't ditch work," Mark said.

Before anyone could comment, Sheriff Hobbs parked his truck and walked over to the group.

"Hi, Sheriff," Jules said. "Sorry to call you out again in the wee hours. Mark's security guy has gone missing. Jake was the last to hear from him on the radio about one-thirty."

Sheriff Hobbs asked, "What was the last communication?"

"He said he saw something unusual, and he was going to have a look. Then there was nothing," Jake said. "Jules and I drove up and down the tree line, and we didn't see anything."

"What's his name and description?"

"Anthony Rizzo. He's been with me for almost ten years. Six-three about two-twenty. If he was in uniform, he was wearing jeans and a black O'Rourke Security jacket," Mark said.

"Any reason to think he's just napping somewhere?"

"Nah. He's not like that. He's my second in command. My hunch is he went after someone." Mark ran his hand through his spiked salt-and-pepper hair.

"Okay. I've got another patrol checking the roads around the resort. We'll find him. Is that his vehicle?" the sheriff asked.

Mark nodded. The men walked toward the black SUV. The sheriff said something into his walkie-talkie.

When there was a lull in the conversation, Jake asked, "Anybody want a ride around the perimeter?"

The sheriff hopped in beside him, and Mark climbed in the back seat.

"I'll be in the office," Jules said.

A little after four, the back door opened, and the three men tramped in. Jules rubbed her eyes and closed her laptop. "Did you find him?"

The sheriff shook his head while she got up to get the coffee maker brewing.

"Nothing," the sheriff said. "It's like he vanished into thin air. I even had patrols check the roads around your property. When the sun comes up, the state police should be here with the helicopter patrol. There's a search and rescue team on their way, too."

"I can muster a few guys if you need help with the search," Mark replied.

"We could use the extra eyes. I have two deputies and a rookie on the day shift I can spare. Let's meet here, and we'll put together a plan," Sheriff Hobbs said. "I'll call my guys in."

"You all can meet in the lodge. Crystal and Mel should be in by five to start breakfast. There's plenty of food and drinks before you start," Jules said.

"I'll put out an alert to my guys." Mark pulled out his cell phone. After a quick call, he set his mug on the table and rose. He left with the sheriff to organize their teams.

"I'm going to head home to check on some things. I'll meet you at the lodge," Jake said.

"I'll be over there in a little bit to help them set up and serve," she said.

Jules followed Jake out the back door. He jogged across the field to his cabin. She walked to hers, saying a silent prayer for the guard. Too many strange things had been happening here lately. Where could Anthony Rizzo have gone?

Around five that evening, Jules sat with her head in her hands at her desk. Roxanne opened the Dutch door, and Bijou woofed.

"Why don't you go home and get some sleep? Emily and I can close up here, and I promise to call you if there's news. You look beat."

"It's been a long day. I can't believe that there's no news on that guard. Where could he be?"

"It'll be okay." Roxanne patted Jules on the shoulder. "Go get some sleep. You're no good to us as the walking dead."

"Thanks, I think." She gave a half-smile. "Come on, Bijou. Let's go for a walk. Though it's more like a zombie walk today. Call me if you hear anything."

Jules and Bijou trotted back to her cabin. She put a bowl of food down and freshened the dog's water bowl. Then she kicked off her tennis shoes and fell, fully dressed, into bed. She hoped there would be better news when she woke up. Two murders, and now this.

Chapter Twenty-Seven

Thursday

The sun streamed in between the cracks of her blinds and woke Jules up. She glanced at her phone. Six o'clock. And no new messages or texts. She hugged Bijou then jumped in the shower.

She grabbed her purse on the way out of the house. "Come on, Bijou. We need to find out what's going on."

Even the dog sensed the urgency and didn't dawdle on their walk to work. Families stirred. Jules waved at a couple heading to the lodge for breakfast. Several cars from Mark O'Rourke's company, the sheriff's car, and a large SUV filled the first two rows of her parking lot.

"Hey, Roxanne, any news?"

"Nope. The guys are over at the lodge planning their next moves. Hey, Bijou."

The terrier wiggled her greeting.

Jules set the leash on her desk. "I'll be back in a little while. I'm going to see what's going on." She slipped out the back door.

Sheriff Hobbs, Deputy Dempsey, Jake, Mark O'Rourke, and two guys from the security firm huddled in the lodge around a back table covered with plates and coffee mugs.

"Good morning, Jules," Sheriff Hobbs said as she approached.

She poured a mug of tea and loaded it with milk.

"Thanks for the hospitality," he said.

Jules sat in the oak chair next to him. "Any luck with the search? And where is Agent Stafford?"

A frown crossed Jake's face, but he didn't say anything.

"He had to go back to Richmond today," Sheriff Hobbs said. "He should be back later today or tomorrow. The state police helicopter is flying around this morning. And we're about to head out in the woods."

Jake started to clear the table. "I'll get those," Jules said. "Is there anything I can do for you all?"

"I'm going with Mark's guys in the woods. Lester's at the barn if you need anything while I'm gone," Jake said.

"Be careful," she whispered.

The men rose and trudged out the door.

Jules hoped they weren't too late in their search. A lot of time had already passed, and she didn't know how she would handle another senseless death. Jules shook off the eerie feeling of dread and busied herself with clearing dishes and wiping down tables. Oblivious to the crisis, other guests ate their breakfasts and chatted. They didn't seem to be bothered by the law enforcement presence. Nobody said anything about it to her, and they didn't seem to be aware of all the sinister things that kept happening around the resort.

Jules retreated to the office, where she rearranged the items on the shelves. She paused to wipe her brow with the back of her hand.

Roxanne flitted into the store from the backroom. She leaned over the counter and stared at her niece. "Okay, missy. You've done all the things that Emily normally does. What gives?"

"It feels better to stay busy. I'm worried about that guard."

"It's not your fault. You didn't do this." Roxanne waggled a finger at her.

"I know, but Ira Perkins was our guest, and all this stemmed from his stay here. And what if J. P. Gross is right? What if I'm bringing more people and the ills of society to the valley? Our goal was always to provide a safe, fun place for folks to enjoy the mountains," Jules let out a heavy sigh.

"He's not right. Our crime rate was much higher when we had boarded-up buildings downtown. People were leaving the area in droves, and there were no jobs. We don't have the drug problems other little rural towns have. What you're doing here is a good thing. You can't listen to the naysayers."

"Thanks. But this not knowing about Anthony's whereabouts is driving me nuts." She put the dust rag away and headed to her desk. Jules spent the next few hours brainstorming ideas for themed events, working on administrative chores, and watching Jack Russell videos on the internet. Her phone rang. She jumped.

"Hey, Jules," Jake said. "They found the guard."

"Is he okay?"

"Yep. He was tied up in the restroom at Honey's fruit stand. One of the staff noticed the door had been kicked in. He found the guard in the bathroom. They took him to the hospital in Charlottesville."

"That's good news." The tension left Jules's shoulders. "Any idea why he was at Honey's?"

"No. Charles said the guard was semi-conscious when the ambulance got there. He followed some guy off your property into the woods. When he got to the field on the other side, somebody jumped him and hit him in the head and overpowered him. Two guys tied him up and forced him into a car. He said they drove him around for a while. And then the next thing he remembered was when they dumped him at the fruit stand."

"And nobody noticed him at Honey's?" Jules asked.

"They were closed yesterday. I'm not sure how long he was tied up there," Jake said.

"I'm so glad they found him." Jules let out a deep breath.

"Mark went with his guys to the hospital. He said he'll call you later. He's gonna increase the manpower on the night patrols for a while. I'm headed home and then to the barn to check on things. Call me if you need me."

She clicked off and put her head on her desk.

Roxanne rushed into the back. "Oh thank goodness they found him at Honey's."

Jules looked up, exhausted.

Her aunt patted her shoulder. "He's okay, and that's good news."

After lunch, Mark O'Rourke strode from the doorway to the front counter in a few steps.

Jules came around the corner. "Hi, Mark. How's Anthony doing?"

"Doing good. He's a trooper. He hopes to be released this evening."

"That's great news. Come into my office." Once there, Jules pointed to the guest chair near her desk and picked up Bijou. "Can I get you anything?"

"No, I'm good. Anthony said he saw a guy in a sweatshirt sneaking around the campers. When he called out to him, the guy ran. Anthony chased him through the woods clear out to the other side, where the runner and another guy got the jump on him."

"I'm glad he's okay." Jules's thoughts immediately flashed to Don Fisher and Tom Hamilton.

"He's anxious to get back to work. We'll have to see what the doctors say about his injury. He got about ten stitches in his head and a couple on his hand and chin. They want to keep an eye on him with the concussion and blood loss. Plus, he was dehydrated when they found him. It'll be a challenge to get him to rest. He's ready to find the jerks who did this." The owner of the security firm paused and twisted in his seat. "We need to talk to you about increasing the patrols here, at least for the next few weeks. I'd feel better if we had a pair on duty."

"I agree. I think we need to have some backup. I'll let my guys know."

"I'm sure the sheriff has told you, but if you see either Don Fisher or his sidekick Hamilton on the property, call the police."

"I know. They haven't been back in daylight in quite a while. They seem to sneak around in the wee hours. Thanks for all your help. And please thank Anthony for us." More annoyed that these two were still tormenting her, Jules was determined that they wouldn't frighten her.

"Will do. I'm sure he'll be back on duty as soon as he can." Mark stood and shook her hand. "I'm headed back to the hospital to check on him."

Jules followed Mark out. He waved to Emily and Roxanne, who were chatting at the front counter. Roxanne smiled her best flirty smile.

"We're going to have two of his guys patrolling each night until further notice. Bijou and I are going to head home."

Roxanne paused for a beat. "I'll let Lester and Jake know."

Jules smiled a half-smile and retreated to her office to get Bijou and her things. As they walked between the Robin Hood and the Sunliner Caravan, Bijou tugged on her leash. She sniffed the grass and moved toward the pink glam camper. Lester had done a nice job of covering the holes from the other night with transplanted sod to even out the landscaping. Bijou tugged harder and almost knocked Jules off balance. The Jack Russell zeroed in on a patch of grass almost under the vintage trailer. The sun glinted off something in the grass and caught Jules's eye.

Bijou fixated on the spot. She tugged and sniffed until Jules followed her to the grassy area.

"What did you find, girl?" Jules picked up an iPhone in a dirty, black case and turned it over. She pressed the button. "Siri, who's phone is this?" She wondered if it belonged to a guest or one of the guys poking around her trailers at night.

The automated voice answered, "This phone belongs to Rich Sanders."

Jules walked back to the office to check the guest records. Sanders didn't ring a bell.

"Back so soon?" Roxanne asked.

"Bijou found a phone in the grass, and I wanted to check the registration list." Jules shook the mouse on the computer at the front counter and waited for it to wake up. "You don't know a Rich Sanders, do you?"

Her aunt shook her head.

"Okay. If anybody comes by looking for a phone, I locked it in my desk."

On the way to her cabin, Jules texted the sheriff and let him know about the recovered phone, in case it was important.

Hunger won out over fatigue. She fixed herself a grilled cheese sandwich and tomato soup. She settled on the couch, where she scanned the MedPro website and dialed the main number. An operator answered.

Jules said, "Hi, this is Terry Jones. May I speak with Rich Sanders, please?"

"One moment." The phone clicked and played a slow version of some eighties tune. The call connected to voice mail. "Hi, this is Rich Sanders. I am out of the office on leave until July first. Please leave a message and I'll return your call when I'm back from vacation. If this is urgent, please dial extension three five three two."

MedPro again. Jules's stomach did a flip-flop.

Chapter Twenty-Eight

Friday

"Jules, Jules," Roxanne yelled from the store. "Your FBI Agent is here."

Jules stepped out of the office and shut the bottom half of the door. Heat crept across her cheeks. "Hi, Agent Stafford. I didn't expect you today." She tried to give her aunt a scowl, but Roxanne only had eyes for Agent Stafford.

"The sheriff sent me over to pick up the phone you found." He returned Roxanne's smile with a high-wattage one.

She ignored her aunt. "I've got it locked in my desk."

Agent Stafford followed Jules into the back office. When Bijou jumped on Agent Stafford, he bent, picked her up, and hugged her. She melted like butter in her new friend's arms. So much for a watchdog.

"Where'd you find it?"

"Between Ira Perkins's trailer and the one where the yard was vandalized. It wasn't near the holes. Closer to the trailer."

"I'm guessing your prints are on it?"

"Yep. I don't usually wear gloves around the campground. The phone belongs to a Rich Sanders."

"That's interesting." He held the paper evidence bag open, and she dropped it in.

"Do you recognize this guy?" He showed her a photo on his phone.

"That's the guy who said he was a reporter, Tom Hamilton."

"No, that's Rich Sanders."

Jules's knees felt wobbly. She sat in her office chair.

Agent Stafford put Bijou on the floor. "A deputy picked him up last night. He was walking along one of the country roads at dusk. He looked a little unsteady on his feet. The deputy thought he'd been drinking. On closer inspection, his clothes had blood on them, so he took him in. His prints came back as Rich Sanders from Alexandria."

"I called MedPro when I found out the name from the lost phone. Friend of Mr. Perkins?"

"He clammed up. He sat and stared at our interrogator, but we're pretty sure he was involved in the incident with the security guard. We'll give him some time to think about whether or not he wants to cooperate. The DNA will come back soon enough from the blood on his clothes, and if it belongs to Anthony Rizzo, he better make up his mind quickly about whether or not he wants to talk."

"Ira Perkins and MedPro keep popping up at my resort. I was hoping we would have been rid of him by now. We've had way too many incidents lately. I've added extra night security."

"Is it affecting business?"

"Not as far as I can tell. We're still at capacity each week. Summer vacation is in full swing. And no cancellations."

"That's good. I'll drop this off at the station and update the team. Call us if you see Don Fisher on the property again. We're pretty sure he's still in the area."

Jules quelled the anxiousness that welled up inside her over Fisher and Hamilton. She and Bijou followed the FBI agent through the store.

Roxanne batted her lashes and smiled at Agent Stafford. Jules scooped up the terrier before she followed her new friend out the door.

Back at her desk, Jules scoured the internet for Rich Sanders. His tweets were few and far between. Most centered around science fiction books and movies. His LinkedIn page detailed his four years of experience as a senior database designer for MedPro. It looked like it was his first job out of college. Rich, Ira, and Don all worked together at the same company, and somehow, they were involved in a scam to extort money from some of their employer's clients. And if Mr. Perkins knew of a scam, why didn't he go to the police early on? Or was he part of it?

The office phone rang twice. When no one answered, she grabbed the receiver. "Fern Valley Luxury Camping Resort. How may I help you?"

"Hi, this is Bethany Miller in the nineteen forties New Moon. We have a clogged toilet that has overflowed. Could you send someone over quickly?"

"I'll have someone there in a minute."

"Thanks. And if they find a Power Ranger or an Avengers action figure, my four-year-old is having a meltdown because they've gone missing."

"I'll let maintenance know. They'll be right over." At least this was a regular service call and not another dead body.

She clicked the walkie-talkie button. "Jake. Lester. We have an overflowing toilet in D5. Can one of you get over there pronto? The mom thinks her kid may have flushed some action figures."

"I've got it," Jake said. "Off to rescue some superheroes."

"Thanks." Jules set the radio on her desk. Normalcy was refreshing for a change.

Jules opened her email and did a doubletake. She had over ninety messages since she'd checked last. She hoped it was a fluke, but most turned out to be suggestions for improvements to the business council. After previewing a handful, she realized she needed a way to keep the council work organized before it inundated her. She created a spreadsheet to track all the ideas and electronic folders to keep up with the correspondence.

An hour and a half and two cups of coffee later, Jules had recorded and responded to all the emails. She added a column to her spreadsheet and categorized each entry. Of the eighty-two items on the list, only three were duplicates. Jules, still charged about her new role, created an email for the board and attached her list. She also made a note to see if they had a central storage location for documents. Then she jotted down a reminder to look at the outdated website. It definitely needed some love.

A few minutes before four-thirty, Roxanne packed up. "See ya later, kiddo.

I'm heading out. I'm having dinner in town."

"Date night?"

"Hmmmm. Maybe. Let's go with dinner with an old friend." Her aunt smiled and trotted out the doorway before Jules could ask any more questions. Roxanne had a mystery date.

Jules's email dinged, and she let out a harrumphing sound when another twenty emails about the business council appeared in her inbox. "Bijou, if this continues, all I'll be doing is council stuff." Jules waded through suggestions for a motorcycle rally, a bike race, a clown festival, a gun show, and a pet expo.

By the time she responded to this last batch, her spreadsheet had over a hundred ideas. Well, at least they wouldn't be at a loss for projects. The first order of business was to get the board to prioritize their plans. She dashed off another email and asked the council's secretary to set up a working board meeting. She shut down her laptop before the next volley of emails landed.

"Well, how about we go see what we have for dinner. You up for some classic TV?"

Bijou raised her head and then ran for the back door.

Jules checked all the locks. "Let's go."

The dog rushed out the doorway and flitted around the grassy area. Bijou growled and chased a June bug toward the barn. They both heard hammering. The little dog's ears perked up, and she tugged on her lead to get inside. Jules unclipped her leash, and she darted in toward the noise.

The hammering stopped. Jake's voice came from the barn. "Hey, Bijou. What brings you out here?"

Jules rounded the corner of the tiny house that was on a flatbed trailer. "This is really taking shape."

"I'm doing the trim and the specialty cuts tonight. This one is the cottage design, so it'll look like something out of *Snow White*, without the thatched roof."

Bijou sniffed around and jumped up on the trailer to explore the inside of the tiny house. She wandered around the downstairs and found a place to curl up near the front door.

Jules wandered around the base and looked at the outside. Then she climbed up and poked around the rooms.

"It looks like Bijou approves. These are going to be a big draw, especially when we have four or five in our little village."

"This should be ready for paint next week. The plumbing and electricity are done. I've drywalled the inside already. Be thinking of how you want to decorate it. If we place these on the pads at the back of the field, the backyard view will be of the woods."

"I like that. We can use the concrete pads that are there and come up with an arrangement that looks like a little neighborhood with some neat landscaping. That field has plenty of space in it. I think we used to house twenty-five or thirty campsites back there."

"This model has a bedroom, loft, and space for a futon. It should be able to accommodate two adults and a couple of kids."

"That's the size of most of the vintage trailers. I think they'll appeal to families and couples looking for a unique retreat. Can't wait until they're finished."

"What are you doing tonight? Big plans?"

"No. Bijou and I were going to see what was in the fridge and binge Netflix."

"Why don't you hang around? I could use an extra hand and a few paws."

"Sounds like fun. Have you eaten?"

"Nope." Jake picked up a hammer and a level and returned to some touch-up work.

"I'll go change and see what I can scrounge up. Be back in a few. Ready, Bijou?"

She lifted her head, looked around, and returned to her napping spot.

"She's okay here."

"I'll leave her leash by the door in case you need it." Jules headed to her cabin to see what she had for a throw-together meal. Maybe dinner with a friend would be a nice change. Roxanne might be on to something.

Chapter Twenty-Nine

Saturday

Jules rolled over and slapped the alarm that rudely reminded her of the time. Eight o'clock. She swung her feet over the bed and winced. Her whole body ached from sawing, nailing, and carrying boards last night with Jake. She dragged herself to the shower and let it pulse hot water everywhere that hurt. After a shower and a double espresso, she started to feel human again.

Last night had been fun. After a picnic dinner that she assembled from fruit, cheeses, crackers, salami, and two oversized brownies, Jake showed her how to measure and cut boards for the trim and moldings. She left a little after midnight. By then, they had finished all of the interior trim work and about half of the outside work. Jules got lost in thinking about color combinations for the interior and exterior. She was leaning toward softer colors, like a warm gray.

After a quick breakfast of oatmeal and a banana, she and Bijou headed to the office. Jules wanted to look through some of her interior design books and some online sites to come up with a theme for the cottage. "Hey, Bijou, what if we did book themes for the tiny houses? Then we could appeal to fans of all ages."

Bijou yipped. Jules took that as agreement. They strolled across the grass and opened the door to find Emily hard at work on the floor, restocking the camping supply shelves.

"Hi, there. You're in early."

"Eight-thirty on the dot," Emily said. "We've had two reservations and a request for sporting equipment already."

Bijou trotted over, sniffed Emily's hair, and checked out the new supplies.

"Thanks. It looks like you've got it all under control. If it's quiet up here, feel free to catch up our social media posts."

Emily returned to organizing the bandages, sunscreen, and toiletries on the bottom shelves.

"We'll be in the back if you need us." Jules grabbed several interior design books off the shelf behind her desk and opened Pinterest to look for some ideas for the first tiny house. "Okay, Bijou. Who lived in a cottage? I've got it. The first one will be the Beatrix Potter. We have lots to work with in her adorable stories. I'm thinking woodland creatures. And I'm going to create a tiny library in each house to match the theme."

Bijou, not really a Peter Rabbit fan, turned around in circles several times before she found the right snoozing spot.

The new project sent a spark through Jules. She forgot all about the muscle aches and tired limbs. She spent the next hours perusing design sites on the internet. She found some cute fabric for curtains and throw pillows.

By the time her stomach reminded her it was past lunchtime, she had assembled several electronic boards filled with furniture, cushions, fabrics, and wall hangings. Her cell phone rang. "Hello, Sheriff Hobbs. How are you?"

"Pretty good. I was wondering if I could bother you to come into town this afternoon. I have some things I wanted to talk to you about."

"How about two-thirty?"

"That's fine. See you then." The sheriff disconnected.

"Hey, Emily. I'm going to run into town for lunch and to see Sheriff Hobbs. Will you be okay here by yourself? Jake and Lester are around if you need them."

"Bijou'll keep me company," the teen said.

Jules had enough time to stop at Lula Belle's for a ham and Swiss sandwich before her appointment with the sheriff. She fished through her purse for her phone on the way out to text Jake. **Can you swing by the office to make sure Emily's OK?**

Not a problem was his quick response.

Jules was leery about leaving her alone with all the lurkers lately.

Jules ate her sandwich in the Jeep and washed it down with raspberry tea. She dusted off the crumbs and did a quick mirror check to make sure everything was in place and nothing was stuck in her teeth.

She entered the sheriff's office and was greeted by a young brunette deputy with her hair pulled up in a loose bun. She sat behind the glass window in the almost empty lobby.

"Hi. I'm Jules Keene. I'm here to see Sheriff Hobbs. We have an appointment at two-thirty."

"I'll let him know you're here. Someone will be out to get you."

Jules tried to get comfortable in one of the plastic chairs. While she was squirming, the heavy door opened.

The sheriff poked his head out. "Come on back." He led her down the hall to his office. The tall man folded himself into his leather desk chair. He leaned forward and rested his crossed arms on the desk. "Have a seat. I wanted to hear about the last reporter who visited you."

Jules slid in the seat across from him. "He came in the store one afternoon acting nervous and wearing a heavy, canvas jacket over a dress shirt. He said his name was Tom Hamilton and that he was a reporter doing a story on Ira Perkins. He wanted to see where he had stayed at the resort."

"Anything else?"

"He was acting weird. I kinda told him we all thought Perkins was a writer and we were excited about his pending book. We walked out to the trailers, and I showed him the camper next to the one Perkins rented."

The sheriff's brow furrowed.

"It was my nineteen fifty-seven glamour camper. He was surprised Perkins rented a place done mostly in pink and high fashion. I guess it backfired on me. Because we had a visitor that evening who dug holes all around that camper. Then later, Bijou found a phone near that trailer."

"Come with me."

Jules followed the sheriff down the hall to a room with a large window facing an interrogation room. The room on her side had several folding chairs and a desk. The austere furnishings of the room on the other side of the one-way mirror included two wooden chairs and a metal table fastened to the floor. Tom Hamilton, in a stained, white dress shirt, sat slumped on the table. His wrists were handcuffed to the table.

"Is that your reporter?"

"Yep. Tom Hamilton."

"The phone you found belongs to him under his real name. We're waiting for his attorney. He's hinted that he might have something to share with us."

"Any chance he'll get out?"

"No. We're still determining how much he was involved with the two murders and kidnapping. He's in here for a while, whether or not he cuts a deal with the district attorney. We've got all kinds of law enforcement looking for his buddy, Don Fisher. He's probably feeling desperate, and the last thing I want is for anyone else to get hurt. Got it?"

"Yes, sir. Can I help with anything else?"

"No. I appreciate you coming by. I wanted to confirm we had your reporter in custody. And tell Roxanne I said hello. We had a nice dinner in town last night."

"Will do, Sheriff." It was Jules's turn to raise her eyebrows. Dinner with a friend. She'd have to corner Roxanne for details. Her aunt was full of surprises. She wanted to get back to get the scoop and catch Jake up on her latest ideas for the tiny house.

She stopped in at the office to check on Emily, who was holding Bijou and scrolling through social media sites on the computer in the store.

"Everything okay?" Jules asked.

"Yep. It's been quiet. Jake came by and kept us company."

"You can head out when you're ready. I'll close up."

"Thanks. I'm going to Charlottesville with friends tonight for a concert." The teenager pulled her purse from behind the counter. "See you next week."

"Have fun at the concert." Jules didn't ask who was performing. She was pretty sure she wouldn't recognize the name anyway. "Come on, Bijou, let's get your leash." She locked the door behind Emily, and Jules, with her four-legged shadow in tow, headed to the back office to straighten up for the night.

They made a stop at home to heat up a veggie pizza. She flipped through photos on her iPad while she waited for the oven. She could have a lot of fun with these houses. She added some new idea photos to a Pinterest board.

Juggling drinks and the plates of pizza, she stepped inside the barn's cool interior to a cacophony of hammering. Bijou darted toward Jake. He stopped and petted the dog.

"Hi. Can you take a break for pizza?" Jules asked.

"Yep. Pizza's always good." He wiped his hands on his jeans. He made a half of a slice disappear. "Lots of progress today. Just about all the trim is done on the front. There's still some left to do on the other sides."

"I found some designs I wanted to show you before I started ordering things."

"Thanks for your help last night." He reached for another slice.

"I had fun. I haven't worked on a project like this since my dad was around. When I was a kid, he dragged me into all kinds of things. I learned how to mix concrete. I tried my hand at laying bricks. We did a lot together." Jules treasured the fond memories, including that lopsided birdhouse he let her design on her own when she was five. She reached for her iced tea. "Okay, don't laugh. I was thinking about going with a cottage literary theme for this in the design."

"*Snow White and the Seven Dwarves*? *Bambi*?"

"All good ideas. I was thinking more like Beatrix Potter. We can do a lot with the characters from her stories."

"It'll look great when you're done with it."

She Googled Beatrix Potter to show him the characters. He looked over her shoulder as she scrolled through a collection of images.

"I was thinking we could build a little neighborhood. Maybe each house could have a different literary theme. I have a feeling that since tiny houses are popular on TV now that folks may want to have a fun getaway in one. You know no deed goes unpunished, right?"

He had a confused look on his face.

"After you finish this one, you'll have to get busy on the next one."

Jake laughed. There was a sparkle in his eyes. Maybe construction was his passion. He had done a good job on the refurbishments, and he was able to fix about anything in the world of vintage trailers. This could be a profitable addition for the resort and an interesting partnership.

Jules picked up her iPad and stepped into the tiny house. "I'm thinking a combination of mossy green, a chocolatey brown for some of the trim, mauve, robin's egg blue, a warm gray, and pale yellow for accents." She pointed to her design boards on her iPad.

"I want to show you something." Jake motioned for her to follow him. "Under the porthole window in the living area, I created a built-in reading nook."

Jules lifted the lid on the bench. "This is perfect for storage, and I love the bookcases that surround it. I'll make this a cozy reading spot. You outdid yourself on this one, Jake. I'll email you this file with the colors. Let me know if you need me to pick up paint or supplies. I'll stop by and get measurements for the cushions and curtains later this week. We'll have to talk about furnishings, too."

"I should have this place cleaned up by lunch tomorrow. Why don't you come by, and we'll measure everything and figure out the details? Thanks for the pizza."

"Sounds good. Come on, Bijou." Jules had a little flutter of butterflies.

Jake was fun to hang out with. She wasn't sure if it was a new project or having something to do besides stream movies by herself on a Saturday night.

Chapter Thirty

Sunday

Jules stretched and rubbed her lower back. She had spent the afternoon with Jake, alternating between crouching and stretching in the tiny house to get furniture measurements of every nook and cranny. The last few hours included ordering a tea table and four chairs, two mattresses, and undersized kitchen appliances. Her back was stiff from all the work and sitting in her desk chair too long.

She checked her totals and her spreadsheet again. According to the calculations, if they could rent it steadily for the rest of the summer and fall, they would break even with their initial investment. And that included splitting the profits with Jake. Finds from flea markets and yard sales could keep costs down.

"Okay, Bijou. That's enough for today. What do you want to do this evening? Quiet night at home or a quick dinner in town?"

The little terrier lifted her head, listening for magic words like "go" and "walk."

"You've been good. Let's go into town. I have a couple of stops I want to make."

Jules parked in front of Between the Covers bookstore, and Bijou pranced in like she owned the place. Bronte, the true owner of the joint, looked down from his perch on the counter. He meowed and yawned but didn't seem too concerned about the dog in his space.

"Hi, Elizabeth. How're things?"

"Fabulous. What can I do for y'all?"

"I'm getting ready to decorate a new unit, and I wanted to know what you had in stock for Beatrix Potter."

The tallish woman smiled. "Let's see, there are some picture books over there in the children's section. I also have a calendar, a biography, and a book about her home."

"We're going to go browse through the stacks if you don't mind."

"No, not a problem. Let me know if you need anything. And if there's something specific you want, I can order it."

Jules and Bijou browsed through the store under the watchful eyes of Bronte. She settled on a biography of the author, some of the little storybooks, and a calendar of her drawings that Jules could frame. She gathered her choices and returned to the counter. "I'll take these for now. But you know I'll be back."

Elizabeth rang up her purchases and put them in a shopping bag. "I'm looking forward to the next business council meeting. Can't wait to hear all the new ideas."

"After we wrap up the Fourth of July festivities, I'd like to do some planning for the fall and the holidays."

"Whatever you come up with will be great. I love the idea of extending the tourist season beyond the summer and fall. See you soon."

Jules and Bijou walked up the sidewalk toward the eateries. "What do you feel like for dinner?"

The Jack Russell seemed more interested in all the scents around her on the sidewalk. She paused to sniff every bench, flowerpot, and street sign.

"I really want something gooey, like lasagna or manicotti, but I'd better get a salad. Let's go see what we can find."

The terrier trotted ahead toward the Good Thyme Bistro.

Jules was glad to get away from thoughts of Don Fisher and Tom Hamilton, even if it was just for the evening. She longed for some sort of normalcy to return to Fern Valley.

They stopped at the hostess station behind the black metal fencing that outlined the patio area.

"Welcome to the Good Thyme Bistro," a tall brunette said. "How many in your party?"

"I'd like to place a to-go order."

"Of course," the teenager replied. "What can we make fresh for you today?"

"How about a chicken Caesar salad with the dressing on the side and an unsweetened iced tea."

"Of course. It'll be about fifteen or twenty minutes. Do you want to wait or come back for it?"

"I'll come back." Jules handed her credit card to the young woman, who rang up her order.

They strolled down the sidewalk in the other direction past the travel agency and an insurance office. The restaurants across the street looked busy. Jules was glad to see so many people out on a warm Sunday evening. At the corner, Bijou tugged on her leash, and Jules followed her past a card store. The dog focused on a silver fire hydrant by the curb. Jules had to tug several times on the leash to get the dog's attention.

A car engine revved. She looked behind her. A small gray car barreled close to the curb toward them. Her adrenaline surged. She scooped up Bijou and stepped back as the car hurtled by, tires jumping the curb near where they had been standing. Her heartbeat thumped a staccato rhythm in her temples.

It was a gray Honda with a male driver.

The driver slammed on the brakes and threw the car in reverse. He looked over his shoulder at her, jammed the car in drive, and then floored the accelerator. He pulled out into traffic amid honks from agitated drivers.

The man across the street on the sidewalk yelled, "You okay?"

Jules waved and sank into a bench about a half-block away in front of KnitWits. She was pretty sure the driver was the infamous Don Fisher.

A couple walked by with a standard black Poodle. Bijou wanted to make a new friend. After the adrenaline rush had faded and the couple with the dog passed by, Jules fished her phone out of her purse and tapped in a text to Sheriff Hobbs about her latest Don Fisher sighting.

She took a deep, calming breath, waiting for her knees to stop wobbling. Only then did she head back to the bistro to pick up her salad. She had lost her appetite, but maybe she would feel like eating once she got home. Jules looked around the Jeep before she and Bijou jumped in, locked the doors, and sped back to the resort. Why could the police not catch this guy?

In the comfort of her home, Jules kicked off her shoes, poured kibble in Bijou's bowl, and settled down in front of the TV with her salad and tea. She felt pretty confident Don Fisher had recognized her and singled her out on the sidewalk. She was way more involved than she wanted to be. Jules glanced over to the door to ensure it was locked. She thought about calling Agent Stafford, but she brushed the concern aside. She doubted Don Fisher would be back after he tried to scare her earlier.

Opening her iPad, she looked over her design boards for the tiny house. She had some items from the last trailer remodel she might use. After throwing a load of laundry in the washer, she started to feel normal again. Don Fisher wasn't going to scare her into hiding in her own house. She grabbed her phone and keys. "Stay here, Bijou. I'll be back in a minute. I want to go check my stash of decorating stuff." Jules kept the extras in the cabin between Lester and Jake's. Maybe there was something she could use in the tiny houses and planning for the new additions kept her mind off of Don Fisher and her other problems.

Turning on the flashlight app on her phone, Jules picked her way past the barn. She walked beside Lester's cabin to the empty one, farther back in the woods. There was enough light from the groundskeeper's floodlight to see almost to the cabin door.

Flipping on all the interior lights, she pulled the door shut behind her. She had metal shelves in the two bedrooms and living room to hold design elements she had used for previous decorating projects. She rummaged through plastic bins in the front room. Pulling out some older pillows, she decided to repurpose them with Peter Rabbit fabric. She added a pair of brass candlesticks with a rabbit design to her growing collection. On a whim, Jules grabbed a candy dish and a pewter bowl to decorate some of the shelves.

Remembering a collection of old books for the reading nook, she wandered to the back bedroom. After going through boxes and bins, Jules paused for a moment to wipe a loose curl from her forehead. Something creaked. Jules chided herself for being jumpy. Then she heard another noise that sounded like footsteps. Then more creaking noises and footsteps. Her heart pounded. She took a deep breath. Was she foolish to think Don Fisher wouldn't come back to try to finish her off?

Jules grabbed a broom from the corner and poked her head out of the door. A shadow crossed into the kitchen. Grabbing the broom handle like a bat, she stepped around the corner past the bathroom. The rational side of her brain told her to find a place to hide and be quiet. The other side said it was now or never, and she was tired of being scared. She let out the fiercest yell she could muster and ran toward the kitchen with her broom ready to strike.

"Hey," Jake yelled. "Jules?" He grabbed the broom handle before she struck him.

"What are you doing here?" she asked breathlessly. "Besides scaring the crap out of me."

"I could ask you the same thing. I saw the door open when I walked by. Nobody is ever in this cabin at night, so I decided to check it out."

"I know I shut that door when I came in." She paused and looked toward the front door. "I wanted to see what I had in storage for the tiny houses." She caught her breath and tried to keep her heart from beating out of her chest.

"I didn't mean to scare you. You wave a mean broom."

She laughed. "Use what you've got. I left the brass candlesticks at the door. They would have been better."

"When I spotted the open door, I thought of what the FBI agent said about people squatting in vacant cabins."

"I didn't think about that. I was knee-deep into design research, and I wanted to check on something." She switched lights off in the back rooms.

She picked up the bowls and candlesticks, and Jake picked up the pillows. Jules paused on the porch to flip off the remaining lights and lock the door.

"Do you have mud on your shoes?"

"No. Why?" she asked.

"It looks like someone scraped mud off on the bottom steps."

She opened the door and put the porch light back on. "That's a lot of dried mud. Someone's been on the porch besides us."

"Stay here." He walked around the perimeter. He approached her a few minutes later from the opposite direction. "One of the back windows is open." He went inside again. The cabin and porch blazed with light while Jake checked the other rooms.

Jules shifted her weight from foot to foot, and, by the time she was considering sitting down, the lights went off and Jake reappeared on the porch. "I shut and locked the window and checked all the others. Nothing looked out of place. I checked the crawl space in the attic. None of the dust up there has been disturbed."

"Maybe it was Lester or one of the guests."

"But why would the window be open?"

"I have no idea. I haven't been in here in a while. I think it was after Perkins's death and the first ransacking of his trailer. I came by to see if there were any matching pillows I could use in the Robin Hood. But I didn't open any windows."

"I haven't been in here since we moved that stuff from the last trailer rehab. I'll check with Lester later." He pulled the door shut and jiggled the handle to ensure it was locked. "I'll check it out tomorrow in the daylight. I'm still curious about the open window. Nothing looked out of place when you were inside?"

"No. The bins and shelves were all where I'd left them. I can manage those pillows. Just stack them here." She extended her arms.

"You sure?"

"I can get it. Thanks." She walked briskly home with her findings. Relieved to be inside, she double-checked the lock on the front door. And now the mud and the open cabin window were more unexplainable things at the resort to add to her list of worries.

Chapter Thirty-One

Monday

Jules overslept. After a brief shower, she scrunched her hair in a ponytail, added a few swipes of mascara, and ran over to the lodge to see if there was any breakfast left. There was, and she left with her arms laden with sustenance.

At the office, she balanced a cup of coffee, a container of bacon and cheese croissants, and a yogurt parfait as she punched in the security code for the office door. Today, she needed to focus on the agenda and activities list for the upcoming business council meeting. The group's website needed an overhaul, too.

"Shut up now!"

Jules froze as the unrecognizable voice reverberated through the office from the store. She dropped her stuff on her desk and tiptoed to the open Dutch door. She peeked over and saw a tall man in a wrinkled black shirt speaking to Roxanne and Emily, who stood close together behind the counter.

"I've had enough. You have something I want, and I want it now. I'm tired of playing around. Both of you stay where I can see your hands." Jules saw only his back, but it had to be Don Fisher. He turned slightly.

She zeroed in on the black gun he waved around. Jules caught her breath. She had to do something before he hurt someone else–or worse.

She slipped away from the door and texted Sheriff Hobbs and Agent

Stafford. **Don Fisher is here. HE HAS A GUN! Send help now.** Taking a deep breath and letting it out slowly, she had to figure out something to do until they answered. She couldn't let him hurt anyone else. Jules got as close to the door as she could to eavesdrop.

"Stay there and don't move. I've had enough of this place. I'm here for my stuff. Ira took it, and I want it back. It was all my idea, and that sniveling little coward tried to horn in on my cash cow."

"What makes you think we have anything from that old goat?" Roxanne leaned forward and stared the man down.

"He took my money, and I tracked him down here. He wouldn't talk. But I showed him who was boss."

"But you didn't get what you wanted," Roxanne said, almost in a whisper.

Don Fisher seemed agitated. Why was Roxanne egging him on? Jules didn't have a way to signal her. Maybe she did. She dialed the office number. Roxanne leaned toward the phone.

"Leave it alone," he sneered. "Right now, I'm your only client, and you're going to help me find what I want."

"The police came in after they found Ira. They took all his stuff. There was nothing left. Go check with the sheriff." Roxanne looked as cool as a cucumber.

Jules was pretty sure her own knees were knocking.

"I'm looking for my money and other stuff. It wasn't on Ira or the reporter."

"How would you know?" Roxanne asked.

Jules willed Roxanne to stop antagonizing him. But maybe it was a good idea to keep him talking.

"My friend checked it out. He pretended to be a reporter and nosed around town. You'd be surprised what people will tell you if they think they're going to be in the news."

"So, what exactly was your gig?" Roxanne moved closer to Emily.

The teen had a wild-eyed look. Jules hoped she wasn't going to pass out.

"I figured out a way to get big money at work without anybody noticing." He puffed out his chest. "It was an easy gold mine. I had all the info, the keys to the kingdom. I just had to make some phone calls. It was way more lucrative than my day job. Quick. Easy. And quite profitable."

"But Ira did notice," Roxanne said.

"It was going so well until he butted in. He wanted a cut to stay quiet. Then when I paid him, he started making noise about what it was worth to me to keep him happy and quiet. That little pipsqueak played both sides. Then, next thing I knew, he'd drained my account. Then the jerk disappeared."

"So, what did you do?" Roxanne's voice was low, and she drew out her syllables. What was her aunt up to?

"What's with the twenty questions, lady? Shut up. I want my money."

"And I'm telling you. I don't have your stuff," she said calmly.

"Shut up. What's with you? That's it. Both of you. Outside. Now. It must be in that trailer since you haven't rented it to someone else yet. Get the key, or I'll have to break the door again."

Jules heard shuffling.

Don Fisher herded Emily and Roxanne out to the front porch.

Jules didn't have much time. He was clearly getting agitated, and, for some reason, Roxanne was baiting him. Jules rushed into the store area and over to the closet. Maybe she could find something in the sporting equipment she could use as a weapon. The bow and arrows were kiddie sets, so she didn't think that would do much damage.

She looked around frantically, and her eyes lit on the shelf of cast iron skillets for campfire s'mores. She grabbed the biggest one she could find and inched closer to the door.

Roxanne and Emily faced Jules.

Don Fisher stood with his back to her. He waved the gun around. "Act natural. I don't want to draw any more attention than I have already. Act cool. Don't speak to anyone. We're going to walk over to the trailer, and you're going to give me what I want." He lowered the gun to his side.

Jules pushed the door open as quietly as she could. She mimed a "be quiet" to her aunt and Emily. Roxanne's head moved slightly, and it looked like she winked. Jules gripped the handle with both hands.

Roxanne asked, "What is it again we're supposed to have? It'll make it easier for us to know what we're searching for."

"You know exactly what he left. I want my money. All of it."

Jules raised the frying pan with both hands and swung it as hard as she could against the back of the man's head. She connected with his skull. His knees wobbled, and he landed on the deck of the porch, hitting his head again. The gun skittered across the porch. He didn't move.

Roxanne retrieved the gun and pointed it at the prone man. "Oh, Jules. We're glad to see you."

Jules giggled nervously. "Quick. We've got to find something to tie him up with in case he comes to."

"Emily, go get the zip ties that are in one of the front counter drawers," Roxanne said.

Jules and Emily managed to zip tie his wrists behind his back. Then with some effort, they looped several around his ankles to prevent him from running away if he woke up. Blood oozed from where she conked him on the head. Jules checked that he was still breathing.

She pulled out her phone and dialed 9-1-1. Explaining what had happened to the operator, Jules asked for an ambulance to be sent over immediately.

Within minutes, emergency vehicles flew in the resort's main entrance. The first was a black SUV, followed by two police cars.

Agent Stafford barely parked his vehicle before he jumped out and ran to the porch. Sheriff Hobbs and a deputy Jules didn't recognize followed suit.

"What happened?" Agent Stafford asked.

"This guy came in threatening us with a gun, and Jules clobbered him with a frying pan," Roxanne said. "He barged in here yelling at Emily and me. Demanding that we hand over his stuff. This is his gun."

The sheriff grabbed the barrel, tilting it down toward the floor. He took it from Roxanne and emptied the bullets.

"Are you okay?" Sheriff Hobbs patted Roxanne's shoulder.

She and Emily nodded.

The deputy checked on Don Fisher and said something into his radio.

"And then you zip-tied him?" Agent Stafford asked.

"I didn't want him to get away again," Jules said.

"I don't think he's going anywhere anytime soon. He's probably concussed," he replied.

Jules thought he was being critical until he cracked a smile.

The ambulance, with lights and sirens blaring, raced through the front gate and stopped short of the split-rail fence. Three EMTs jumped out. Carrying a plastic box that looked like it held fishing tackle, they dashed to the porch.

They worked on Don Fisher for a while. He stirred and looked around like he didn't know where he was. Then the EMTs brought the gurney and hauled him to the ambulance. After the deputy shooed some of Jules's guests back toward their trailers, he followed the ambulance to the hospital.

Sheriff Hobbs took a couple of pictures of the porch. The blood had begun to congeal where Don Fisher's head had been. "Why don't we go inside and talk. I'm sure everyone could use a cup of coffee. Jules, you may want to get someone over here to clean this up."

She called Jake. In hushed tones, she explained briefly what had happened and asked him to get Lester or Mel to come over to get the blood off the front porch. She followed the special agent inside.

"Jules, mind if we use your office?" Sheriff Hobbs asked.

"No, help yourself."

The sheriff and the FBI agent talked to Emily and Roxanne. Then it was Jules's turn. Her knees still felt wobbly, but she was relieved they had finally apprehended Don Fisher.

"I need you to fill in some of the missing pieces," Sheriff Hobbs said. "Tell us everything related to Don Fisher from this morning."

She pulled up the guest chair next to her desk. "I came in late this morning. Actually, that's my coffee and breakfast on the desk. When I came in through the back door, I heard a man threatening Roxanne and Emily. It was the green-truck guy. And he had a gun."

"Why didn't you wait for us?" Agent Stafford asked.

"I texted you both, but when I didn't get an answer, I had to figure out another plan. This was an emergency. He was taking Emily and my aunt to the trailer by gunpoint. He sounded agitated and desperate, and I didn't want him to hurt them."

"So, you clunked him on the head with a frying pan?" the sheriff asked.

"It was the only thing close to a weapon I could get my hands on. And it worked."

"It did indeed," Sheriff Hobbs said. "He won't be feeling great for a while."

"So, what's next for Fisher?" Jules asked.

"He'll be in police custody while he's at the hospital, and when he's released, he'll go to jail. We have enough charges pending that he's not going to get out for a long time."

"He kept saying he wanted his money. He was convinced Perkins had left something of his here. I only found that one batch of cash."

"The rest of what was left was in the account Ira created in the Cayman Islands. Ira only had a small portion of the money here," Agent Stafford said.

"Don Fisher said Perkins was blackmailing him." Jules took a sip of her drink.

"That's how it started. Then he figured out a way to siphon off Fisher's money. Fisher got the bright idea to change his cash to bitcoin to hide it on the dark web, but Perkins somehow got wind of it and found a way to steal it. Then Ira moved the money to an offshore account. He left Fisher high and dry. And Fisher wasn't too happy after doing all the dirty work and not reaping any of the spoils," Agent Stafford said.

"And the other short guy who said he was a reporter?" Jules asked.

"Rich Sanders worked with Don Fisher and Ira Perkins. He was friends with Don and seemed to help him occasionally. Fisher paid him for side jobs. He sang like a canary after a couple of days in jail. He was more than willing to point the finger at his buddy when he was facing jail time," Sheriff Hobbs said.

"I'm glad it's finally over. I'd really like to get back to running my resort and forget all about Ira Perkins blackmailing sick people. Do you all need anything else? I want to check on my team and get the porch cleaned."

"We're done here," Sheriff Hobbs said.

Jules followed him through the store.

"I'll call you later." The sheriff and Roxanne had a moment where they stared at each other.

During the quiet, Jules had an a-ha moment. Suddenly, she felt like the third wheel, so she slipped out the front door.

On the porch, Jake dumped a bucket of water on a soapy spot. He used a broom to sweep the suds and excess water off the side. "This should dry soon. Good as new."

"Thanks, Jake," Jules said. "I'm hoping that's the end of Ira Perkins and his exploits."

The FBI agent and the other law enforcement officers left as quickly as they arrived.

Jules enjoyed the solitude for a few moments until Jake broke her train of thought. "If you're okay with it, I'm going to have a couple of my buddies come over. I want to move the Beatrix Potter in place and get it fastened down. I'll do the final work on it when it's anchored in place. Our first tiny house will be ready for decorating."

"Come by tonight, and we can do a walk-through, and if you want, we can go to Pop's to celebrate. My treat," he said with a boyish grin.

"Sounds like a plan. I'd like that."

Roxanne breezed out the front doorway. "Jules, I'm going to head into town for lunch with some friends. Are you all okay here? That buzzard almost made me miss my lunch date."

Maybe things were starting to get back to normal. And she had a real date with Jake.

Roxanne Mallory's Skillet S'mores Recipe

Ingredients

- 1 tablespoon butter
- 24 ounces of semi-sweet chocolate (or other chocolate of your choice)
- 15-20 large marshmallows
- 1 package of plain graham crackers.

Instructions

Melt the butter in the skillet over the fire. Make sure to cover the skillet surface with butter. Fill the skillet with the chocolate chips. Cover the chips with the marshmallows. Heat for 7-10 minutes until the marshmallows are toasted. Remove from the fire and use the graham crackers to dip the s'mores. Be careful. The skillet is hot.

To make this a colorful spring dessert, substitute Peeps for the marshmallows. You can also substitute chocolate caramel candies to change up the flavor.

If you'd like to make these in an oven, preheat the oven to 450° F. Put your skillet in the oven for 5-7 minutes. Remove the skillet and follow the instructions above.

Lula Belle's Renowned Pimento Spread

Ingredients

- 1 8-ounce package of cream cheese
- 1/3 cup of your favorite mayonnaise (Duke's is popular in the south)
- 2 cups of shredded cheddar cheese (Extra sharp is best)
- 1 dash of garlic powder
- 1 4-ounce jar of diced pimentos

Instructions

Use an electric mixer to beat the cream cheese. Medium speed works best. Mix until it's creamy. Add the cheddar cheese and continue to beat until the mixture is fluffy. Add the mayo and garlic powder. Drain the pimentos and stir them into the mix.

Cover the mix and chill in the refrigerator for an hour. This makes about 2.5 cups of spread.

If you want to spice it up, dice 3-4 jalapeno peppers and throw them in the mix before you chill it.

Lula Belle's Famous Virginia Cheese Sticks

Ingredients

- 1 teaspoon water
- ½ teaspoon vegetable oil
- 2 teaspoons unsalted butter
- ¾ cup shredded sharp cheddar cheese
- 1/3 cup shredded Parmesan cheese
- ½ teaspoon paprika
- 1 pinch cayenne pepper
- ¼ teaspoon salt
- ½ cup flour

Instructions

Cover a baking sheet with foil and grease it with the vegetable oil. In a medium mixing bowl, add butter, cheddar cheese, Parmesan cheese, paprika, cayenne pepper, and salt. Mix thoroughly.

Add flour and sprinkle in the water. Mix the dough.

Press the dough into a flattened pancake and wrap in plastic wrap. Refrigerate the dough for 30 minutes. Preheat your oven to 375° F.

Roll your cheese dough on a floured work surface to about an eighth of an inch thickness. Cut your dough into strips (about 1.5 inches long). A pizza cutter may be easier to use than a knife. Arrange them on your baking sheet. You can decorate the dough by drawing lines or punching holes.

Bake for about 15 minutes (until crackers are crispy).

Crystal Carson's Chocolate-chip Pancakes

Ingredients

- 1 ¼ cup flour
- 2 eggs
- 1 cup milk
- 4 tablespoon butter (melted)
- 1 tablespoon sugar
- ¾ tablespoon vanilla
- ¼ tablespoon cinnamon
- 1 tablespoon baking powder
- ¼ tablespoon salt
- ½ to ¾ cup of chocolate chips

Instructions

Preheat your griddle or skillet. Combine the dry ingredients (except for the chocolate chips) in a large bowl. Add in the wet ingredients and mix until your batter is smooth. Stir in the chocolate chips.

Spoon your batter on your griddle for the size pancakes desired. Cook for a minute. When it bubbles, flip the pancake and cook the other side for a minute.

For gooier pancakes, add ½ cup of mini marshmallows when you add the chocolate chips. You can also substitute butterscotch or other chips for the chocolate ones.

Donna Ford's Dark Chocolate Peanut Candy

Ingredients

- 1 16-ounce jar dry-roasted, unsalted peanuts
- 2 ounces chocolate bark squares
- 1 12-ounce package dark chocolate morsels
- 1 4-ounce package German chocolate baking squares
- 1 teaspoon vanilla extract

Instructions

Break all of the bark/baking squares into smaller pieces. Combine all the ingredients in a slow cooker. Cover and cook on low for two hours. Stir your candy occasionally.

Drop mixture by the tablespoon onto wax paper. Let cool until candy is firm.

If you want to change it up, you can use fresh, roasted peanuts. Donna Ford gets hers from Suffolk, Virginia. (You can also add different flavors of morsels or mini marshmallows for variety.)

Mel Carson's Quick Bacon and Cheese Quiche

Ingredients

- 1 refrigerated pie crust – Follow the directions on the box
- 4 eggs, beaten
- 1 cup milk or half-and-half creamer
- ¼ teaspoon salt
- ¼ teaspoon pepper
- 8 slices crispy, cooked bacon or turkey bacon
- 1 cup shredded Cheddar cheese
- ¼ cup grated Parmesan cheese
- 1 tablespoon chopped onions

Instructions

Preheat your oven to 350° F. Follow the instructions on the package for your prepared pie crust.

In a bowl, mix the milk/creamer, eggs, pepper, and salt.

Layer the bacon, cheese, and onion in your crust. Pour the egg mixture on top. Bake for 50 minutes. Let this stand for about 5 minutes before you cut it.

You can substitute ham for the bacon if you like.

Crystal Carson's Gooey Cinnamon Buns

Ingredients

- 1 package (about .25 ounces) active, dry yeast
- ½ cup warm water
- ½ cup milk
- 4 cups all-purpose flour
- ½ cup butter
- ¼ cup white sugar
- 1 teaspoon salt
- 1 ½ cups brown sugar
- 1 cup chopped pecans
- 1 tablespoon ground cinnamon
- 2 eggs (beaten)

Instructions

In a small bowl, mix 1 teaspoon white sugar and the yeast in warm water. Let it stand for about 10 minutes. Warm the milk to bubbling in a saucepan. Mix in ¼ cup regular sugar, ¼ cup butter, and salt. Stir until melted. Let this mixture cool.

In another, larger bowl, combine the yeast mixture, milk, eggs, and 1 ½ cup flour. Stir well. Then add the remaining flour. When the dough forms, put it on a lightly floured surface and knead for eight minutes.

Lightly oil a large bowl and place the dough inside. Coat the dough with the oil. Cover with a damp cloth and let it rise in a warm place for an hour.

Melt ¾ cup butter in a small saucepan at medium heat. Stir in the brown sugar. Whisk until smooth. Pour into a greased 9x13 baking pan. Sprinkle in half of the pecans. Melt the remaining butter. Combine the remaining brown sugar, pecans, and cinnamon. Set this aside.

Roll your dough into a large rectangle. Brush with 2 tablespoons of melted butter, leaving a half-inch border around the rectangle. Sprinkle in the brown sugar/pecan mix.

Start a long side of the rectangle and roll up the dough. Pinch the seam to seal. Brush with remaining butter. With a knife, cut the roll into 15 pieces. Put the cut side down in the prepared pan. Cover and let rise for an hour.

Preheat the oven to 375° F. Bake the rolls for 25-30 minutes until golden brown. Cool and move them to a serving platter.

Acknowledgments

Writing is a long, solitary effort, and I want to thank my family and friends who provided all the love and support for this book and my writing endeavors—Stan Weidner for all the hours spent as roadie, photographer, and partner in crime, my parents (Micky and Sandy Baker) who instilled in me a lifelong love of reading, Cortney Cain for her amazing feedback, Meagan and Jocelyn Cain, my pop-culture gurus, and Bill Cain for always keeping everyone in stitches. For all the encouragement and support, I'd like to thank my Bethia UMC family. And many thanks to Joy Pfister and her wonderful crew at Studio FBJ.

Many thanks to Dan Minton, Terry Dewberry, Cristina Allen, Shawn Flippo, and Faith Flippo for answering all my police procedural questions.

Thank you, to my agent, Dawn Dowdle, for all her help and support in navigating the writing and publishing world. And a huge thank you to Shawn Reilly Simmons, Verena Rose, and Harriette Sackler, the infamous Dames of Detection, and everyone at Level Best Books for giving Jules and Bijou a home.

I am so grateful for my talented Sisters in Crime, Guppy, and James River Writer friends. Your support is invaluable. Jayne Ormerod, Mary Burton, Sherry Harris, and Barb Goffman—I cannot thank you ladies enough for all the great advice!

And thanks to the best critiquers around: Susan Campbell, Frances Aylor, Catherine Brennan, Amy Lilly, K. L. Murphy, Sandie Warwick, Marjorie Bagby, and Mary Dutta.

About the Author

Through the years, Heather Weidner has been a cop's kid, technical writer, editor, college professor, software tester, and IT manager. *Vintage Trailers and Blackmailers* is the first in her cozy mystery series, the Jules Keene Glamping Mysteries. She also writes the Delanie Fitzgerald mystery series set in Virginia (*Secret Lives and Private Eyes, The Tulip Shirt Murders,* and *Glitter, Glam, and Contraband).*

Her short stories appear in the *Virginia is for Mysteries* series, *50 Shades of Cabernet, Deadly Southern Charm,* and *Murder by the* Glass, and her novellas appear in The Mutt Mysteries series.

She is a member of Sisters in Crime and active in Central Virginia, Chessie, and Guppies Chapters, International Thriller Writers, and James River Writers.

Originally from Virginia Beach, Heather has been a mystery fan since Scooby-Doo and Nancy Drew. She lives in Central Virginia with her husband and a pair of Jack Russell terriers.

AUTHOR WEBSITE: http://HeatherWeidner.com

SOCIAL MEDIA HANDLES:

Website and Blog: http://www.heatherweidner.com

Twitter: https://twitter.com/HeatherWeidner1

Facebook: https://www.facebook.com/HeatherWeidnerAuthor

Instagram: https://www.instagram.com/heather_mystery_writer/

Goodreads: https://www.goodreads.com/author/show/8121854.Heather_Weidner

Amazon Authors: http://www.amazon.com/-/e/B00HOYR0MQ

Pinterest: https://www.pinterest.com/HeatherBWeidner/

LinkedIn: https://www.linkedin.com/in/heather-weidner-0064b233?trk=hp-identity-name

BookBub: https://www.bookbub.com/authors/heather-weidner-d6430278-c5c9-4b10-b911-340828fc7003

AllAuthor: https://allauthor.com/profile/heatherweidner/

YouTube: https://www.youtube.com/channel/UCyBjyB0zz-M1DaM-rU1bXGA?view_as=subscriber

Also by Heather Weidner

The Delanie Fitzgerald Mysteries (*Secret Lives and Private Eyes, The Tulip Shirt Murders,* and *Glitter, Glam, and Contraband*)

Short Stories in *Murder by the Glass, Deadly Southern Charm, 50 Shades of Cabernet, Virginia is for Mysteries, Virginia is for Mysteries II*

Novellas in the Mutt Mysteries series (*To Fetch a Thief, To Fetch a Scoundrel, To Fetch a Villain,* and *To Fetch a Killer*)

Printed in the USA
CPSIA information can be obtained
at www.ICGtesting.com
LVHW041747260924
792228LV00001B/151

9 781685 120368